CLICK

L. Smyth was born in Somerset in 1993. As a journalist, she has written for the *Financial Times*, *The Times Literary Supplement*, *The Daily Telegraph* and *Prospect*. Since 2018 she has worked as a podcast writer. She lives in London.

CLICK

L. SMYTH

KILLER
READS

A division of HarperCollins*Publishers*

www.harpercollins.co.uk

KillerReads
an imprint of HarperCollins*Publishers* Ltd
1 London Bridge Street
London SE1 9GF

www.harpercollins.co.uk

This paperback edition 2019

First published in Great Britain in ebook format by HarperCollins*Publishers* 2019

Extracts from the poem 'Marina' are reprinted by permission of
Faber & Faber Ltd from 'The Ariel Poems' by T.S. Eliot

A catalogue record for this book
is available from the British Library

ISBN: 978-0-00-831411-8

Set in Minion by
Palimpsest Book Production Limited, Falkirk, Stirlingshire

Printed and bound by CPI Group (UK) Ltd, Croydon, CR0 4YY

MIX
Paper from
responsible sources
FSC C007454

For my grandparents – Mary, George, Nick and Bill; and for Great Uncle Bob

PROLOGUE

*The first time I saw Marina was in October 2013. The last time I
saw her was three months later.*

*It seems strange to put it like that. It still surprises me – despite
having had years to think about it – how short that time frame is.
Sometimes it is assumed that the oldest relationships are the most
influential, and that those who know us for the longest periods are
those who shape us most significantly. But often the opposite is true.
It is the short, intense relationships which have the strongest impacts
on us, and only those who flit in and out of our lives who have the
power to make us profoundly different. The time spent with them
is so brief that each moment in their company becomes effortlessly
memorable. The feelings and smells and images that they evoke
worm into our brains and we find ourselves returning to them
compulsively – trying to pin them down, trying to understand their
effects.*

*I still don't understand what happened with Marina. I don't
understand the effect that our friendship had on either of us. The
more I think about her, the more she eludes me.*

But it would be wrong to say that I don't remember anything about her. I remember everything extremely clearly, to the extent where I feel as though I know her well. I remember the way her eyes curled at the sides when she smiled; the way they narrowed with suspicion in seminars; the way she smoked with the cigarette balanced in the middle of her mouth. I remember the sound of her voice too: soft and low on the phone, deep and loud in large groups, slightly nasal with an upward inflection when she spoke to boys. My memory of her is so vivid that even hearing her name provokes a kind of frenzy in me. Without warning my mind fogs over, casts back, and it is like the last four years never happened. We are both eighteen again, stood outside the library, rolling our eyes at the other students.

Over the last few years I have been good at restraining myself. I have cut myself off from that life. I do not keep in touch with anyone from university. I have removed all traces of myself, online and elsewhere, so that they won't be able to find me. I have tried to ensure that I am forgotten, so that every piece of my history is forgotten. And then I can forget it myself.

But recently she has started to reinsert herself into my thoughts. I see someone in the street with the same gait, or the same curl in the bottom of their hair, and my stomach lurches. I catch a whiff of her perfume – a sort of honey blossom scent – and my palms begin to sweat, I feel light-headed, convinced that she is in the vicinity.

It feels different this time. The newspaper headlines, the flashes of her face across the TV screens … I can't help but suspect that everything is about to come to light. She is catching up with me. I need to set the record straight before someone else gets there first. I need to tell the story, as it was, from the beginning.

PART I

PART 1

CHAPTER ONE

October 2013

i.

Marina and I met during our first term at Northam: a tiny elite university in rural England. At that stage I had been living on the campus for about three weeks, and I felt like I was on the brink of insanity. If that sounds flippant, narcissistic or entitled – good. I was eighteen years old. I was angry all the time and I hated university. Everything about it had fallen short of my expectations, from my room (which was small and dusty) to the nearby city (dull) to my teachers (likewise) to my floormates (shrill or condescending, often both). My course was limited in scope, heavy in reading, and there was a snippy, competitive atmosphere among my classmates which prevented us from becoming friends.

That last point I found especially disheartening. I had grown up in a small town with hardly any people in it – I had few friends, no siblings and my parents were antisocial – and I saw university as the point at which my life would really begin. There I would finally meet people who spoke the same language that I did. I would meet a group of people with conflicting opinions.

I would have my mind wrenched open, would stretch my perceptions beyond what I had been taught, and I would learn – really learn – how other people saw things.

In reality everything was the same. The existing hierarchies and prejudices remained intact behind a screen of diversity. Conversations were either flat or gratingly pretentious. Everyone spoke about irrelevant topics in a language that I didn't understand, and dismissed my contributions with a load of obscure statistics.

I'd told myself that I wouldn't start drinking alone, but with that form of self-medication out of the window, there seemed only one good option left. I grabbed my laptop from my desk. I sat on my bed in my cold, damp room. For hours on end, I scrolled down my newsfeed.

The autumn of 2013 was the moment of the social media boom. True, certain giants had established themselves earlier in the millennium – by the time the iPhone came out in 2007, Facebook and Google were already a daily ritual. But in 2013 the market suddenly exploded, and a flurry of new apps and features arrived to steal your attention. The result of this – especially if you were a university student with little to do during the day – was that you were constantly glued to your devices.

I was no exception obviously. I had the full English: Snapchat, Facebook, Instagram, Twitter, etc – and my eyes were permanently locked to a screen. Sometimes this would mean that I was doing something productive (reading an article, writing an email) but mostly I was watching the digital lives of others. I was reading their statuses. I was reading their wall posts. I was studying their photographs, even the ones they weren't tagged in. I was analysing their social lives in microscopic detail, tracing through their friend networks to see who their good-looking friends were going out with, what their interests were, what their cousin's ex-partners looked like now.

When I did this time would soften and dissolve, so that I

eventually forgot that it was passing. My surroundings would disappear. Then my sense of physical boundaries: having skin; a body. All that I would eventually become conscious of was the white rectangular heat of the laptop light on my face and the cold sensation of plastic or glass under my fingers. I would spiral from Facebook to Instagram to Twitter, back to Facebook, across to Instagram, looping and circling around again, refreshing the page impatiently, impatiently refreshing it again, rearranging the tabs, clicking on clicking off, tapping on tapping off, tapping back on and spinning back around again until some instinct caused me to wrench my eyes away and – stop. I was concerned by how much time I spent doing this, but I was also aware that there was a kind of satisfying fluidity to it. The Internet felt like a space which I could navigate freely.

Needless to say, I hardly posted anything on my own profile. That wasn't the point. The point was that I could watch what other people were doing. I could watch my new peers. In this way it acted as a kind of sedative, a dose of virtual sugar, a way to fill my head with fug and so distract myself from reality. I could roll the mouse down my newsfeed for hours, and the photographs, the witty comments and the tags would keep coming. It was a numbing distraction, like watching a film or reading a novel.

But there was also a weird element of inclusion to it. Looking at those lives onscreen – I didn't feel excluded in a way that I did from the people around me, or from the narratives I read or watched on TV. There was something interactive about watching social media conversations. I felt – perhaps because I could control exactly what I saw next – that I could become part of their lives. I felt that there, on the Internet, I was in the midst of a picturesque youth.

I mention all this because in the context of such a culture, obviously I knew about Marina before I met her face-to-face. I discovered her on my course Facebook group. The group was

7

something that one of the university admins had invited us all to join in the weeks before the start of term, ostensibly so that 'general files' such as the reading list could be found in a convenient place. This was the official line. The tacit agreement was that these groups were for the purpose of Facebook stalking. They were a preview into the lives of potential friends.

What was therefore surprising was not that I knew who Marina was before meeting her, but that I didn't know more about her. Her profile gave little away: I was surprised to see no cover photo, and no listed interests. All that I could ascertain from the small icon of the profile picture was that she had a curtain of blonde hair and a petite frame. She was leaning against a car with her head twisted sideways, her back turned towards the camera.

It was for this reason, I think, that Marina stuck in my mind. She had the sort of filtered virtual aura which suggested she was glamorous, and it was heightened by the fact that her profile was so private. She seemed to be above the boastful social media culture, to care little about it and – in being that way inclined – exuded a sophistication which I envied. To put it bluntly, she was the kind of friend I wanted to have.

It would be wrong to give the idea that I was desperate for company. I wasn't always alone. There were often people I could spend time with at Northam, and I was fine at cementing rapport individually if I tried. But groups of people made me uncomfortable. Somehow I felt lonelier among them than I did on my own.

Probably this was due to my upbringing. I was an only child, and had been homeschooled for a few years before my A levels. In that time I had established a sense of independence that made me feel – naively – that I was in control of my existence. My tutor was a complete pushover, and my parents preferred to defer teenage-patrol duties to her than try to control me themselves. The result was that I ran riot and no one noticed. It was blissful.

Returning to school at sixteen was naturally a shock. I couldn't believe that I'd have to adhere to a social order that I hadn't devised myself. I couldn't believe that I'd have to turn up on time, or pretend like I cared about other people's small-talk problems. But in the short-term, I also wanted to fit in – so I put on a mask of cool politeness and feigned interest in whatever they said. People said I was polite. Really I found them boring.

I hoped that there would come a time where I wouldn't be feigning interest. I looked forward to a future where I would be able to have conversations with people – one-on-one – that were conversations I actually wanted to have.

There was something in that glimpse of Marina that made me think that she would understand this position. I felt that she was set apart from others – that she didn't live according to their customs. She, like me, could perhaps manipulate her face to seem interested in conversations that she didn't really care about. She, like me, perhaps made hilariously sarcastic asides that other people didn't pick up on. I was interested in seeing whether she lived up to this expectation and – if so – what her real thoughts and ideas were. So that's why I looked out for her in those first few weeks of term. That's why I made a note of her Facebook page, added it to my bookmarks, checked it every day.

In the initial seminars and lectures, I also kept an eye out for Marina. I would shuffle into the theatre, waiting for others to pass, eagerly noting whenever someone blonde or slight or vaguely short walked by. But it was never her. On a second glance I'd notice that they were in fact too tall, or their legs too stumpy; otherwise I'd glimpse a notebook and see a different name scrawled on the front. Soon I began to assume that 'Marina' had decided not to come to Northam after all. She must have received another offer from somewhere else at the last minute – or she'd been added to the group by mistake.

The days sloped by. I went to lectures and then retreated to my room. I looked at what other people were doing online and felt depressed about my state of isolation. Nothing, it seemed, was going to make me happy, to subdue that swell of anxiety – the suspicion that I was wasting my potential.

ii.

It was a Wednesday when it happened, that much I remember. I was feeling groggy that day, having spent the previous evening at a fresher's event, and then in my room with some random guy whose name I have thankfully forgotten. At around two in the afternoon – unable to bear the stale smell of salt-sweat any longer – I decided to go to a lecture. I showered, dressed, left my building, crossed the campus, and then sat down in the corner of the theatre. The lecture itself was uninteresting. I sat through it passively; looking at the clock; glancing at my phone under the desk; scribbling notes for show.

When it had finished I walked down towards the exit. I was about to leave when I heard the voice of the professor: 'That's not quite how it works, Marina.'

Slowly I turned my head.

A girl of about five foot six was stood at the lectern. Her back was turned, but I could see that she had long blonde hair, slightly curled at the ends. Her head was cocked to the side. Now it shook vehemently.

'I'm sorry, I know how it sounds,' the professor continued, 'but my hands are tied.'

'Hands tied how?'

'This isn't suitable for discussion now.'

'Hands tied how?' she said again.

He lifted his head and looked cautiously around. His glasses tilted up from the end of his nose.

'If you've already transferred to a different subject,' he said, 'then you can't transfer back. That's all there is to it, I can't help you.'

I looked at the professor closely for a moment. He was a man of about sixty, with a protruding stomach and a sweaty flat face like a coin. Usually he wore an ironic expression – raised brow, curled lip, a smug glint in his eye. Yet his features seemed to have lost their composure. His mouth moved with sudden jerks, his eyebrows twitched; below them his eyes looked hollow and unfocused. He seemed unnerved by the girl in front of him – the girl whose face I couldn't see, whose words I couldn't quite hear.

I edged forwards, pretending to pack files into my bag.

'You *can* help me. Of course you can. You're the course convenor.'

'No. It's not that simple.'

'Why?'

'I shouldn't have to explain.'

'You're a lecturer. It's your job to explain. And anyway,' she shrugged slightly, 'I deserve an explanation. You of all people know that.'

The professor laughed in a forced, shallow manner: lightly at the back of his throat. The sound echoed around the room. I watched him push a hand through patchy hair, embarrassed and smiling. Then he glanced around again and caught my eye. At that moment his expression shifted: his features stabilized, became authoritative, patient, ironic.

'*Well* I've said all that I can tell you,' the professor's voice was now resonant and calm. 'Which *is*, that if you have any concerns then they should be sent to me in an email, copying in the head of department.'

Marina began to object, but before she could trap him in further conversation he cut her off, muttering darkly about pressing engagements. He gathered his papers together and lifted his overcoat onto his back. Then he smiled tersely at her, at me, and shuffled out the door.

Marina bent down to pick up her satchel from the floor and swung it over her shoulder. Then she sighed theatrically and turned around – and I saw her face for the first time.

11

It was slimmer than I'd expected, with high cheekbones and a slightly pointed chin. Those sharp shapes, mixed with her snub little nose, gave her an almost goblin-like appearance, and yet they were balanced out by a smattering of freckles and a full, bow-like mouth. Now, even though she was frowning – her brow furrowed, her mouth knitted into a downwards curve – the expression was childish somehow. There was an air of innocence, of mischief about her.

As she walked past me, she looked right into my face and her frown deepened.

Her eyes were green, I noticed, with small flecks of gold in them.

Alone in the lecture hall I reflected on the confrontation I'd just seen. Marina's blunt manner amazed me. At school, those who engaged in backchat with the teachers were mostly layabouts without much wit, whose interjections consistently fell short of the mark. I'd often felt a prudish satisfaction watching their snark dissolve into humiliated silence: the corners of their mouths drooping, their eyes turning to the table.

With Marina it wasn't like that. She seemed not only to be tolerated but respected by the professor. His reaction had not been reproachful or even impatient, but nervous. It was as though he suspected that she had the power to publicly humiliate him in some way. He had solicited her approval even while he was rebuking her.

iii.

I thought about this as I walked down the corridor until I realized I was in front of the pinboard. I looked up at the timetable showing the times and places of all the seminars, scanned them quickly. I wondered how many clashed with my commitments. Might I be able to turn up to some of them, just to see if she was there? Then I thought: that is impractical. She'd said she wasn't on the English course. There was no reason to think that she'd be attending any of the other seminars.

A better bet would be to find her outside of lectures: in the library for example. I went to the library, but she wasn't there. Not in the open downstairs area. Not in the creepy silent room. Not on the nooks of the upper floor by the archives. She wasn't in the café, nor the dining area, nor the bar. She wasn't in the campus shop.

On my way back to my room, I took a detour to the other side of campus, towards the bougie accommodation. Two girls were sat on a bench, and I overheard one of them complaining to her friend about having sunburned the 'rooves' of her feet while on holiday in St-Tropez.

'Rosa,' the other girl said, 'Is rooves actually a word?'

'Obviously it's a word. It's the tops of houses.'

'Or feet?'

'Or feet.'

I glanced up towards the tops of the buildings. They were slate grey and dusty in the autumn sunlight. High in a window I noticed the outline of a silhouette: a pair of hands adjusting a string, the slow mechanical movement of the curtain moving upwards to reveal a blue midriff. Instinctively I ducked behind a lamp post, and then – a second later – peered out again. The window was now ajar. A small hand was dangling out, clutching a cigarette.

I could hear someone laughing loudly. A slim almond-shaped fingernail tapped the butt of the cigarette, and sprinkles of ash fell from the sky.

It was her, I was sure of it.

I bent forward, squinting, and saw a trickle of wavy blonde hair spill across the sill. A head turned, and took a drag from the cigarette. It could feasibly be her, I reasoned, noting the outline of her side profile, comparing it to my mental copy of her profile picture. But she moved too quickly to draw any solid conclusions. Her features blurred together, made her look anonymous.

Abruptly the window snapped shut and the cigarette fell from the sill. It danced through the air down all four floors and landed near me on the concrete. I stared at the blunted end. There was a gentle smudge of lipstick along the butt.

For a second, I thought about picking it up. Then I became aware of a stilted silence nearby.

Turning, I saw that the two girls on the bench had stopped their conversation and were staring at me. Their faces registered a certain amusement, as well as a certain distaste. I realized suddenly how weird I looked. Sheepishly I emerged from the lamp-post and walked past them silently, expressionlessly, without even glancing in their direction.

The next day I walked past that window, and the day after that, but the blinds were drawn.

I didn't see anyone there again.

***

I dreamed of Northam again last night. The open window. The gentle night breeze. Marina smiling down at me. Her mouth forming the words, her neck snapping back in a fit of laughter.

The dreams are always silent. I don't hear her laughter. I don't hear her say the words. But I always know exactly what she is saying. I know how her voice sounds saying it. And I know exactly what her laughter sounds like: the notes quickly rising to a shriek.

I look cautiously around, check that no one is watching. Then I flip the newspaper, curling my shoulders inwards and craning my neck down to peer at her face. I look at her snub chin, the almonds of her eyes, ripe berry of her mouth. I see there is a lock of hair in her face. I reach my hand out. I attempt to brush it away with the tip of my finger.

14

The following week I turned up five minutes early to the professor's lecture. I hovered at the end of the corridor – the one leading to the theatre – and scanned the crowd waiting outside. I couldn't see her at first, it was so busy and loud – all the faces blurred into one another – and so I edged forward, past the bent knees and bulging rucksacks and forearms crossed over folders. I avoided eye contact with those I vaguely knew, pulling my hair over my face.

Soon there was a commotion behind me: the professor.

He bustled through the group of students, papers waving theatrically in his hand, a murmuring of 'excuse me' as he pushed his way forward. Then, at the door, he wavered. I watched him intently. There was a strained look on his face, a kind of suppressed smirk. He looked as though he might have been rehearsing a line in his head. But he said nothing, only glanced sideways briefly, then straightened his shoulders and walked into the lecture hall.

My eyes tracked across in the direction of his glance. She was sat against the wall, reading a book. I noticed she was wearing the same style of dress as the week before, but a deeper shade of blue. Her hair was in a low, neat bun at the nape of her neck and her face was knotted into a little frown. She flipped over a page in the novel and raised an ironic eyebrow.

At that moment the crowd began to trickle into the lecture hall, and she stood up. I watched the dark blue fabric lift and drop as her legs unfolded and straightened. She began to move towards the theatre with them, and I followed where she was going, keeping a good distance behind. There was a spare seat next to her. Avoiding eye contact, I shuffled in and sat down.

Around us I heard the familiar hum of student voices – those awkward few minutes before the start of a lecture which are never quite long enough to make conversation. I stared at my hands. I wondered how to introduce myself. I wondered what I could say that would sound natural. I had never been good at introductory conversations: the 'hello' itself was fine, but the segue into small talk always felt stilted. I was terrified of the inevitable silences that would follow and so would pre-emptively fill them with vacuous babble – babble that I found impossible to sustain, so my sentences trailed out, and I would end up awkwardly cutting myself off … Anyway, I kept my mouth shut.

The lecture began. I paid attention this time, partly because the title irritated me: 'Female novelists in the nineteenth century.' That categorization was annoying. I had never been a fan of what-was-called women's fiction, in the same way that I'd never been a fan of what-were-called women's magazines. I liked the idea instead that literature transcended the boundaries of gender, and thought that to lump together the work of (in this instance) Gaskell and Eliot into a 'women's literature' category was to strip them of a creative freedom that male novelists were automatically afforded. That said, I mostly read men.

There was also a particular reason – a particular detail – which jolted me to pay attention that day. It was a sound bite I happened to pick up on in the first five minutes. After introducing the topic of the lecture, the professor said: 'Now, who exactly, made up the readership of lady novelists during this period?'

Not female novelists, as the lecture title indicated, or even women novelists, as I might have found acceptable – but *lady* novelists. Nice ladies. Polite genteel women who behaved themselves. Every time he casually dropped it in, I felt my face flush and my throat constrict in anger.

Now he peered over at the students in the front row, and tapped the pen against the lectern. I resisted the urge to charge to the front of the lecture hall, grab the pen and shove it up his nose.

'A particularly *in*teresting detail,' he continued, 'in fact I should say, a particularly contro*versial* detail featured in the writings of both lady novelists is the—'

Someone cut in: 'Women.'

The interruption jolted me alert. I felt a prickle of panic at the nape of my neck. The professor stopped speaking.

'Pardon?'

I looked around. A hundred eyes were now staring towards my row, wide circles of panic and irritation. I thought for a moment that Marina had spoken, but when I turned towards her, I saw that she was looking back at me.

I realized, with horror, that the voice had been mine.

The room spun. To steady myself I turned my eyes away from Marina and looked forwards. The professor had stopped talking. He was squinting in my direction through his glasses. His eyes flicked from me to Marina, seemingly attempting to establish who, exactly, had interrupted him.

He cleared his throat.

'Pardon?' he said.

In my periphery I saw Marina fix her gaze upon me. My lower lip felt numb. What the hell was I going to say now? Why had I put myself in this situation? I brought my hands together under the table, laced my fingers so tightly that my knuckles ached.

Suddenly another voice piped up. I recognized a cool, affirmative tone.

'They're not lady novelists,' Marina corrected confidently. 'They're women.'

The professor rolled his eyes.

'Marina, if you have an issue, please send an email and copy in—'

'If you've bothered to make us sit through a lecture specifically about quote unquote gender and the novel then surely it's worth explaining some of these terms. Otherwise just stick to the one you've used in the title.'

My toes scrunched in my shoes. I felt excruciatingly hot. The backs of my knees were slick with sweat, my face unstable. Under the damp of my fringe I looked in Marina's direction. She was looking straight ahead, not registering my presence. Her mouth was curled in the very corner: in what almost looked like a smile. She seemed … pleased.

The professor, on the other hand, was uncomfortable. His forehead was a blotchy red. His cheeks were pink and seemed to expand with the silence, pushing the collar of his shirt tight against porcine jowls. Now he scratched them, laughed breathily and said: 'For your information there is an entire section on this in the reading material provided.'

'Then—'

'Marina, for the moment I would like to just get on with it …'

'Well to be honest—'

'*Marina.*'

Another, shorter, silence as the professor jigged from one foot to the other. I glanced around. Other students looked either bored or riveted. They chewed their nails. The professor rustled his papers and continued on a different tack: 'If you'd like to discuss it having *read* the secondary material then there may be an opportunity at a later date. In the *meantime*' – here he leaned a large, flat hand into the lectern – 'I would like to just get on with it. And if anyone else has a similar issue, please wait until the end to raise it with me.'

***

That's when it started, I think. That was the first time that I became aware of it happening: my body folding in on itself, the hardened core at the centre of my identity dissolving and becoming replaced by something else … something corruptible and soft; unfamiliar. Until that lecture I hadn't been aware of it, but I'd always had a fear of being found out. To some extent I still have it. It is not just that I am worried that someone will discover an unpleasant secret of mine and reveal it to the world. It's more specific than that. It is, I suppose, a fear which stems from me. It's a sense that I'm not completely in control of my own actions; that, by accident or otherwise, I will be the principal agent in my own downfall. When I'm not paying attention, drawing a tight restrictive circle around myself, I'll say something tactless or do something stupid, which will reveal my true nature as incompetent. Or evil.

I think again about the headlines in recent days – the torrid accusations, the glimpses of my face, the glimpses of my name. All of it makes me question myself. I am worried about what they are saying. I am worried about how they are depicting me. I am worried about whether that representation will cause me to lose sight of who I am again, that it will make me do something that I don't understand.

***

It was that moment in the lecture when my self-doubt began to set in, I'm sure of it. Before then I had always thought of myself as someone reserved and watchful. I was a person with control over their inner thoughts and emotions. Though my silence unnerved people around me, I had always felt bolstered by it.

But because of that lecture slippage, I felt that my sense of self-preservation was gone. I had acted so out of character, and with such potentially humiliating consequences, that I couldn't understand what sort of person I was anymore.

I scared myself.

v.

I was relieved when the lecture ended. My stomach hurt, the skin between my fingers was clammy. I no longer had any desire to talk to Marina. All I wanted was to leave. I gathered up my things, packed them into my bag and walked down the stairs out of the lecture hall. I went towards the toilets. There was an unused disabled one around the corner which I knew was always empty. I would be able to collect myself there.

I stood at the sink and splashed my cheeks with cold water. It hit my skin and fell back into the basin, leaving reddish marks. I dabbed at them with the edges of my sleeve. Then I turned to the mirror and studied my profile. My immediate reaction was one of embarrassment: how *contrived* I looked. Since I had arrived at university I'd made a conscious effort to wear more make-up every day: a mask to accompany my new identity. But now, in the shallow light of the bathroom, it was patently obvious how ridiculous it looked. The dark, sweaty sheen of foundation drooped around my jawbone; there was an ugly blue smear underneath my eyes. My lips looked bright and my teeth yellow.

In the past I had refrained from wearing lots of make-up, mainly because I thought that my face possessed a sort of masculine quality that meant I couldn't decorate it without it looking try-hard. Here I realized it was more than that: the make-up seemed to expose rather than conceal; it brought out every pore, every wrinkle, every hideous bulbous feature. I rolled a piece of hand towel off the dispenser and began to mop away the product. With every wipe, I felt a calm sift through my body. I felt that I was effacing the features, the morning: the memories of the lecture.

The door creaked open behind me and I stiffened. A small, slim silhouette slipped in and approached the sink. She stood next to me, and as she bent forward I saw the curl in the bottom of her hair. I remained still, like she couldn't see me.

For a few minutes we pretended not to recognize each other. We stood in silence, me removing my make-up, she adjusting hers. Then, suddenly, she said: 'Aren't you going to say thank you?'

It was delivered as a statement, not a question. I turned to look at her. She was still staring straight ahead, towards the mirror, so her tiny face was turned to the side. I noted how small her nose was, how her top lip puckered up towards it like a wave.

'Sorry?' I croaked.

Her eyes shot out at me from under a curl of her fringe. They caught the light streaming from the window.

'Fine,' she said, wincing, then looking back at the mirror. 'But next time have some backbone. At least have something to *say*, if you call out the professor like that. It's just embarrassing otherwise.'

Her little hand flicked up and down across her eyelashes, wiggling the brush. I watched the tiny threads of black thicken into clumps, the green crescents behind them darken in the shade. Briefly I wondered why she wore so much make-up, whether she looked the same without it.

There was a silence. To fill it I said, idiotically: 'I'm Eva.'

'Marina.'

I saw myself shift awkwardly in the mirror. There were questions written all over my face. I wanted to ask what she thought of me for interrupting the professor. I wanted to ask how she felt confronting him herself, yelling out in the middle of a lecture. I wanted to ask what her issue was with him. But these seemed like stupid, clumsy things to say at that moment so I changed tack.

'Sorry, I didn't know that you studied this subject.'

'What makes you think that?' she said.

I thought of the way she had looked at me when I first saw her, and the effort of not bringing that up made me flustered.

'Well,' I coughed a little. 'I haven't really seen you here before.'

She groaned. 'It's a long story.'

At this point I was standing diagonally behind her, leaning against the sink. I watched her fingers smudge along the corners of her eyes. The crease along her brow deepened. Her eyes narrowed. Then they turned slowly to look at me.

There was a cool frankness in her expression, as though she

21

were expecting me to ask her something. I sensed that now – now was my chance.

What is it that causes us to confess things to strangers? And why, in a confined, gossipy place like Northam, would Marina tell me of her problems, of her saga with the professor? Sometimes it is possible to establish a certain affinity with someone in a matter of seconds. Something about the way they move or speak or dress seems to offer a glimpse of their underlying personality which – due to some correspondence in our own personalities – invites us to reveal certain things.

Despite my quiet nature, I was not used to extracting confidences from people, and so for a while I assumed that it was a connection of this kind which had caused Marina to speak to me. I thought – foolishly I'm sure – that my lecture outburst had caused her to recognize me as a kindred spirit. She had seen past my nervous exterior to the potentially interesting friend beneath. She had wanted to extract that person. She had wanted to help me come out of my shell.

Now I know the opposite is true. She hadn't wanted that at all. Instead she had seen how much conviction I lacked, and recognized in it an opportunity.

I was someone who, quietly, shared many of her opinions, but had no confidence to contradict her where they diverged. I would be there to bolster her brilliance, that was all, a sickly weed next to a burgeoning flower, and by feeding off my energy she would emerge more beautiful, more charismatic. Without allowing me to realize it, she would steal all of my secret characteristics, all my good arguments and ideas. She would scrape them away and use them for herself, leaving me as an empty, silent husk – someone with no voice and no personality.

***

I stood there silently, studying her eyes and mouth and cheeks. There was another silence as she bent forward and pulled another eye pencil out of her pocket. I thought about the structure of bones under her face.

Then: 'I have a long time,' I offered.

She looked back at me in the mirror, squinting with suspicion. She rubbed the pencil along the insides of her under-eyes.

'Well,' she said suddenly. 'It's to do with Montgomery.'

Her fingers continued to move around her face, rubbing the pencil along the tops of her eyelids, smeared the kohl with her fingertips. As she did so, she gave me the background.

Marina had known Professor Montgomery for some time, she said, as a family acquaintance. Her father was an academic too, and they had entertained a rivalry since their university days. She had seen the professor at family parties and symposiums that her father hosted, and he had always seemed pleasant, in a small talk kind of way. Then, when she applied to Northam – originally for languages – she had been offered a scholarship to study the course with English literature. She guessed that the professor had had something to do with it, but that hadn't put her off at the time. It would have been stupid to turn it down. The tuition fees had risen, and besides, 'English is fine.'

But when she arrived she had found the professor insufferable. He was strangely controlling – always asking her to see him in his study, always giving her extra assignments. She felt that he was overfamiliar in his manner, vain about his professional success (constantly name-dropping other academics), and even his arguments were heavy-handed and boring. There was too much historical speculation, she said, and not enough of genuine interest. Those were the exact words that she used: *genuine interest*. As she said them she reached across to grab a piece of towel from the dispenser behind me.

A few weeks into term, she'd stopped going to English lectures altogether. She asked the board to switch to languages full-time.

But the scholarship was contingent on her taking English as well, and so she had had to go to the professor directly to ask for permission. Having reviewed her attendance record, the professor was now waging a 'petty' war against her – neither allowing her to return to his course, nor to keep her scholarship only doing languages. Marina shook her head. It was just politics, she said, a way for him to exert power over her, and so to spite him, she was going to the lectures and seminars until she got her way. She said that she hated how nepotistic the place was, and how everyone in the humanities department pandered to the professor. She hated especially how one *eminent academic* – here she put her fingers in quotation marks – could have a monopoly like that in the twenty-first century.

'Anyway, that's the long and short of it,' she said, making a grimace. 'Unbelievably tedious.'

I wasn't sure whether that description was supposed to refer to the story, the people in it, or her take on the situation. Whichever it was, it didn't apply to her. She was a fantastic speaker: vivacious and precise. I wondered where she had learned to speak like this, so confidently and unapologetically.

'How many languages do you know?' I asked, somewhat out of the blue.

'Enough to get by.'

'French?'

No reply.

'What about like … Russian, Chinese?'

She nodded primly. I couldn't tell whether or not she was lying. Either she was a selfeffacing genius or a narcissistic fantasist – and whichever it was, I felt unable to ask more questions.

There was another lull in the conversation. I stood there awkwardly and began to run imaginary sentences through my head.

Suddenly Marina said: 'What are you doing this evening?'

The question had come out of nowhere. It was unclear whether it was a leading conversation or a piece of small talk.

'Nothing,' I managed.

'There's a house party down the road I'm going to.'

A prickle of anticipation shot through me.

'Maybe you should come,' she added.

The conversation was too perfect, surreally perfect, and it made me, for a moment, feel detached from myself. It was like I was watching a film of my life rather than participating in it. I tried to act accordingly: keep my face stable, not too eager.

'Sure.'

I passed my phone across to her. My hand was shaking slightly. As she bent her head forward, I looked at her roots. Natural blonde. I studied the small translucent curls along the top of her crown, admired the way they framed her forehead.

She said would add me on Facebook and message the details later. Then she smiled, drew her bag over her shoulder and left.

I remember clearly how I felt once she had gone. Everything seemed to be in sharper focus. I looked at myself in the mirror again and this time my appearance had changed: my features were more pronounced, my face slimmer. My eyes had an interesting bright spark in them.

I walked back to my room dopily, registering details I hadn't seen before – the way the grey clouds sloped into the horizon beyond the buildings. The way the silver willows curved into the lake, the way their thin branches dragged in the water. It was a beautiful campus, in its own way, I decided. The buildings had all been painted an unimaginative shade of brown, yes – and, yes, they were boringly arranged: a long rigid line of rectangles, like a queue for something that would never arrive. Demolition, for example. It was not exactly inspiring, and yet looking at it then I thought it had a pleasing symmetry and simplicity. Perhaps

Northam offered a new opportunity after all. Perhaps I was on the cusp of something exciting.

In my room I looked at the small damp bed, the desk beside it. The clock read 3.51. I suspected that the party would start at around nine, which meant I should arrive at around ten, and that meant I now had a maximum of five hours to compose myself. I would just peek at Facebook, I told myself, and then shower and decide what to wear.

I lifted the lid of my laptop. Just a few minutes.

Two minutes later I looked at the clock and saw that it was now eight in the evening. I refreshed my Facebook page. There was still no message from Marina; no friend request, nothing. I paused.

I wondered whether she had forgotten, whether she had even been sincere in the first place. Maybe it was for the best, I reasoned. What kind of person invites someone to a party after meeting them in a toilet anyway? My mother would have a field day.

At the thought of my mother, I felt a wave of rebellious energy. I bit the bullet and sent Marina a friend request.

The minutes ticked by. I waited for her to accept. Nothing.

So I began to draft an accompanying message. Even in the first sentence I was aware of how weird I sounded: '*I'm Eva, the girl from the toilet earlier ...*' – it was difficult for me to carry on past that. Everything I wrote either sounded too eager and blunt: '*so is there a party going on tonight???*', or falsely casual: '*what's the deal with the ...*' I typed them out over and over again, deleting, redrafting and then eventually settling for the first thing I had written. I added in extra details, such as where I was living, where we could meet and what I could bring. I cringed at how long it was but forced myself to hit send anyway.

Ten minutes crawled by and no response came.

Now it was quarter to ten. I walked to the campus corner shop and bought a bottle of wine. It was one of those cheap bottles with a screw cap, a label depicting a pastel cartoon of some berries, and garish Italian font scrawled all over it in an unsuccessful attempt to make it look drinkable. I thought about guzzling it down right there in the middle of the pavement, just to get it over with. But before I could wrench off the lid, my phone vibrated in my pocket. Marina's name flashed across the screen.

yeah there now
58 st clements

Was that supposed to be an invitation?

I hovered in the lamplight. I thought about going back to my room. Then I thought: fuck it. I unscrewed the cap of the wine, took a large swig, and began walking towards St Clements before I had time to think about turning around.

***

Someone is watching me.

He is sat a few tables away, beside the bookcase marked T-V. It is dusky over there, there is not much light. But I can still see his eyes staring out at me from the darkness.

At first I wasn't entirely sure that it was me that he was watching. I thought that I was imagining it, or perhaps that he was looking at the clock behind me – but now it has become impossible to think otherwise. Every time I look up, his eyes burn into mine. I can feel them settle on me again when I look down. Now he is actually grinning: a slash of yellow teeth, like a slice of lemon. I can see him getting up. He packs his books into a satchel. He begins walking towards me. I feel panic. My hands grab at the stack of newspapers and clasp them into to my chest.

'Hello,' he says, approaching my desk. 'Are you all right?'

His voice is calm and low, with the hint of an accent.

'Oi, I asked you a question. Are you all right?'

Slowly I nod.

'You look familiar,' he says. 'Have we met?'

27

A beat goes by – then: no, I tell him. No we don't know each other.

'*Are you sure?*' *he says again.*

No. I've never seen him in my life.

'*Well, are you from around here?*'

I say nothing.

'*You're not, I can tell.*'

I say nothing.

'*Maybe you want to see the local sights. We can go for a drink if you want.*'

Silence.

'*Does that sound nice? Do you maybe fancy going for a drink? Or a coffee?*'

No, I tell him.

'*We could go to the pub. I know a nice place around the corner.*'

No, I'm fine.

*He makes a face, like I've confused or upset him. '*Why were you staring at me if you weren't interested?*'*

I look back at the screen. I wasn't staring at him.

'*Yes you were. Sat over here giving me the eyes.*'

I continue to stare at the screen. The black screensaver descends, the cursor flickers. I hold the mouse and wait for him to go away. He hovers for a few minutes, puts his hands into the pockets of his squeaky leather jacket. I feel a sudden, dreadful certainty he is going to touch me.

But he doesn't.

Instead he sighs, shakes his head, murmurs something and turns away. I hear him walking in the direction of the exit. I wait a long time before turning to look after him.

When I see that he is gone, I pull my sleeves over my knuckles, straighten my neck. I pull my skirt down so that the fabric is no longer rucked up beneath my upper thighs.

Upper thighs. My breathing tightens. I squeeze my eyes shut and try not to think about it.

Henry was about six foot four, with slim, quick features and a head of sharp blonde hair. He wore an expensive long coat, which moved like a blade of grass. I watched it sway gently in the breeze as he leaned against the doorway, frowning at me.

After the long walk to the house party, guided by limited 3G (signal is patchy in the Northam area), I had perched my empty bottle on the garden wall and knocked at the door. Henry had opened it.

He was a composed drunk, but an irritable one, and in any case he was drunk. He looked me over, tightened his jaw. I was struck by its sharp angle. Everything about him was elegant.

Eventually he said: 'Hello?'

'Hello – I'm with Marina,' I stuttered. The wine slurred my words. I wished I could make them sound less apologetic.

Henry didn't respond to this information at first. He looked pensive, as though he were trying to place the name. Then his eyes bloomed into large, black orchids and he nodded.

'Oh right, hi – Henry.' He gestured towards himself. 'She's just over here … She's in the …' He turned his back, and his coat flapped up to expose a glimpse of silky paisley shirt as he walked away.

'I'm E—' I began.

But before I could finish my sentence I was being swept into the hallway. Cigarette smoke drifted into my nostrils and eyes; strobe lights flashed wildly from the room next door; a strange kind of music thudded into my ears along with the ceaseless chatter of the people around me. I swirled through them into the house party.

What struck me first was not the noise or the smell but the number of *people*. The corridor was littered with people, people people people. They were leaning against bannisters, slouching on the ground beneath the window with cigarettes in their

29

drooping hands, jiggling beer bottles while shuffling awkwardly to the music, or dancing madly before suddenly steeling themselves and leaning flat against the wallpaper. I scuttled past – trying to keep Henry in my sights as he sliced ahead of me at an impatient clip – and caught fragments of their conversations. 'So Heidegger, I think actually, let's be honest, when it comes down to it, is maybe not that wrong?'

'Not sure about that mate.'

'No – not crime. It's *grime* and punishment. It's an event I'm running.'

Oh right, I thought, squinting through them for Henry's figure, so it's *this* kind of party. The kind of party where you stood out unless you were wearing pyjama bottoms and some sort of naff glitter on your face; where everyone pretended not to know each other; where everyone talked about politics in a knowing, strident fashion. The sort of party where you could, potentially, disagree with someone without offending them.

I walked past the sitting room, through the hall, past the bathroom, past the coat hooks, down the corridor. When I finally reached the kitchen at the end of it I realized two things: 1) I had now lost Henry. 2) I badly needed a drink.

Drink, as it turned out, was not in short supply. Half-empty bottles were strewn around the counter; screw-top spirits sat on the shelves; cups full of strange, ugly scented liquid tilted precariously on the edges of tables. A suspicious queue for the loo suggested that it was another kind of hit that everyone here was after, so I suspected none of the alcohol would be missed.

Still, I couldn't quite bring myself to steal anything. I somehow felt self-conscious, and – despite the wine fog– weirdly out of place. I knew this was ridiculous. I knew that I looked more stupid and awkward just hovering there, not talking to anyone or drinking anything – but it felt wrong to swan into someone's house and take their stuff. I couldn't just swipe something. What if someone saw? I wanted people to like me. I wanted Marina to like me.

A figure walked past in a long black sequinned jacket, a single black feather dangling from one of his ears. 'Yeah no I think she's in my seminar,' I heard him say. 'Nice girl. Bit easy though.'

There was the safety issue too, I thought. Even in the nightclubs in my hometown, I had always made sure to push a thumb over the lip of my bottle in case it was spiked. Now, in this unfamiliar company, I didn't want to risk my chances. No – I needed to get away from them. All these people. I needed air.

I went through a kitchen side door which led to the outside. It was very dark. I felt the notoriously cold Northam wind pinch at my cheeks, and immediately began to feel better.

I walked around pretending to be looking for something, and eventually wandered to the corner of the courtyard, where wicker chairs were spread out along the lawn and thin people in colourful clothes smoked and talked. They flicked their ash into a water feature and propped their feet on garish plastic toadstools. I took it all in. The garden was surprisingly big, I thought, for a student house. I guessed that it housed around four. I wondered where the residents were.

That was when I heard the familiar sharp voice, now slightly nasal: 'Henry, it's not *true*. And it's not even your opinion, it's some shit you've memorized from *The Spectator*.'

Marina was lying on the grass a few metres away, one leg spread loosely over the other. She was holding a cigarette between a pinched thumb and forefinger. Her hair fanned out over the shoes of the girl sat behind her – a girl who wore a turquoise velvet jumpsuit, who was staring mutely at the garden wall.

Henry was rolling a cigarette between graceful long fingers. At this slight from Marina he frowned.

'Er no, *Vanity Fair*,' he corrected. 'Not that the source is the point. The point is the argument. It's about the way that women bear life – men don't feel the responsibility that women do. They

31

have the freedom to be funny, because the shelf life on sperm is endless. They aren't reminded of the heavy burden of … life all the time.'

Marina snorted. 'Even for you that's terrible.'

'Even for me?'

'Doubtless you're a prime example of the superior male comedian.'

'Doubtless.'

'With your endless sperm and liberated mind.'

'You said it, not me.'

'Honestly, that's the sort of thing that'll be viewed in like two hundred years' time as a twenty-first century curiosity.' She stretched her leg towards him. 'Some bored robot will be scanning through the clickbait archives, then they'll come across that article and think—'

Henry put the cigarette into the corner of his mouth.

'Think what?'

'Millennials,' Marina said drily. 'Something about capitalism.'

She stretched out her leg across the grass, lifted it, and lightly kicked his jaw with the edge of her toe. The cigarette fell. I watched it roll gently across the grass, still burning. There was a lull in conversation.

Henry's eyes tracked slowly from the cigarette to Marina's toe. They tracked up to her ankle; to the blue edge of her skirt that skimmed the front of her calf. They hovered there for a second. Then he stared her in the face, rolled his eyes theatrically. Marina laughed.

The girl behind her stood up, dusted the grass off the velvet of her lap, and walked past me into the house.

I remained in the shadows for a moment, watching Henry and Marina talk. I considered their sharp reclining figures against the pink and yellow glow of the fairy lights.

Theirs wasn't a romantic dynamic, I thought. It was sexual, definitely, but in a way that was kind of performative, which made me think they had never and would never have sex. They flirted artificially, like actors in a film. Or perhaps as though they were operated by a marionette master. Yes that was it: it was like someone was twitching their strings, tweaking fingers to cause jerky head movements at a suspiciously appropriate moment. The right movement and the right comment at the unnaturally perfect time.

'But what do you even *mean* by that exactly?'

Henry's face was lit up by the glow of the moon, and as he turned briefly away from Marina to take a sip from his drink, his lips parted to reveal a set of gleaming trapezium teeth.

Now he said it again: 'But what do you *mean* Marina?'

Hearing his voice, with its insistent, droll intonation, made me reconsider the pair in another light. Henry's voice, specifically, seemed out of kilter with his languid movements. Now I noticed it I realized that everything he said was a bit mannered, like he had rehearsed the words in his head a few times before speaking them. I leaned forward a little, eager to catch the tic.

'Oh for god's sake,' said Marina. 'All I'm saying is you sound like a fucking idiot. Just … stop being so pretentious, it makes me cringe.'

Marina wasn't like that. When I heard her speak I felt that she was doing so impulsively. There was a lightness, an easiness in her voice and mannerisms. She had something that Henry lacked, a kind of authenticity.

As if sensing this observation, at that point Henry's head turned towards me. He narrowed his eyes.

'Oh,' he said. He reached for a Heineken bottle on the grass. 'Mari is this your pal? I meant to bring her over here.'

Marina didn't look up. She was staring at her cigarette.

'Sure,' she said absently.

Henry stared at me with disapproval. He took a long swig from his beer.

'Sorry,' he said, unapologetically. 'Who are you again?'

'I'm ... Eva.'

'Eva Hutchings,' Marina mumbled, and then – as though the name had jogged her back to consciousness, as though she had said it and then realized why she knew it – she looked up. Recognition flashed across her face. 'Oh – you! Hello.'

She rolled over onto her stomach and stretched out a slim arm to pat the grass beside her. Henry said nothing. I edged forwards and sat down obediently.

'Eva ...' she mused. 'Eva from the lecture.'

'Yeah.'

'When did you get here?'

'Just—'

'I suppose you've met Henry.'

I looked across at him, and his eyes moved somewhere behind me.

'Yup,' he said, a new cigarette dangling out of his mouth.

Marina's eyes flicked to Henry and then flicked back to me. In that gesture I recognized something conspiratorial, like a silent code was passing between us. Henry opened his mouth again, but before he could say anything Marina turned to me.

'Hang on – I don't have a drink. Eva, have you – no ... Henry, you know where my vodka is.'

'Er,' Henry said.

'Can you just get it?'

Henry looked at her meaningfully. His features seemed to enlarge and slope down his face, like a melting waxwork.

A silence followed which I found myself eager to fill, but as usual I couldn't think of anything to say. I blinked the smoke out of my eyes. I plucked at the grass.

Finally Henry shrugged. 'Fine,' he said.

He stood up slowly and headed towards the light of the kitchen. I watched his coat billowing behind him. I listened to his footsteps across the grass.

When he was gone, Marina drew a hip flask from the coat lying in front of her, and poured the contents into two used cups. She pushed one into my hand. The liquid was a light grey colour, sort of cloudy, like dishwater. I took a sip, felt it slide into the back of my mouth and then crackle unpleasantly down my throat.

'What *is* that?' I choked.

'Oh don't.' She made a dismissive gesture. 'I'm sorry about him. There's no one else here who will entertain his shit.'

She was talking about Henry, I realized. Perhaps she thought I had said 'who' instead of 'what'.

'Why do you then?' I said. 'Entertain him, I mean.'

My mouth was returning, gradually, to a normal temperature. My tongue curved around the inside of my teeth. It now had a rough texture.

'What?'

'Why do you entertain him? If you don't like Henry, then why do you entertain him?'

She eyed me cautiously, and then took a swig directly from the hip flask. I became dimly aware of someone talking far away from us. There was a squawk from inside the kitchen, the sound of a bottle smashing.

'Henry's an old family friend,' she said with a slight smirk, as though being an 'old family friend' were something unflattering. 'I guess I know everyone else here through him.'

This wasn't exactly an answer, but I was interested to hear what she might reveal about herself: what sort of colour she might add to my mental portrait of her. She spoke for a while about Henry, about how irritating she found him. I remember her saying how he was 'contrived' and that he always recycled other people's opinions. Then she did a very good impression of him talking about gender.

'It's the responsibility women have, to bear *life*,' she said, keeping her neck very straight, whipping her head around with her mouth pulled down at the corners. I laughed a lot, probably more than was appropriate. Furtively, I took a large mouthful of the liquid in my cup.

Marina was *so good* at impersonations. That seems an essential thing about her, now, whenever I think back on those days. She was a very good observer of people. She knew exactly how to capture mannerisms, subtle facial expressions, idiosyncratic modulations of voice and then project them for comic effect. Now I watched her eyes widening, her head shifting to the side and then glaring at me in disbelief, just as Henry had earlier. I took another large mouthful of my drink – too large this time – and choked a little. It was wonderful being in her company.

After finishing the contents of the hip flask, we headed back into the house and the familiar smell of vodka and vomit began to drift into my nostrils. Monotonous beats pulsed in my ears. The people along the corridors were now slouching almost horizontally, long eyelids drooping down their faces. They smiled lazily at us, sometimes they called 'Marina!', but she only responded distantly, dismissively even. She would twitch her mouth into what almost resembled a smile; mouth a word that could have been a 'hello' but might also have been a yawn. She did not stop for any of them. She kept walking forwards, forwards and forwards.

I followed.

We walked past the sitting room, where about fifteen silhouettes were shuffling around under the strobe lights, even less energetically than they had been earlier. Looking at their sloping silhouettes there reminded me, for some reason, of a passage I'd read somewhere about purgatory. We walked past the toilet, for which the queue had diminished. Several people were sprawled outside the doorway, their limbs dragging across the carpet. Peering closer I recognized one of them. It was Henry.

Marina bent forwards and gave him a hard rap on the shoulder. He jolted to consciousness, his grey eyes springing open – and blinking, then, for several seconds, as though readjusting to the scene. When he recognized Marina, he ran a hand through his hair and smiled warily.

'Hey.'

'You've got something of mine,' she said. 'I forgot.'

The smile vanished. 'Mmm?'

'You've got something,' she repeated, sharply this time. 'I need it back.'

She turned to me, frowning.

'Stay here,' she said.

She knelt down next to Henry, then swung his arm over her shoulder, crouched forward and stood up. He bowed over her, and though she was only a slip of a human, slim and ethereal really, in that instant she seemed to me stocky. Very secure. Slowly she began to pivot towards the bathroom door. She leaned him against the frame, bent forward towards the handle and opened it, stepping inside with him.

He protested mildly: 'No, Marina, it's fine. It's fine, I'll get it later. Mari—'

'Shut up.'

They stood together, very close, inside the tiny bathroom. She balanced Henry against the sink, then glanced at me. Briefly I wondered if she cared what I thought of the situation, whether she knew that I'd made the connection, that I'd seen the tiny sachet in his hand. But before I could say anything – before I could examine her expression – she reached forward and slammed the door shut in my face. I heard it lock, and then their conversation became muffled by music.

It was time to go home.

***

I don't know what to make of that memory now. It's troubling to think about. I can recall very clearly the way Marina behaved towards Henry – how aggressively she spoke to him, how aggressively she handled him, how quickly she flipped from lavishing me with attention to not even registering my presence – and I know that it signifies something. But I can't quite put my finger on what. Often memory works like that – you go to it to find a revelation, and it gives you the opposite: confirmation that you are missing something.

vii.

Throughout our months of friendship, the idea that Marina's dalliance with drugs was an addiction didn't cross my mind. It still seems an inappropriate term, and I flinch at it – *addiction*. It just wasn't a word which applied to people our age, and everyone in that group, however wild they seemed, was cushioned by a kind of middle-class assurance that it was a pose. It was, as even our parents called it, *an experimental phase* – a rite of passage, not an act of sincere rebellion. After university we would grow out of it: get serious jobs, get sober (except on weekends) and get on with our lives. But that was the thing about Marina. She really wasn't like us, as far as all that was concerned. She always took things too far.

The next day I awoke with a thick fog in my head. There were tiny red threads along the insides of my eyelids; my mouth contained a strong, acrid flavour and my cheeks had puffed up into two wrinkly, stiff blobs under my eyelids. In short, I had a hangover.

A lecture was scheduled for that afternoon, and I knew without opening my eyes that I wasn't going to get out of bed for it. I also didn't have to open my eyes to know that it was an unseasonably warm day. There was a kind of burning sensation in the room: the air was oppressive and thick, it heaved with sweat and the hot stench of alcoholic breath. I rolled over and plunged my face into the cold pillow, let it rest there for a moment. Then my hand crawled out to the side of the bed. I grasped the phone. I turned my head to the side, put my other hand over a light patch on the glass and noted the time. It was 12 p.m.. I had missed the lecture anyway.

On the plus side, I had several Facebook notifications. Marina had accepted my friend request. She had sent me a short message apologizing for abandoning me the night before. She asked if I might be free later that day:

> i have to get something in town but we cd have brunch after

She wrote just like that: all in lower case, with no punctuation. It always bothered me – still bothers me – how someone so eloquent face-to-face could be so careless in their virtual correspondence. I was the opposite. I liked to observe rather than participate in verbal interactions and then, given a pen or a keyboard, I would write long, adjective-packed sentences which often came across as – yes indeed – contrived or expository. Thus:

> Hi. No, don't worry about it! Sometime this afternoon would work. I'm still in bed at the moment. What time were you thinking?

I hit 'send' without reading over it.

Usually I would review my messages – scan them for spelling mistakes, read them aloud, wonder how the other person would feel receiving them; what they would think about me. I was meticulous. But on this occasion I was too hungover, too lazy and fuggy-headed for it to matter until it had already been sent.

I lay there on the bed with my neck craned to the side, staring at the screen. The little dots wiggled in the corner; then they stopped. I waited for a few seconds for them to start moving again but nothing happened, so to kill time I went onto my profile. I flicked through my photos and wondered whether I came across as cool and aloof or friendless. There was a fine line I knew, and at that point in my life I often thought about it. Another thing I thought about was whether I was more or less narcissistic than other people. For example, was it more vain to fill your Facebook profile with self-promotional statuses and selfies, or to meticulously cultivate it so that you came across as 'unbothered' – like you didn't care about what you looked like? Like you hardly checked Facebook, despite the fact that actually you rarely did anything else?

My own profile offered no reassuring answers, so I looked at Marina's for comparison. She had barely commented on any of her posts, and her photos were all uploaded by other people. I flicked through them back to 2010. In each one she was either alone, or looking away from the camera; away from the people around her. This seemed to confirm something I had suspected already, but on recognizing it I felt somehow dissatisfied. If she was always this antisocial, why did she attract so many people? Where did they come from? Also, why hadn't she been more embarrassing at school?

A notification popped up in the corner of the screen. It was a message from Marina. I felt a jolt – like she had somehow intuited that I was stalking her photos. But in fact she had sent me her number and a confirmation of the meeting time:

yeah like 3

Strange time for 'brunch', I thought. I glanced at the clock on the screen. It was now 1.15. I tossed the phone aside and buried myself in the pillow. I counted to four. In, out. In, out.

Silently I willed myself to get up. I pushed my head further into the pillow and then – after a beat – brought my palms up underneath my shoulders and lifted myself into a cat pose. Not too bad.

Another second went by and then I forced my body to move forwards and upwards. I watched my arms stretch out underneath me, mysteriously strong and agile, my legs crouched and straightened, and while performing those movements I suddenly felt as though I were watching someone else, as though my constituent body parts were acting separately to me. My hands picked up a towel and I wrapped myself in it. It felt alien, but cold and nice against my skin. My fingers reached out to the door handle, grabbed the grainy metal – that, too, seemed peculiar. Then my back was straightening and my feet were padding across the corridor towards the shower. This was a shower that I shared with six other people – one of whom now came out of his room, waved at me and made an arch comment about my scanty state of dress. I pretended not to see him.

In the shower cubicle, I took off the towel and stepped towards the spray. The water fell out in thin, tepid drips. I stuck my tongue into the stream. It was slimy, tasted faintly of sulphur. I dunked in my face, then my whole body. I began to feel alert.

At three o'clock, I met Marina for lunch in a small café in town. She was sat on one of the outside tables, wearing a grey fur coat and holding a large plastic water bottle. There was a bag at her feet with folders poking out of it. As I approached the table she tucked her phone into the bag, then leaned forward and waved towards me. Her eyes were smudged but her lipstick was carefully applied, and when she smiled her mouth opened fully. It reminded me of a crab emerging from its shell.

'I'm exhausted,' she said. 'I haven't slept.'

I replied: 'Me neither,' though it was obviously a lie.

'I'm sorry about last night anyway, Henry wanted to talk about something and I was stuck in that bathroom for ages.'

I made a swift comment about not even realizing she'd gone

– also a lie, but easier to stick to than 'me neither'. I was relieved she hadn't chased up my 'me neither'. Instead she gave me a grateful smile and then we started talking about Northam.

The meeting went well. Very well, in fact. It quickly emerged that we thought along similar lines, and that we were finding the experience of university similarly disagreeable. We both railed about the idiotic structure of the course, the boorishness of other people in our class, the anticlimax of Northam in general. She, like me, had expected it to be more liberating. She said that she had turned down an opportunity to work on a film set with a family friend in order to come here. She said that she had wanted to be educated before getting a job – she had wanted to revel in the 'experience for its own sake'. But now, confronted with the reality, she had started to regret the decision to come to Northam at all.

'I mean this is an *institution*, not an academy,' she said. 'It's full of people who view education as just a stepping stone. Look at the way the course is set up. Look at how closely the careers department is intertwined with everything the academic department does. Look at the way we're instructed – I don't know – to do group presentations so we can put 'teamwork' on our CVs. It's depressing. Sometimes that alone is enough to make me want to drop out.'

I couldn't say much to that. I tepidly responded with a counter-question.

'But overall, it's not quite …'

The corner of her mouth lifted. 'What?'

'You're not going to drop out.'

'No. I've thought about it … No.'

She looked around then, grabbed an ashtray from the table next to us and drew a packet of cigarettes from her bag, then put one in her mouth. I looked at the way it balanced there while she lit it. I thought about the passage of the smoke drifting past her lips, down her throat and into her lungs.

Then she looked up and saw me staring at her.

'Would you like one?' she asked.

'Oh.' I looked down at my hands. 'No thanks, I don't smoke.'

'Suit yourself.'

Later on Marina would often chastise me for being 'repressed' – but I always knew she enjoyed the fact that I wasn't like her. Even that gesture of refusing the cigarette had seemed to satisfy her, like I'd confirmed a judgement that she held against me. Where Marina was fun, I was reserved. Where she was cavalier, I was cautious. Where she was given to making grand statements, I offered a mumbling appraisal of both sides before ultimately agreeing with her. I think that's how it looked, at least.

Smoke continued to drift around us, gradually travelling outwards to the surrounding tables where families were sat with their prams and soft drinks. A group of young women on the adjacent table were tucking into a roast. When Marina saw them, she lounged sideways and dangled her arm over the back of the chair. I sat with my hands in the middle of my lap, one foot pressed hard on top of the other under the table.

About five minutes into our conversation, the waiter came over and asked if Marina would put out her cigarette. It was clear from the first few words what he was going to say, but she only stared at him innocently, and continued to smoke until he'd finished giving a full explanation. There were people eating nearby, he said (his eyebrows raised, his hands rubbing anxiously against one another) – yes, there were people eating nearby and her smoke was unpleasant for them. He was awfully sorry, really he was, but would she mind … would she mind just while they had their meals? Otherwise there were tables further away.

Marina held his gaze. She sucked for a few seconds, raised her fingers to the stalk and finally plucked it from her mouth.

'Of course,' she said, exhaling a long plume.

Then she stubbed it in the ashtray in front of him.

It was like something from a film. I started to laugh quietly, discreetly, in a way that I hoped would show Marina I found her funny without offending the waiter.

It didn't work. When I looked up I saw that the waiter was glaring at me. His look was so hostile – so accusing – that my apologetic reflexes kicked in and unthinkingly I blurted: 'I'm sorry.'

He shook his head and walked away.

Marina laughed at that.

'What did you do that for?' she said.

'Sorry?'

'It doesn't say no smoking.'

'Oh. Yeah. Sorry.'

'Don't apologize,' she said. 'Definitely don't apologize for *me*.'

Over the next few weeks we began to see each other more and more. We met for breaks outside the library, where I would stand with her as she smoked and talked, usually about the other people in our class. We sat together in seminars. We sat together in lectures. Then we started to cut lectures and just go to seminars instead. Then we started to skip the PhD-taught seminars – going to just one a week, the one led by the professor – and discussed the set books on our own.

Marina had some pretty weird ideas about literature. She thought that everything had a central meaning, and that you could pinpoint the 'message' of a novel or a play according to the intentions of the main character. Helpfully, she said, quite often the main character was a stand-in for the author. Thus *King Lear* was 'about Shakespeare's fear of early-onset dementia'; *Anna Karenina* was about 'Tolstoy's commitment issues' etc. I never quite knew what she was on about, or whether she was actually joking, but she was entertaining to listen to nonetheless.

After the library Marina would often come to my room. Initially I lamented that I hadn't put up posters or photos to make my life look interesting. But she seemed to like the fact that

I was so anonymous, like a blank slate that she could draw all over. We would drink two or three bottles of wine there throughout the afternoon, and then head out to a party at one of her second year friends' houses.

I say 'friends'. The truth is that I never had meaningful conversations with any of them, and from what I recall Marina rarely spoke to them either. We'd spend a lot of time at parties at the fringes of conversation, smoking by ourselves, nudging each other, exchanging subtle looks. She didn't really engage with other people – not fully. Even when she was at the centre of a big group, Marina seemed to be separate, superior, floating above everyone else – like a performer in a play. And, like a haughty actress, she regularly grew impatient with her fans.

'Who's that?' I asked once, having seen her ignore a wave from a guy in Henry's house.

'Ugh, Robin,' she said. 'Henry's housemate. He's a dick. I can't be bothered to do the stop-and-chat.'

Hearing her rebuff other people like this could have made me paranoid, but in fact, predictably, it had the opposite effect. It made me pleased. It struck me that for all her online popularity, for all her apparent charm and attractiveness, I was the only person who she ever really wanted to hang around with on a regular basis. When she was not with me, she was alone.

I liked that about her.

***

The librarian gives me an odd look. I have been in here for too long. Perhaps I am acting strangely, perhaps my face looks strained, perhaps I am making peculiar subconscious noises. Or maybe she knows. Maybe she recognizes me.

I pick at the skin between my fingers, watch the dry flakes break off and scatter onto the desk. It is already starting to get dark outside. I can see the tree swaying outside, the branches swooping forward to tap against the glass. They look and sound like fingers. I turn back to the desk. I flip over the newspaper so that the picture is hidden.

I don't want to see her anymore. I don't want to be near her.

CHAPTER TWO

Early November

i.

One day Marina decided that we would go to the beach. It was at this point early November – the sky was grey, a thick seasonal mist had settled over the campus, and the temperature was dipping to zero. I couldn't imagine that a seaside outing was going to be especially pleasant. But true to form I didn't bring this up, and my opinion wouldn't have mattered. Marina said that she wanted to see the sea. She said that she was going to hire a car so that we could drive there.

I thought this was a lavish investment, considering we could just take the train, but I kept my mouth shut.

'I know it seems unnecessary,' said Marina, 'but I like to drive.'

Marina was like that: if she wanted to do something a certain way, then she would do it irrespective of the practicalities or cost. I learned not to ask questions about her spending.

We went to a hire shop. The man behind the desk wore a name badge which said on it 'Graham'. He called us both 'Madam' – this was very funny – and asked Marina which model she would like to take out.

Marina surveyed the selection of cars. After a while she settled for a convertible.

'Oh?' said Graham with surprise. Then he composed himself: 'Certainly, Madam.'

Once we were strapped in, Marina turned up the music to 'very loud' and careered off down the road. The soundtrack of choice was early noughties R&B – she particularly liked Kelis and Khia – and I felt that there was a strange disconnect between the sinuous country roads, so English and so wholesome, and the thumping American lyrics coming out of the speakers. Marina seemed to enjoy this. When we reached a red traffic light, I remember her winding down the window and mouthing to the male driver next to us: 'Lick it now, lick it good.' He turned and tipped his flat cap at us.

Soon the clouds lifted and, against expectation, cool sunshine appeared in short misty bursts. Marina took this as sufficient encouragement to put the roof down, so roughly half an hour into our journey she swung the wheel and pulled into a layby. I remember her tiny green eyes darting to the rear-view mirror, her hands sliding over the plastic of the gearstick, a slim finger pushing the button below the radio control. The roof lifted up, tilted forwards and began to roll back.

'So you're from Walford,' she said, as a fresh bout of wind blasted us across the cheeks. 'What's that like?'

It was the first time she'd asked me anything about my background and I struggled to find an answer. What was *Walford* like? My small, provincial town with the river running through the centre, with its functional concrete bridges, with its dusty Victorian buildings and neon supermarkets, with its tragic pubs? I thought of tweed and suede, rubber wellingtons. I thought of my mother's voice, reproachfully correcting me: '*Actually*, Walford museum has the oldest cauldron collection in England.' And I paused to think of something clever to say – some witty riff on this, some funny description to impress her – but there was really no way to spruce up Walford.

'Dull,' I said.

Marina laughed. 'What's the school in Walford – there's that posh one.'

'Wolsingham.'

'Yes! Wolsingham Girls! Is that where you went?'

I dug my fingers into my seatbelt. I didn't want to tell her about the homeschooling. And I worried that if I told her where I'd really gone to school afterwards Marina might know someone who would tell her that I had. So I said: 'Yes.'

'Oh,' she said. 'So wait, hang on, you must know the Dukes?'

'Mmm.'

'What do you mean mm? They would have been … Like the year above you, maybe two years above. You must know Matilda.'

'Oh. Yeah. I know of her.'

I had heard of Matilda Duke. Her family owned a large estate nearby – somewhere west of Durham – and in the early noughties the BBC had made a documentary about how her father, Bart, made money to maintain it. Bart was posh and swore a lot, which was considered hilarious, and I knew that he was thought of as a 'prize guest' on the Walford dinner party circuit. But I knew little about Matilda. She was at another school, so I'd never met her. I doubt she would have spoken to me anyway.

'She's actually surprisingly nice,' Marina was saying. 'I mean, her voice is annoying but once you get past that she has some great anecdotal material. She's always been pretty … experimental.'

Marina went on to talk about how she knew the Dukes through her stepmother – they were related in some obscure way – and then went on to dissect Matilda's personality without pausing for a response from me. I let go of my seatbelt, relaxed my shoulders.

'She's not actually as quote unquote *wild* as people think she is. She has few inhibitions in some ways but seems pretty prudish when you hear her talking about other people ...'

Five minutes later she had come full circle and was talking about Matilda's voice again.

'It sounds like she's eating a peach,' Marina said. 'Uverrything she shaysh is like she's trying to keep the shaliva in her mouth.' She turned and pointed at me, waiting for me to pick up the impression.

'It would almost be Sean Connery,' I said. 'Except there's too much plum in there. It's more like ...'

'You don't have to be *posh* to be privileged.'

'Joanna Lumley,' I said.

'Very good ... Hey, I wonder if she's still doing those adverts.'

I settled back into my seat. The conversation was over: I had dodged the bullet. And I was right to relax: Marina never asked about Walford again.

We reached the beach and found a parking spot at the top of the hill. It was a tight space, so I got out while Marina parked. Then she climbed out and, without putting the roof back on, pressed a button on the keys to lock the car. The lights flashed twice: *beep beep.*

I stared at her. 'Aren't you ...?'

She turned to me defiantly.

'Aren't I what?'

'Aren't you worried someone might ... I don't know, steal it?'

'What are you talking about?'

'The car. We should probably put the roof up.' I paused. 'Shouldn't we?'

Marina waved her hand dismissively – a swift, sharp movement, like she was swatting a fly.

'Eva, this isn't Walford,' she said sarcastically. 'Crime levels aren't nearly as high here.'

Not for the first time, I felt ashamed of my provincial background; of my unworldliness, of my ultra-cautious temperament.

I was so neurotic. Also I was freezing from the journey. I pulled the collar of my coat tighter around my chin.

'OK,' I said.

Marina laughed. 'Come on,' she tugged my arm. 'It's going to be fun.'

It was fun. We drank beer and made sandcastles. We bought a disposable barbecue and piled it with meat, and bananas stuffed with chunks of Mars bar. I dug my toes into the wet sand, and through mouthfuls of charred chicken leg, asked Marina questions about her life before Northam. She spoke about feeling deprived of a 'Generic Family Experience', because her parents were divorced; because her mother had died when she was young. She spoke about her father experimenting with Buddhist philosophy, about how his investments had somehow benefited from the financial crash, about the 'laughable' attempts at poetry she had published in her teens. I pulled my coat fiercely around my neck. I drank a lot of beer. Marina drank a lot too, and I didn't try to stop her.

It was getting late, and we were both quite drunk, when Marina slid off her coat and said that she was going to swim. She started to take off her other clothes. Then she ran into the sea. I didn't join her because it was freezing, plus I felt a little self-conscious about a birthmark on my upper thigh. But I watched her, and I noticed everything. Marina's skin was smooth and pale. Her underwear had a zigzag stripe. I studied her as she sprinted into the surf.

I remember, now, sensing a slow spread of anxiety as her silhouette charged into the high grey waves. The long slow curls sweeping across her back. Her small, fragile shoulders flinching as the cold water smacked against her stomach. The waves rising and falling, crashing onto her head, flattening her hair dark against her scalp. She seemed so vulnerable. She disguised it well – she did not scream – but I could see that she was fragile out there.

51

Later she emerged from the water, wrapped a towel around herself and sat beside me on the sand. 'Pussy,' she said. 'It's not even that cold.'

In the moonlight, the tiny golden hairs on her stomach stood straight, and there were goose pimples along her arms. She was shivering.

When we returned to the car it was raining. The seats were soaked through. The gearstick was slick with black raindrops.

'Fuck,' said Marina, expressionlessly. 'That's a shame.'

I said nothing.

We laid our coats over the seats and got inside. As soon as we sat down I could feel damp seep through to my underwear and so to distract myself, I smoked a spliff with the window slightly open. We drove home in a drunk daze. Marina was actually better at driving when drunk, or maybe it just seemed that way because I felt more relaxed. I really did. I was cold and wet and shivering, but I was also unusually happy.

Marina looked at me sceptically.

'You're quiet,' she said. There was a note of accusation in her voice.

I told her my clothes were wet – that I was cold.

'You can shower at my house,' said Marina. 'I'll lend you some clothes.'

The following morning Marina returned the car, alone, and I forgot to ask about Graham and the rain damage. I still don't know how much she had to pay for it.

ii.

There were a lot of things I forgot to ask Marina, now I think about it. The questions I did put to her were always beside the point somehow – too vague or too specific to elucidate what she was ever really thinking. I wish I'd fastened onto some of the other leads instead. I wish I'd asked where she was on certain days; how certain things made her feel. But there's no use in regretting all that. I don't know how much I can trust of what she told me anyway.

The conversational pattern of our friendship was this: I asked her questions about herself; she asked me questions about grand ideas. I'd say: 'What was your mother like?' and she'd reply, e.g.: 'Do you think that life is a simulation?' I got the impression that she only ever asked me questions so that she could answer them herself. If I gave a response that she disagreed with, which was rare, she'd brush it off and complain that I didn't understand. She'd say that I didn't 'speak her language'.

Marina was opinionated. Her thoughts were hard-boiled, polished facts with no room for negotiation. I, on the other hand, had only a clutch of half-baked conclusions. I understood ideas, but I had no clue about how to settle on one at any given time – how you might say that something was *more true* than something else and actually mean it. My thoughts lay in my head in a series of unconnected fragments – like shattered glass – and I couldn't piece them together to see what the original construction had looked like.

Sometimes I pretended this disconnect didn't matter, but I knew it did. I didn't want relativism. I wanted to find a definitive interpretation for everything.

When it came to writing my own essays, my conclusions would always say something admiring about the 'unreadability of the text', as though being confusing were a badge of literary merit. I would explain various theories and then wind up making a non-committal comment like: 'Milton holds up a mirror to the reader'. I knew this was probably a cop out, the verbal equivalent of knowingly tapping the side of my nose – but expressing my ignorance was the closest I could come to saying something true.

Once I asked Marina what she thought of that line about Milton.

'Unhelpful,' she said. 'Irresponsible, in fact.'

I agreed that it would be better to think of an actual argument – but what?

'*Paradise Lost* is about someone struggling to come to terms with their sexuality in an oppressively homophobic environment,' she added bluntly. 'Lucifer rejects the heteronormative values pressed upon him by society – aka God, embodied by Adam and Eve – and is subsequently dealt the punishment of expulsion. He has to go and face his demons.'

'Literally demons,' I said.

'Then he starts complaining about the decor of hell and saying stuff like: "Better to reign in hell than serve in heaven." It's obvious – high camp. Put that.'

Her argument was always a bit off, but I found her conviction refreshing. The fact that she had so much confidence meant she could speak freely about any number of topics. She didn't get tangled up in questions of political correctness or historical accuracy, as I did – she just charged on. And even if I wasn't always sure that what she said was appropriate, or (when you unpacked it) made sense, there was something comforting about being close to someone who scoffed at the very notion of self-doubt. It made me believe that I, too, would one day have an opinion about something.

Looking back now, I think it was this self-conviction which caused Marina to be disliked by other people at Northam. There was something cold and uncompromising about her. It put them off, especially other girls.

Did Marina notice this? I think so. Did she mind? Unclear. She had a way of speaking to people that indicated she found them tedious, yes – but at the same time she always seemed to be seeking them out. When we went out to clubs or bars, she would always make some excuse to introduce herself to strangers. She would saunter over and ask for a lighter, or hang next to them with a sultry, bored expression on her face, waiting for a moment to sarcastically chip into their conversations.

I was so convinced by her self-confidence back then that I didn't consider that this might be a sign of loneliness. In fact, I interpreted it as a personal insult. Her behaviour made me suspicious, paranoid even, like she was looking for an opportunity to get away from me.

iii.

I can't keep putting it off.

The way I've written everything here, it makes it seem as though Marina dominated my first term at Northam. It is true that my memory of that time, like so many other things, is now clogged up with thoughts of her. I find it hard to picture any events where she wasn't there – I can't even clearly remember the moments where I was alone. But the truth is that there is another side to it. There were other things that happened. The other events, the events with the professor ... I should address those.

In my initial glimpse of Marina with the professor, I'd recognized for the first time that there was something stagey about him. It wasn't that he was lecherous exactly, but his authoritative persona, as someone who knew everything and whose self-confidence was unshakeable, struck me as unconvincing. I had seen him once without the mask on. Now, in the times I'd seen him since, it always seemed like he was trying to prove himself, like he was attempting to perform a part that he wasn't at all suited to. Many people were like that at Northam – but the professor was the worst offender.

Or the second worst.

When I walked around campus, I'd sometimes see the professor with Henry. Their heads would be buried together in conversation in the café, locking eyes, nodding seriously. At other times they would exchange papers at the end of a lecture in an underhand fashion – Henry would slip the sheets sideways onto the lectern and give a perfunctory nod. It was like he thought he was on a mission for MI5 and not at 'Renaissance Rhetoric' in northern England. Once, when our first year seminar overran by ten minutes, Henry opened the door without knocking and ducked his head in. He looked panicked when he saw his mistake, muttering: 'Wrong room.' But I saw him go back in afterwards, when he thought no one could see him.

I heard from Marina that Henry was getting a head start on his dissertation. This was the cause of their clandestine meetings, she explained. She said that he was seeking advice from the professor about which areas of research might propel his chances of getting into Cambridge or Yale for a PhD. Early tuition was frowned upon, and since he was only a second year, it made sense for them to keep it hushed up.

'To be honest though I don't know why Henry bothers,' Marina said to me. 'It's not that big a deal what kind of work you do anyway. References are what really matter. Professor Montgomery will pull strings to get him where he wants to go.'

This I found hard to believe. Then I remembered Marina's scholarship.

The professor's favouritism made me uncomfortable. I didn't like the way Marina spoke about it either: she simultaneously criticized the 'nepotistic structures' of university, but was clearly complicit in it, in the fact she wanted to keep her scholarship. It hurt my head to think about this, so I tried not to.

Instead I deflected my dissatisfaction onto Henry and the professor. Conspiracy theories about them raced through my mind. One day I put one of them to Marina.

'Do you think …?'

'Do I think what?'

'Henry and Montgomery …' I said. I waggled my eyebrows, attempting to appear breezy and flippant.

'Nah,' Marina retorted, somewhat irritably. 'For one thing, he's definitely into girls.'

'Who, Henry?'

'God knows about him.'

'Then Montgomery?'

'Yes,' she said. 'He's got a wife but ... to be honest, there are always other women. He was always accompanied by a "friend" to events, even when I was a kid. There would always be something dangling off his arm.'

This seemed to me so unlikely that I recoiled.

'Ew,' I said. 'Who would ... where did he even find them?'

'Everywhere,' she said.

'But where?'

'*Everywhere*, Eva. That's how it *works*. He just ... some people are like that. Women get desperate when they're older.'

'Does his wife know?'

'No idea.'

I would try to push the conversation a little further then, try to dig a little bit more about the circumstances in which Marina and Montgomery knew each other, what he'd been like at those parties and out of office hours, but she would never dwell on the topic for long. It was fair, I guess, because I was so needy in my questioning.

'You absorb too much popular culture,' Marina said to me once. 'That's your problem. You see a story in everything. You've got so much wasted mental energy. Life isn't a novel, *Eva*. We're not in *The Secret* fucking *History*.'

This made me laugh so much that I started choking.

CHAPTER THREE

November 2013

i.

It was about halfway through the term when Marina managed to switch back to English. This seismic shift was mentioned to me suddenly, almost as an aside – in such a way that I didn't spend much time investigating the causes. That seems funny to me now. From what I remember, the solution appeared to have had something to do with Charlton. Charlton was a prestigious 'college' in the US where her father worked in some vague over-seeing capacity. She had written to the administrators there explaining her situation, and they had – allegedly – offered her the opportunity to transfer. Once Northam got wind of it, they had mysteriously done a U-turn, throwing the professor's counterarguments out the window.

The professor no longer objected to Marina's presence in the room. He didn't huff and puff or send her away when we came to his seminar. He didn't even send her to the back of the room. Instead he largely ignored her. Fortunately for me, we were even allowed to sit side-by-side, as we were now, listening to him talk.

'I hope you've all brought the Oxford edition as instructed,' he said tartly. 'The Cambridge edition is, frankly, an insult to academic publishing and a detriment to Marlowe's legacy. As if it's not enough that he died in a pointless duel. Four hundred years later he also has *amateurs* butchering the text.'

After smiling indulgently at his own joke, the professor walked over to the blind and pulled it up swiftly. A striped rectangle of light fell over his face. I watched it diminish, gradually, as he walked back to his armchair and sat down again. The leather squeaked under his tweed.

'Turn to Act III.'

I often thought that the professor's office looked like a cartoon version of the real thing. Bookshelves full of dusty tomes lined every wall. Armchairs hunched around a well-worn coffee table; old paperweights and stacks of crinkled A4 covered every surface. Apart from a flattened laptop in the corner – which honestly looked like a prop – there was no modern technology in there, and the lighting was so dim that it was hard to see the letters on a page. Surely this atmosphere couldn't espouse anything productive? Surely he couldn't be reading all those books and writing all those papers in here on his own? Once Marina joked to me that if you tapped on a book on the shelf, it opened up into a backroom full of strippers and porn films.

Now the professor scratched his inner thigh, shunted his crotch forward in his chair and began to speak. A copy of Marlowe's *Doctor Faustus* lay on his lap.

'Before we begin,' he said, 'it's important to note that the name of the protagonist is for all intents and purposes pronounced *four-stuss*, not fow-stuss.'

Marina and I exchanged glances.

'There is a wealth of evidence to support this, before any of you attempt to disagree,' his eyes flashed in our direction, 'starting with the assonance in the first scene: "the form of Faustus' fortunes good or bad". There is also the spelling in Henslowe's diary: "f-or-s-t-u-s". "Fow-stuss" is a modern corruption dating from Goethe.'

Marina's mouth began to twitch. We had been out the night before – with Henry and his housemate Robin. Marina found Robin hard to deal with because he didn't find her funny. She had done a very good impression of the professor – spreading her legs and coughing and hacking – which had made me laugh a lot. Henry had laughed too. He'd even taken a video on his phone, which Marina had told him to delete – but Robin remained stony-faced. At this slight, Marina disappeared, and when she'd returned an hour later she looked completely out of it, muttering angsty hateful things about Henry and the professor and saying that she felt sick. I had taken her home, nursed her, scooped vomit out of her hair and wiped her face with a cool cloth.

'Faustus is not Marlowe's finest play, but it is unquestionably his most celebrated, and most frequently adapted. I'm sure you're all familiar with Wilde's *Dorian Gray*, and ...'

Now Marina was tetchy. When she was hungover she found other people impossibly irritating, and this irritability clouded her judgement. She would interrupt in a trembling shrill voice and make a point that didn't tarry at all with the conversation. Sensing this coming, I felt prematurely annoyed at her.

Marina and I were sat together in the middle of the study, right in the eyeline of the professor. She stank of alcohol sweat. I could see her fringe smeared across her forehead. She was nibbling her thumbs. It was clear that she was waiting for the professor to slip-up, to say something outrageous or unreasonable which she could contradict.

But he carried on, in silky tones: 'Faustus is a highly conflicted character, and it is indeed a highly conflicted play ...'

She was getting agitated, definitely. Lightly I kicked her – a signal of discouragement. She returned it with a scowl.

'Caught between farcical comedy, and the deepest kind of torment: confronting your own mortality. Marlowe's atheism is a much-debated question, of course, after he was *framed* by Thomas Kyd, and it is a much-debated play ...'

Marina had now begun to loudly nibble the corner of her pen. She tapped it against the front of her teeth. A second went past and then, having received no response, she began scratching the nib against the plastic tabletop. It made a light, barely perceptible but nevertheless distracting sound, which caused the professor to stop mid-sentence.

'Marina,' he said.

Marina carried on scratching, her head tilted slightly.

'Marina,' the professor repeated. 'Is there anything you'd like to get off your chest?'

Marina stopped. She lifted her head up and glared at him.

'Well?' he said.

She cleared her throat, paused.

'I was wondering why you were using the A-text,' she said eventually. 'There are two versions of Faustus. Why did you set us the shorter version?'

This was a bit weird, to be fair. The professor stared back at her, a vaguely amused expression on his face.

'I was working around to that,' he shot back. He licked his fingertips and then turned a few pages in his folder. 'The notes pertaining to the A-text are here in front of me. Would you like me to read them now?'

There was an awkward silence.

Marina looked down at her desk. 'No I'm all right, thanks.'

The professor turned back to the class and opened his mouth to speak – but then, at that moment, Marina suddenly let out an enormous, theatrical yawn, an interruption so immature and melodramatic that the professor stopped himself. Everyone else stopped what they were doing too: writing, typing, tapping, texting – and looked up.

The professor looked startled.

'Will you please just—' he began, but before he had time to

finish, Marina had stood up, packed all her things into her bag and abruptly stridden out of the room.

I watched the unwashed wave of blonde hair skittling down her back, her silhouette disappearing into the hallway.

The door slammed behind her.

***

Thinking about this now, I see that I was naive about Marina at that time. Everyone else accepted that there was something seriously wrong with her. There were rumours about her mental health: rumours I wilfully ignored.

When she left the seminar that day, I could sense that people were whispering about her. Some of them shook their heads. They widened their eyes at each other. I hate to think what they might have been saying. But at the time I blocked out my ears, so I can't verify any of it now.

***

The professor's eyes scanned the crowd and then they fell on me.

'Perhaps you should ...'

'Yes,' I said.

I packed up my things and went to the bathroom – the disabled just down the hall. I knew that she'd be in there.

On opening the door just a crack, I saw the damp grey of the walls, the image of her face reflected in the mirror. She looked awful. Disturbingly so. The expression on her face was entirely unfamiliar. I can't describe it properly, even now. There was something haunted, something ghostly about it. There isn't a suitable adjective, it just made her look ... dead.

'What's wrong?' I said.

'Nothing.'

'Then what was that all about?'

'Nothing.'

'Well,' I paused and wondered how best to put the question to her. 'I wonder if you should maybe ...'

'I should what?'

'You can't—'

Her eyes shot towards me. 'I can't what?'

We glared at each other for several moments. The expression on her face had changed – now it was nameable: she looked defensive.

I wanted to say to her: *you can't expect to be the centre of attention all the time. You can't throw a tantrum when you're not given credit that you don't deserve.* But there was something in her look which advised me against it. There was an unspoken regulation in our relationship. I could only speak when she allowed it; when she approved of what I was saying. Although I felt justified, completely *in the right* — I still couldn't bring myself to speak against her. In that moment, that regulation between us seemed more important than anything else.

And so I said nothing. I shrugged, looked at the floor and left the room. I walked back to my accommodation block. Alone.

ii.

When I was in my room I lay in bed and looked at my laptop. While I scrolled through social media feeds, I thought about our conversation. That led me to click on her profile again. I went straight to her photos, put them in a separate tab, and began to flick through. But this time rather than concentrating on how artsy and beautiful she looked, or how many likes each photo had accrued, I noticed her habits of virtual response.

One of the things I'd admired about Marina was that she didn't care about her online status – I loved how she was above it. The way that she ignored her timeline activity but still had loads of tagged pictures, etc, had struck me as classy and aspirational, yes. But there was something else: it fundamentally justified her behaviour towards me. I took her abuse because I accepted that that was who she was. She was mean because she didn't solicit or give approval. From me or to me. From anyone or to anyone. Online or offline.

But now I noticed, looking at her online activity more closely, that there was something she did do regularly. She might not have commented, tagged, or uploaded anything. She might not have liked posts. But she did like comments. She only liked the witty comments, made by people whose profiles – I hovered my mouse over the names – were as stylish and elusive as hers. Far from being detached, her profile was carefully monitored. It was not that she was above being vain – she was just vain about seeming vain.

I closed the lid of my laptop. I went to sleep.

iii.

The next day when Marina apologized, I accepted straight away, and we never spoke about the seminar incident again. We went to the same parties, drank in the same groups, and she even still came to my room from time to time. But it was different after that. My perception of her had changed. My behaviour towards her was less encouraging. And rather than look at her as an equal, I started to watch her from a distance, analytically, like I had watched my friends at school.

Things she said and did struck me as increasingly peculiar. Her relationship with the professor, for example.

Marina's schtick with the professor struck me as odd in a different way to Henry's. Theirs was a power game played without any clear rules or intentions. Why had he offered her a scholarship in the first place? Why had he been toying with her? And why had she been so insistent on studying his subject if she hated him so much anyway? Marina was always irritated when I tried to bring this up, brushing off the issue as tedious.

'It's not something that we have to talk about,' she said once. 'I just hate Montgomery, it's not interesting.'

But the fact that she disliked him so much was exactly what *was* interesting to me. It didn't make sense as to why she was following him around. She hated him – and yet she was making a huge fuss about transferring back to do his course. She'd insisted that we skipped everything except for his seminars. What point had she been trying to prove?

'I wasn't necessarily trying to prove a point,' Marina would say. 'It's just unacceptable that students should be treated like that.'

This would stimulate another rant about the structure of university – how the institution was a nepotistic hotbed, etc – and I would tune out, silently reminding myself not to bring it up again. Marina's complaints about university now came across as spoilt, boring and repetitive. It struck me as embarrassingly lacking in self-awareness to complain about nepotism when she was fighting so hard to maintain a scholarship that her dad had (probably) orchestrated for her. And she didn't deserve the scholarship anyway – she was so careless with money, so careless about work, so careless about everything.

'Look, it's a long story, you wouldn't understand.'

Then there was the issue of exclusivity. As time wore on, and her excuses became increasingly evasive, I began to suspect that there was another reason that Marina was avoiding this subject with me. It was like she didn't want to talk about the professor to me because my knowledge would somehow encroach on her home life. This struck me as a class thing – like I couldn't be trusted with any insider knowledge because I hadn't grown up riding ponies and quaffing Veuve Cliquot in the Home Counties. Because I took things seriously, like work and money, and so did my family.

Sure, Marina's father was a lecturer, but he had a pot of inheritance money which allowed him to make cushy investments. From Marina's anecdotes it seemed like he hardly did anything at all, excepting a few token lectures. Marina, Henry and the professor had their own community – of leisurely jobs and moneyed 'mind-improvement' – and this was not a community to which I was invited. They enjoyed their private political machinations exactly because they were private.

I resented them for it.

iv.

One day, towards the end of November, I was sat in the library working on an essay. There was a deadline at the end of term. I was in the middle of trying to think of a convincing argument – actually, any argument – when I heard Marina speaking.

'Eva.'

I ignored her.

'Eva,' she repeated, tapping on the desk. 'I need your help with something.'

I looked up at her warily. There was that familiar expression: half mischievous; half angry.

'What is it?' I said. The words came out dull and flat, ruder than I'd intended.

'Well,' she said. 'I'll just cut to it, because I'm not sure if we have much time.'

She told me, with exactly the level of bluntness that had been promised, that she wanted to break into the professor's office. He was out meeting Henry at a coffee shop, and she knew that he'd left it unlocked. Wouldn't it be funny to just go in there for a bit? Wouldn't it be funny to steal his copy of *Doctor Faustus*?

I was unconvinced by the idea that it would be funny at all. I couldn't even understand where the plan had come from. And I couldn't understand why – after the whole debacle with her course had been resolved – Marina was still intent on upsetting Montgomery. I opened my mouth and was about to say exactly this, when I caught sight of Marina's expression. She looked very sad, needy – almost like she was trying to tell me something. I closed my mouth.

'On second thoughts,' she said, 'it actually doesn't matter if you want to come or not. I'm going on my own whatever happens.'

'Er … OK.'

She made a series of short, frustrated hand gestures to indicate she disapproved of this reaction.

'It's just such an effort trying to get you to have fun,' she fumed. 'This is what first year should be about, Eva – taking risks. That is what you'll remember in years to come. Not slaving away on an essay which doesn't have a conclusion. It won't even contribute to your final grade.'

There was nothing much I could say to defend myself there.

'Well sure,' I conceded. 'It's not like we're going to get jobs when we graduate.'

'Exactly. Your degree won't count for anything in the long or short-term. The only thing you're paying for – that's *thirty grand* by the way – is access to experiences. You're entitled to have as pointlessly good a time as possible here. And this heist – it will be anecdotal gold.'

There was truth in what she was saying – and even if her plan was insane, I was flattered by the attention that she was giving to me. I liked listening to her spell out her arguments. I liked watching her having to persuade me. I scrunched my nose, feigning disapproval, then slowly I put my book down.

'Well … maybe,' I said.

Marina lit up. She snatched the corner of my notebook then, jolting my hand, so that the pen I was holding skidded and drew a thick black line across the page.

'Not maybe,' she said. 'Definitely. I'll help you pack up your stuff.'

Once I was packed up, we walked quickly out of the library, out down the stairs and out into the rain. Marina ran a few yards ahead of me, her coat flapping behind her, her hair sprawling out at all angles, and I ran to catch up, pulling the shoulders of my jacket over my head like a hood. We ran across the campus, past the crowds of people, past the umbrellas. I felt the sheets of rain lashing across my face, the puddles splishing under my shoes. It was exciting, an adventure.

We entered a lecture building through an automatic glass door and, conscious of attracting attention, slowed our pace as we approached his study. Then we stood there for a moment, partly obscured by a little nook: a dipped-in hexagonal section of the wall, in which were hung a series of noticeboards. I looked uncertainly at Marina.

She was thumbing her chin with one hand, gesturing to the door with the other.

'Ah well – ah, here we are,' she said, in a perfect impression of the professor. 'Here we go then.'

We shook off our coats and folded them, still damp, under our arms. I saw that our rainsoaked feet had left small trails along the floor. Without saying anything, I grabbed Marina by the arm and gestured to them quickly – a panicked flick of the hand.

'It's fine,' she murmured, laughing. 'Just wipe your feet here.'

She swatted to a piece of rough carpet. I did as she said. Then – without giving me a second to prepare myself – Marina leaned forward, lifted her little hand into a fist and knocked lightly on the door. There was no answer.

We waited for a second: two, three. She knocked again, harder – still nothing. We waited for a few more seconds, allowing a crowd to pass, then Marina jumped forward, forcefully twisted the knob and pulled us both inside.

My feet tripped a little over each other. The door clicked shut behind us.

The professor's office was empty. The lights were off. The armchair sat slumped in front of the window, the high back casting a shadow over one corner of his desk. I could see that he wasn't in there, but in this semi-darkness – the main light off, the rain drilling against the window – everything seemed too quiet. I couldn't quite believe he wasn't there. Each of our footsteps clacked loudly on the floor.

I immediately regretted my decision to come with her. What point was there to it anyway? Why steal a book, why steal anything? I thought about turning around to leave. But turning to Marina, I saw she was – of course – still smiling and I didn't want to leave without her. Her pupils were very wide.

'Get the book,' she whispered, nudging me sideways. 'It's on the shelf.'

There was an edginess in her manner. Something which made me think twice about doing what she said.

'But why?' I said.

'What do you mean why?'

'I just …' I thought it was childish.

'Can't you imagine next time we have a seminar and he can't dig it out? It will be funny. You do that and I'll get on his computer.'

She registered my expression and rolled her eyes. Why were her pupils so wide?

'What's wrong with you today?' she said. 'This is just to fuck with him. Come on, he's not due back for at least another half hour.'

Marina went over to his computer and began to tap into his keyboard. It was a loud tapping, obnoxiously loud, so loud that I felt sure you would be able to hear it from outside. My heart beat wildly in my chest.

'Come *on* Eve.'

I crept over to the bookshelves, stood there awkwardly. I looked over the dusty tomes, scanning each title for *Doctor Faustus*. Every time I heard footsteps outside going past, I'd flinch with fear.

Marina, on the other hand, was unconcerned. She stood behind the computer with square shoulders and a confident, determined posture. Like a warrior going into battle. Every time I turned

69

around to get some reassurance she would be staring straight ahead, ignoring me. Her eyes were transfixed.

'Marina,' I whispered. She did not respond.

This was not, I decided, at all fun.

I turned my eyes back towards the bookshelf, studied each of the spines and it was then – there! – that I saw it. Well thumbed, a fraying cover, Post-its sticking out at all angles. I snatched it off the shelf, pinching the pages between my fingertips, and waved it towards her.

She was still looking at the screen but she now looked perturbed.

'Marina,' I said sharply.

She looked up, saw what I was holding, and smiled. But it was a tight smile, like she was thinking about something else. Then she opened her mouth – as though preparing to say something – and quickly shut it again. Her eyes flicked to the door.

There were sounds coming from outside: shuffling footsteps and two low distinctive voices. I could tell who they belonged to, even if the words were muffled. One voice, with its careful drawl, a long slow syllable petering out at the end of each sentence, was Henry. And the other, slightly higher, more nervous, more peppy … the other was the professor. And he was getting closer.

Marina and I stared at each other, our eyes wide and frozen. The doorknob rattled. There was the sound of someone putting a key in a lock. The doorknob twisted again and stuttered. I could still hear the professor's voice – louder now, more distinctive.

'Oh,' I heard him say. 'Hold on, sorry, Henry, I must have forgotten to … lock this bloody thing …'

My brain said: MOVE – I put the book down and made my way towards a store cupboard. I tried to pull it open, I tried again, but no – it was locked. In my periphery I saw a shape – Marina – slip effortlessly into a cupboard closer to the window.

The voice was louder now: 'Right, yes. Thanks very much, I'll see you on Thursday. Take care.'

I heard the lock slowly twisting in the other direction. Then it stopped. There was a sigh and I heard him taking the keys out again.

Light on my feet, I ran to another cupboard and tried it and – yes! This time it flew open. I felt dizzy with relief. Ducking my head down, I crouched inside and pulled the door shut with a careful click, just as the office door creaked open.

The sound of footsteps first. Then a long, wide shadow spread into the room.

Through the slats of the cupboard I had quite a clear view of the professor. His silhouette was wide and imposing. I had to stifle a giggle as it passed over the doorway. It slid over the carpet. It slid over my face inside the cupboard and hovered there. I blinked nervously, focusing on the professor's figure, watching him bend in front of his desk.

He stood for a long time in front of his computer. His face was lit up by the light of the screen: concerned expression, a lip curling. He looked up and around, slowly, at the objects in the room. Eventually his gaze settled on his desk – on the book. I recognized the copy of *Doctor Faustus* and felt a chill down my neck as his hand moved towards it. He ran his finger along the spine and picked it up.

A moment went by. With one hand, he placed his laptop under his arm. With the other, he carried the book towards the shelf. He put it back, then turned as though to leave. I held my breath, sure that he was going to see me through the cupboard grate: sure that I would laugh or sneeze, that I would breathe too loudly, that I would do something to make him pause and wrench the door open.

But he didn't. He didn't see me at all.

Instead his stooped figure moved towards the door. I heard it open and shut. The key scraped into the lock. Then the clack of footsteps again, all the way down the corridor.

He was gone.

A few moments went by and I told myself to breathe. I could hear footsteps of other people outside. I could hear the muffled chatter of people walking past. I could hear the rain, lighter now, still tickling the window pane.

'Marina,' I whispered.

There came no reply.

I edged out of the cupboard, a feeling of dread and paranoia prickling my scalp.

Tentatively I knocked on Marina's cupboard. Silence.

I tried again, my hands shaking.

Still silence.

For a terrible second I had the rash thought that she'd somehow abandoned me. I believed that in those moments I'd spent looking away she had somehow found a way to escape …

But then I knocked a third time, and I heard faint laughing from inside the slats. It became louder and louder. Suddenly Marina burst out.

'*That*,' she said, 'was hilarious.'

She clutched her chest and laughed harder, tilting her eyes up to the ceiling. Her pupils were really very wide.

'Yeah,' I said wearily.

'God it was funny. Did you see how confused he was by the book?'

'Yeah.'

'Such a fucking dolt.'

A scatter of footsteps rushed past then, causing me to jump. Marina laughed, falling backwards, pointing towards me, clapping her face with a wild hand.

That was it – I'd had enough.

'Let's get out of here,' I said. I looked around. 'How do we get out?'

I turned to the door and saw, in the small crack between the door and the wall, the outline of the lock bar. We were stuck.

I repeated: 'How the hell do we get out? Fuck!'

Marina rolled her eyes.

'Calm *down* dear,' she said. 'It's the ground floor. How do you *think* we get out?'

She walked to the window behind the desk, stuck her hands underneath it and began to shunt up the frame. It opened fully and she climbed onto the ledge. I watched her hoist herself up, knees scraping the corner of the ledge, her little figure crouching then squatting, lifting up to balance on her arches. She hesitated for a second. Then she fell – quickly, gracefully – out and down. I didn't wait to hear her hit the bottom before I followed.

The fall was not far, but it was far enough to hurt. I tumbled down forwards in what felt like slow motion, my hands stretched out away from me, a scatter of wild fragmentary images flying in front of my eyes: faces and shoes and bricks, windows and grass. I saw the buildings of Northam in the distance – the library, the main hall, Marina's accommodation block – before landing with a squelchy thud. As I did so my arms skidded out and I felt my palm catch on something sharp. It dug into the flesh, piercing the skin. I closed my eyes for a few seconds. Then I looked up and saw a stream of light. It was coming from an open window above me.

I whispered: 'Marina', but got no response.

'Marina,' I said again.

I scrunched my hand into a tight fist to mitigate the pain, and lifted my head up. It took me a second to acclimatize, then I realized that I was alone. I looked at the students walking past, clutching files. None of them could see me, for I was obscured by a hedge. But I could see them, and none of them were her.

I brought myself to my knees, gathered my bag close to me, and stared out beyond them – out towards the central campus, out towards the lake. I brushed my fringe out of my eyes and focused, looking into the darkening distance.

It was then that I saw her. I was sure it was her. The slim

silhouette running out into the rain, the arms flung open wide. The bag bobbing up and down on her back as her legs moved faster, her arms spread wider, the colours of her hair, clothes, body all blurring into one. She was shrinking, disappearing. And now that I was concentrating, now that I could really see her, I thought I could hear her laugh: a shrill piercing note echoing across the campus.

The truth of the situation struck me then with a violent force. Marina, I realized, could afford to take risks like this – but I couldn't. She could afford to be on the professor's bad side. She could afford to be expelled, just as she could afford to ruin her clothes or ruin hire cars. She could afford to fuck up her education, to view it all as a game. These were things that I could not afford. I wasn't from the sort of background that could support such cavalier behaviour. I didn't have money to ruin my clothes and buy replacements. What's more – I didn't *want* to ruin them. I didn't want disposables. I wanted things that I really *wanted*, things that I could look after long-term.

For a few seconds I sat there in the mud. Then – after the last of the students trailed in – I stood up. My legs felt shaky, but my hand was not as bad as I'd thought – the pain disappeared within a few paces. That was lucky. I walked back to my accommodation alone, my knees sodden with mud and my palms and elbows freezing and bloody. When I finally got to my room, there was a queue for the communal shower. I sat on my bed, wrapped in a towel, staring at my mud-caked ankles and my mud-caked clothes.

I thought about her silhouette running away from me. I could still hear the sound of her laughter, echoing across the lake.

V.

It was after then that our friendship really began to disintegrate. I don't believe I was to blame for this. Marina was increasingly volatile and rude, often barging into conversations unannounced,

74

shutting them down abruptly, and then demanding attention via some other method. She would simper and snivel. She would wrinkle her nose at *everything*. She would constantly try to embarrass me.

'Evie,' she'd say after some snide comment, coming over to stroke my hair. 'Where have you *been*?' Then she'd tangle her fingers through my roots, begin threading a plait, start talking about how it was 'funny' that I'd started to dye it. She'd pick a piece of lint off my jumper and claim it was dandruff, say how that was 'sweet'.

Her behaviour was grating, yes, but it's true that I didn't behave kindly during those final weeks of term. I felt a need to point out how annoying she was – how hypocritical and boring she was – and not discreetly, but in a goading, humiliating fashion. I would wait for her to start speaking, and then I'd butt in with a counter-question. I would lead her to raise her voice, then I'd coolly interject with a superior line of thought. I wanted to make her fearful. I wanted her to question herself. I wanted to make her unsure of her own personality.

One of the first things that I had started to call her out on, for example, was her hastiness in making judgements about people. She might have had a confident manner but her language was always extreme. She seemed to think that people were either inherently good or inherently bad – by their very *nature* – whereas at that time I tended to see people as being essentially blank, with a palette of character traits which changed according to mood or social context. I had neuroscience to support me on this; Marina had instinct. It irritated me that whenever we met a new person, they could never simply be nice, or reliable or fun according to Marina. They had to have a reluctant upside, and an extreme downside.

'Rebecca Barnes makes some OK points in seminars,' she would say, 'but I've *never met anyone* with a more convoluted way of expressing themselves. She uses so many qualifiers. There is no point in making a good point if it means other people have to weave their way around your sentences to understand it.'

Where before I would laugh and agree, now I began to object. I said that I thought that, actually, Rebecca Barnes had some good insights and communicated them nicely. Anyway, I liked that she made contributions to the seminar. It was good to have someone to interrupt the silences.

Marina snorted when I said that, wrinkling her light freckled nose.

'Well yeah, you're right,' she replied. 'At least she makes a contribution in the first place.'

She always laughed softly, sweetly, after putting me down – as though my weaknesses were endearing character quirks. Once it had made me embarrassed. Now it made me want to hit her. But I smiled and laughed back through gritted teeth anyway – letting the laugh carry on for a second longer than was natural – just long enough to hint at how I really felt – and then we moved on to some other topic.

We were good at moving on like that. The truth is that we knew so little about each other that there were always safe conversation topics to return to – things we couldn't disagree on. We could always teach the other about ourselves. We'd talk about our lives before we met: our former teachers, our schoolfriends, our families.

I loved hearing about Marina's family. Even now, while there's a strong instinct warning me against it, I also feel excited at the possibility of describing it here. I can't help it. I still get a buzz out of it. Her life story has always been, will always be, exciting to me.

I'll start with the content – the story. Marina and I were both only children, but the similarities end there. Excepting my home-schooling experience (about which I'm pretty sure I never told her) my upbringing had been dull. Hers, by contrast, was exceptional: a soap opera of Dickensian proportions. Her mother was a socialite who had been a bridesmaid at Princess Margaret's daughter's wedding. Her father, a loveable scallywag from 'similar stock', had made a fortune in the city before crashing out to become a semi-famous academic. They'd married at 25 and divorced at 29, after her father ran off with his 'floozy' research assistant. After that her mother had taken Marina to live with her in the Cotswolds. But then when Marina was 6, she had died of lung cancer and so Marina had been left motherless, forced to return to the home of her father and her new stepmother.

'The hussy and her keeper.'

The plot was enough to hook me in. But Marina's way of narrating elevated it to new pastures. She was enthralling, unpredictable, funny. She made her life seem not tragic but like a dark comedy. She said that she wasn't aggrieved by the loss of her mother, but 'better off for it'. In fact, she said, her mother had 'deserved' to die because of her irresponsible lifestyle.

'Too many cigarettes,' she would utter, striking a new one from the pack. 'Too much booze. No wonder Dad left her, she was practically incontinent before I could walk.'

Her father, rather than a philandering traitor, seemed charmingly scatterbrained. Marina clearly adored him. She said that they were 'two peas in a pod', that her life had improved significantly after moving in with him. He had – she explained – 'no filter after a drink'. I'd sit openmouthed as she told me the things he'd done. How he used to pick her up from school in an Elvis Presley costume; how he'd once confronted Tony Blair about the Iraq war while he was the keynote speaker at a banking event. Once, at a prestigious film party, he had jumped on stage while Phil Collins was performing and sung 'You Can't Hurry Love' to Marina in the crowd.

It strikes me as funny, embarrassing even, that I didn't question how much of this was true. Even when I googled her stepmother and discovered that she was not some 'floozy' but a dour academic – I didn't think to ask Marina for an explanation.

I just assumed that my prejudices had jumped to the conclusion that she would be young, because that was the sort of woman men left their wives for. I felt ashamed at that. And when I looked up pictures of Princess Margaret's daughter's wedding and saw that none of the bridesmaids could have been Marina's mother, I just assumed I'd got the wrong wedding, or otherwise that I'd misremembered the details of what she told me. My casual knowledge of the royal family surely paled in comparison to hers.

That's how it was. I might have disbelieved everything else she told me, but the story of her family remained intact. It was wholly, uncomplicatedly, indisputably factual. However much we had argued before, however much I'd decided that I hated her, I would always fall silent when she spoke about it. I would listen to her intently, swallowing every word, never questioning anything.

These conversations were only light reprieves, however. The rest of the time we conducted polite, restrained small talk, or read stuff aloud while we got drunk, so as to distract ourselves from the heavy silences. I had a sense that soon, very soon, an outburst would punctuate the streams of nicety and the tensions would erupt, causing a chasm in our friendship.

CHAPTER FOUR

December 2013

i.

It came to a head on the night of Henry's birthday party. Henry's twenty-first birthday fell about two weeks before the end of term and he threw a lavish celebration in its honour. This was evidently true – it was a birthday bash – but Henry deflected. He claimed, tenuously, that the party was to celebrate the upcoming Christmas holiday instead.

It should be noted that Henry 'didn't celebrate birthdays'.

'What is age though, really?' he'd said to me once, contemptuously, while on a cokefuelled bender. 'The entire concept of *becoming a year older* is void. *To exist is to change, to change is to mature, to mature is to go on creating oneself endlessly.* I mean look at that star, Eva. It takes light eight minutes to travel from the closest star to Earth. That means that you're looking at that star now – eight minutes ago. And so the star might be dead. I'm paraphrasing here, but the conclusion is that we might be dead. And so what is time? Time doesn't exist. Time doesn't exist, so it doesn't make *sense* to celebrate birthdays. It's … well, not just tacky – it's fundamentally against my philosophical principles.'

He'd thrown me a look of disdain then, as though imagining all the tacky birthday parties I might have hosted over the course of my sad, bourgeois life.

The truth was I had never hosted any sort of party. I couldn't stand the idea. Even attending them made me feel exposed. I drank too much and said too little, and I couldn't dance, however drunk, without feeling self-conscious.

I was therefore less surprised by the fact that Henry had thrown what was effectively a birthday party than by the fact I had been invited. Objectively I wasn't a great addition, and I had the strong impression that Henry didn't like me. Whatever, I went.

Henry's house was one of Northam's less dingy student abodes. It had unusually large, airy windows, Danish light fittings and expensive cream carpets. Henry and his housemates had done their best to disguise this by buying cheap furniture which made the place seem more shabby and unclean than it really was. In the hall, there was a mouldy coat stand and a half-cracked mirror. In the kitchen, manky fridge magnets lay scattered along the surfaces, all bearing 'ironically' tacky slogans like: 'A balanced diet is a glass of wine in both hands', and: 'If we can send one man to the moon, why can't we send them all there?' In the sitting room, two long, brown divans curled along the carpet in front of a pair of moth-eaten curtains. They cast a dull shadow over the room – a room that was now littered with cigarette butts and empty bottles. I sat next to Marina on a torn up armchair, smoking a spliff. My head rolled backwards over the upholstery. I wasn't thinking about anything.

'Calm *down* dear.'

Soon enough I clocked that Marina had been talking. She was talking not to me – but to a group of people on the other side of the room. I listened in and was instantly annoyed. She had used that sarcastic phrase – 'calm down dear' – in the professor's study before we'd escaped. Before she had abandoned me. Why was she bringing it up now? I blinked and turned to look at her. She was sat very upright in her chair.

There was a delirious smirk on her face.

'Britain wants to knock those trade barriers down. An opening Britain is the *ideal* partner for an opening China.'

She spoke in an exaggerated RP accent, with her mouth pinched into a tight line and her chin drawn deep into her neck. I watched as she leant forward slightly on every other syllable, then widened her eyes so that they shone with false earnest. I realized then what she was doing.

It was an impression of David Cameron.

'Might I add,' she continued, 'that Eva's drunk red face currently bears a rather strong resemblance to that of my dear dear colleague Boris.'

I didn't laugh. No one else did either. A couple of people left the room to get drinks.

Marina tried to continue for a few more sentences, but her features kept jerking out of joint and she kept fluffing her line. Finally she threw back her head, laughing alone. Her hair spread out over the back of the sofa. I felt it brush gently against my ear.

'David Cameron is awful,' she said. 'I mean, naturally I'd vote for him over Ed Miliband, but he's still awful.'

I felt her words work their way around my brain. A slow but certain feeling of disgust penetrated my giddy head-fog, and I heard myself pointing out that she'd previously identified as a Labour voter. Marina explained that she was more *inclined* to vote Labour 'ideologically', but she couldn't take Ed Miliband seriously.

'Besides,' she said, 'my constituency is Tory, so it wouldn't make a difference.'

I felt a sharp stab of indignation. I didn't like this fatalistic streak – this shrug of complacency. Still, I could see that everyone else was leaving the room, likely as a result of her embarrassing performance, and so it seemed pointless to tear her down. There was no point without an audience. I marinated in the silence for a minute, let myself return to calm. Then, once everyone else had gone, I heard Marina switch on her autopilot. She started talking about the other people at the party.

'God, they're so boring,' she said. 'I'm so bored. It's like no one wants to have a political discussion in here.' After a few swift character assassinations, she concluded: 'They only ever talk about people.'

My toes clenched in my shoes. Marina lit her cigarette, shrugged and carried on: 'Small minds discuss people; average minds discuss events; great minds discuss ideas.'

This was a line I had heard before. It was something that Marina often liked to murmur under her breath, sometimes flicking her ash, in order to seem casually profound. I had fallen for it at first. It was a smart piece of rhetoric. It helped, too, the way she tended to look at me when she said it: a flash of conspiratorial warmth, twisting her mouth into a smile. But the charm had waned over the last few utterances – and now I just found it annoying. The quote wasn't true. It was elitist, pretentious rubbish. I asked her where she'd heard it.

'I don't know,' she shrugged, irritated. 'It's something my father says.'

No, I told her, it wasn't something her *father* said. It was something that Eleanor Roosevelt had said, or was supposed to have said, once, to someone, somewhere – actually there was no evidence for it. I knew this because I had googled it two days before, anticipating this interaction.

She frowned. Her eyes sharpened into small green darts.

'Who cares? It doesn't matter who said it. It's true.'

Was it? I asked her. Or was it a lazy piece of spin – the kind of simplification that someone like Henry was likely to parrot?

Silence.

As the silence lengthened, a tension stretched between us. She wiped her fringe away from her forehead. Her eyes were hypnotic, with a kind of unsettling melancholy quality. For a second I thought about holding my tongue – but then I took one look at her smug, smiling mouth and something inside me snapped.

Surely the greatest people, I continued, beyond the merely 'great' – did not cut off conversational avenues just so that they could lie around in their ivory towers theorizing. And besides – 'There's no need.'

And *besides*, she was just talking about people at this party. She spoke about other people constantly, in fact. Whether through impressions or in bitchy appraisals she was always comparing herself to other people, competing, shouting over, or dismissing them. It was her go-to topic of conversation. Yes. Of all people, she belonged to that supposedly inferior bracket who 'talked about people'.

Now I was gathering momentum.

'It's pathetic,' I said, louder, 'how much it means to you to exert superiority over others. You go on about Rebecca Barnes because you're threatened by how much Montgomery respects her opinion. You go on about – I don't know – how Henry regurgitates other people's ideas and can't think for himself, because you don't read as widely as him. You thrive off the idea that you're superior to *other people*, but the truth is you can't stop thinking about them. You're nothing without—'

'Oh wow,' someone said. 'Finally.'

I stopped, astonished, and looked over towards the door. Henry was stood in the doorway. He was clutching a bottle in one hand and an imperious cigarette in the other. He hovered there for a moment, then – as the silence lengthened again – he walked into the room. I watched the long lines of his coat, the swift movements of his shiny black feet, as he approached Marina and took off from where I had left off: 'She's not wrong, Marina. You do spend a lot of time talking about other people. I've just turned 21, so here's a tip from an old soul. Stop being so fucking patronizing. It's embarrassing and annoying for everyone. While I'm at it, your impressions really aren't that funny. It's just about fine when you do it every now and then but, for gods' sake, it's awful when you cut in like just now.'

Marina stared at Henry incredulously. Then her stare moved, slowly, to me. The green eyes widened accusingly. My glance shifted from Marina to Henry, Henry to Marina. They stared back at me. They waited.

I felt a knot roll in my stomach –panic and dread, but also something newly defined: indignation. I was right. Henry was siding with me. He was still condescending, still inappropriately aggressive, still void of self-awareness – but he was siding with me.

Marina and I stared at each other for several minutes, both refusing to blink. Then finally she looked to the floor, grasped both the arms of the chair and pushed herself up.

She said that she had to pick up something from her car.

I watched her shadow move into the square light of the doorway. Then it shrank, and she disappeared.

Henry and I remained together alone, silent for a moment. I was still sat on the sofa; he stood leaning against the armchair opposite. He took a drag from his cigarette. Then he shook his head slowly. Two long plumes came out from his nostrils and curled around his head.

'I don't understand why you put up with her,' he said.

He was staring into space, with a vacant expression, apparently unbothered. But the intimacy of the conversation alarmed me. I looked into my drink.

'What kind of comment is that?' I said.

'You know what I mean.'

'I don't think I do,' I said. 'She's a good … she's a good friend.'

Henry laughed at that, and when I looked up I saw that his head was thrown back in amusement. I noted the shape of his throat: the sharp arrow of Adam's apple pointing into the air. I took another large swig of my drink.

'Oh come on, don't pretend like you don't know. What I mean is ... Why do you put up with how she treats you?'

He sat down in the armchair, stretched his hand along the back of the cushion. There was a small smile on his face. He seemed more relaxed, more genuine now that Marina wasn't there. He looked up. His eyes were lighter.

'That's pretty rich from you,' I said.

Henry shrugged. 'We don't pretend to be friends.'

'Right.'

His hands dove into his pockets, and produced a tiny bag of white powder. He pinched it open and poured some of the contents onto the table.

'You're often so direct that I can't tell whether you're joking or not,' I said.

'We're not talking about me.' He pressed the powder with a credit card and then cut it into thin white lines. 'We're talking about Marina. She always cuts you off. It's a bit weird.'

I focused on a tiny piece of powder. 'I don't know what you're talking about.'

'Yes you do. And you should be straightforward – face up to it. You should speak more.'

He cocked his head to the side and smiled gently. Then he gestured towards the table with the card. I saw the flash of the Coutts emblem; below it a set of white streaks. They shimmered on the blue surface. I thought of the sea. I shook my head. He shrugged, drew a twenty from his pocket, dipped his head forwards and dove downwards. His face slid along the table like a rolling pin, and there was a loud, squeaky sniff as the line shot up his nose.

I sat there limply. I thought about getting out my phone.

'You sure you don't want any?'

'No thanks.'

Generally speaking, I no longer felt that awkward when they did this. I no longer felt conspicuous not participating. It hadn't been an issue since the first time Marina had asked me to do it, when I'd said no and confirmed that it wasn't my kind of thing. (*Good*, Marina had said. It was a hassle for me to share their supply.) But in that moment with Henry, I felt differently. I knew that this situation had a particular charge. I knew from the way that he kept glancing at me that if I said yes, then and there, that it might change the nature of our relationship.

He kept leaning forwards, and his voice had a gentle lilt.

'Sure?' he asked again.

I sipped my beer, nodded, and the jerky, sudden movement of my head immediately caused me to feel nauseous. The room seemed to swerve, the pores of the ceiling enlarged and came very near to my face, and then, I realized, so was Henry. He was holding a rolled £20 note towards me. The edges of his nostrils were shiny. I could smell something like petrol. And I knew in that moment that I was about to do something I would regret.

Afterwards, I stood up and gave the note back to him. It was slippery and smooth under my fingers. They touched his as I passed it back over.

'All right?' Henry said.

I nodded. I felt very, very funny. The room was swaying and I was moving with it. Everything was bright and good. Short hot bursts of air erupted from my nose and the breath on my upper lip was causing it to lift at the edges. That was a nice feeling. That was such a nice feeling that a large smile broke out over my face. I had so much energy all of a sudden! I lit a cigarette but it wasn't enough – I needed to spread my arms. I flung them out across my body.

'You sure you're all right?' Henry said.

Wow he was beautiful. He looked so beautiful.

I nodded again. I bent down giddily and put the cigarette into the ashtray. I flexed my fingers into a star shape. The music thudded in my ears and the floor seemed like water. Henry was a long looming figure, coming very close to me. I looked slightly past him, noticed the figures in the corridor. Lovely party humans! Then I leaned forward, reached my hand around his neck, and brought my face close to his. His mouth looked funny from this angle: a series of wavy little lines. I couldn't distinguish between them and his chin. I pulled his face in further.

His breath was warm on my cheek. His eyes were like the moon. I thought about laughing or taking a photo or telling him that but instead …

I kissed him.

He was reluctant, passive, at first. His body felt cold and stiff and his lips didn't move. This was not the expected reaction. In fact I was momentarily so amused by this lack of enthusiasm that I started thinking of ways that I could recount it to Marina. He was frigid after all, he was a robot man, he was … then I came to and realized that no, wait, he actually was reacting now. His mouth began to move; then it began to feel warm. Gradually his head leaned forward, his long fingers slid around my neck.

I dimly processed the situation, almost as a third-party observer. What were we doing now? Why was this happening? It was so *weird*!

It was then that I sensed a familiar presence in the corner of the room. I pulled away abruptly, it all felt too abrupt, and as I reeled backwards and readjusted my eyes the scene began to fall into place again: the sharp edges of Henry's face, the look of confusion in his eyes staring past me, the curl of his fringe over his eyebrow, the brown shabby sofa and the swell of the ceiling.

My eyes tracked across the ceiling, studying the pores in the paint, blinking, refocusing until I could identify the silhouette in the doorway. Short and secure, with two arms folded over the abdomen. A smile wavered on my lips.

'Marina.'

She turned and disappeared.

'Marina!'

My voice sounded strangely nasal, and so much louder than I expected, echoing down the corridor.

Listening to it I felt a dark, warm pull deep in my stomach. I started to laugh.

ii.

Over the next few days I hardly left my bed at all. My hangover was excruciating – a dull, persistent headache and a nausea which made me sweat and shake all over. Those physical symptoms were exacerbated by the shameful memory of the party. But why did I feel ashamed? It wasn't that I had expected anything to come from kissing Henry. The kiss itself was so random as to be inscrutable. As I thought about it, turning the image in my head over and over again, I found it impossible to even pinpoint specific details about it: what I had felt towards him at the time, what he had looked like, what my hands had been doing.

I couldn't understand why any of it had happened.

Now my hands moved towards my phone. No messages. I drew up the lid of my laptop and pushed myself into a sitting position. I began to scroll through photos of Henry. He was undeniably very handsome. His eyes were round and deep and dark; his face was masculine and angular; his mouth was attractively taut. Yet even captured in this 2D format, there was something off about him. He was too controlled. That rigidity had a frigidity, a kind of standoffishness.

Well – what then? Did kissing someone always mean that you were sexually attracted to them, or was it just the impulse to *do something* that had overwhelmed me, that had gradually been building up over the weeks of following Marina around?

Yes, I decided, that was the reason – plus the drugs – and when I discovered that the kiss had not affected Henry either, my convictions were strengthened. I saw him again in the corridor after a seminar. He gave me a curt, dismissive nod, made some disinterested small talk, and then drew a packet of cigarettes from his pocket and left. It was clear that he thought no more and no less of me. It was as though the evening hadn't happened.

Predictably, however, it had affected Marina.

I had been trying to contact her for three days when I finally saw her outside the lecture theatre. I had been texting her, calling her, Facebooking her – at first in a casual tone, then semi-apologetic, then disguised as a joke, then openly desperate. Three days in the timescale of a student is a long time. There is so little structure to the day that each minute seems like an hour, especially when you're waiting for someone to contact you. Marina and I were used to spending nearly every hour together and her absence seemed alien, unnerving.

So when I saw her outside the lecture theatre, I felt such a twisted mix of hurt and anger and nervousness that I didn't know what to say. I had spent so long looking at pictures of her online that in my mind she had almost become an abstraction – her physical presence made me feel overwhelmed.

I saw her move towards me. Her small arms were curved out in an arc, her long wavy hair spread out down her back and then she leaned forward into a hug. I flinched a little at the unexpected physical contact, but she drew me in further towards her, wrapping her arms tightly around my abdomen. The gentleness, the intimacy of the gesture moved me. I relaxed into the hug, put my arms around her.

'What's wrong with your phone?' I said, murmuring into her hair. 'I thought you'd been kidnapped.'

There was a moment of silence before she drew her face back to look at me. There was no warmth in her face. She wore a cold, cruel smirk. We detached from each other quickly.

'So,' she said flatly. 'Did you have *fun* on Saturday night?'

I stared at her.

'Did you?' she said again. Her voice was cold and expressionless.

For something to do I looked down at my nails. 'I guess so.'

'You and Henry ...' she said, and nudged me with sharp little elbows.

I wanted to ask her where she had been for the last few days, why she had been ignoring me, whether she had a problem with Henry or with me or whether it was something else. Her sharp little eyes glared into mine. Steadily I held her gaze.

I said: 'No, it was nothing.'

'Oh come on.'

'No, it really was nothing.'

'How long have you been interested in him?' She nudged me again, this time lodging her elbows deep into my ribs. 'Did your crush develop straightaway – at the first party? Was it *un coup de foudre*, or has it been slowly developing?'

I wasn't embarrassed. Despite the forceful bluff of her tone, there was an uneasy look on her face that made me feel powerful. Her pupils looked a little dilated, and she wore a wavering expression. She was unconvincing.

'I'm not interested in him,' I repeated. 'It's just something that happened. He was high, I think and I was ... well, drunk.'

'I was thinking that it's funny, because you've never been in a room with him alone before.'

'So?'

Just then the professor strode past, and the crowd began to shuffle into the lecture hall. We followed them cautiously.

'So?' I repeated, once we had sat down.

Before she could answer – if she was going to answer –the professor cleared his throat, loaded up the PowerPoint and began to speak from his lecture notes. She shrugged and turned away.

I sat through the lecture anxiously, twiddling my thumbs. Every so often I glanced at Marina. She was disturbingly quiet. Her lips were pursed tight. She looked intently at the PowerPoint projected on the front wall.

After weeks of having to restrain Marina – of feeling on edge whenever she was in the company of the professor – perhaps this quietness should have relaxed me. Instead it made me feel anxious. It made me feel like there was something going on in her brain that I could not access, that she was shutting off from me.

After the lecture ended she did not pack her bags and march out, like she usually did. She sat next to me and stared straight ahead at the table. Her eyes had a glazed expression.

'Marina,' I murmured. 'Are you OK?'

She pursed her mouth into a grimace.

'What's going on?' I said.

'Nothing's going on.'

'Yes there is. Is it Henry? Is it me and …?'

She laughed and bit the edge of her pen. 'It's nothing to do with you,' she snorted. '*You*.'

I felt something inside me snap. It was clear, in the bitter intonation of that word – *you* – what it was that she really thought of me. She thought that I was pathetic, ridiculous, insignificant.

'Then,' I attempted to contain my anger, 'what is it to do with?' I dug my fingernails into my palm. 'And if it's not to do with me, then why are you ignoring me? Why are you bringing *me* into it by overanalysing what happened with Henry? Just tell me what the problem is.'

'Why couldn't you just tell me that you had feelings for Henry?' she snapped suddenly. 'It's not like I mind. I think it's weird that you didn't say anything before.'

'I didn't say anything,' my voice wavered, 'because nothing was going on. I don't feel that way about him. I was just out of it, I—'

'There's no need to be so coy about it, Eva. I really don't care if you like Henry, but I'd have appreciated the heads-up. I could have helped … shape his opinion of you.' She curled a stray piece of hair around her finger, then looked up at me from under her fringe. In that moment she looked ugly and cruel.

I felt a cold whip of anger. 'You mince about like some grand intellectual,' I erupted. 'You think you're so fucking sophisticated

91

because your dad does something *so feted* for a living and you've acquired some of that language and self-importance by being around him. But when it comes down to it you're *nothing*. All you care about is being at the core of every conversation, the object of everyone's desire, the centre of attention all the fucking time. All you add up to is someone who wants to be ... wanted.'

A silence fell. I watched Marina turn away from me for a moment. Then she wiped her fringe from her eyes, and looked up at me again. I saw that she was smiling.

'Why are you so defensive?' she said.

'Because I'm fucking sick of you. I'm sick of the way you flounce around pretending to be some grand feminist when your entire existence depends on impressing people, usually men, with your fake knowledge and your fake confidence and your fake looks. Either I have to follow you like a lapdog, or you ignore me.'

She shook her head and laughed mirthlessly. 'You sound hysterical,' she said. 'I can't speak to you like this.'

'Oh *hysterical*.'

'Grow up.'

'As soon as I do something that you don't like, you shut me down—'

She turned and sighed. 'You're so ...' she said.

'What?' I practically shouted.

'You're disappointing,' she said. 'Just another needy bitch.' Then she leant forward into her rucksack, and pulled a notebook out. She began scribbling something down.

'What are you doing?' I asked her.

She carried on scribbling. I felt the urge to say something else.

'Marina I—'

'Fuck off, *Eva*.'

That mention of my name eradicated any shred of self-control I had left.

It wasn't just that I no longer admired her, I realized. It wasn't that I no longer passively liked her – or even that I passively disliked her. I actively hated her. She suddenly appeared to me not as someone to look up to or be friends with, but an ugly hard obstacle – a *thing* that was having a corrupting effect on my life. I wanted to hurt her: obliterate her. I jammed all my things into my bag and swung it over my shoulder.

Then I gave her a hard, vicious shove that knocked her sideways in her chair, and walked quickly out of the lecture theatre.

***

For a while, when I thought back on that memory of pushing Marina it seemed to me quite funny. The sight of her heaving sideways, her long blonde hair swinging upwards and down, her body swaying out of control – it was comical. I liked thinking about the way I'd wiped that smirk off her face, just for a moment. I liked remembering how I had stood up for myself.

Now the thought of it appals me. Writing it down makes my joints ache and my fingers tense over the keys. I just wish that I had handled the situation better. I wish I had said something to make her act differently, to make her reveal what was really going on in her head.

I have always had a superstition about language, about the alchemic forces of conversation, and although I know, rationally, that it is not really true, I sort of believe that given the right tone and the right placement of words that it is possible to draw out the secrets of the universe. Words, more than anything, can influence the forces at work in the world. If you can manipulate a conversation, you can manipulate anything.

Since I heard about what happened to Marina, I find myself constantly returning to that conversation. I think about all the other things I could have said to make her talk to me; all the ways I could have trapped her in a web of words. Instead I put myself first. I was clumsy and selfish and melodramatic.

From that moment until the Christmas holidays, I didn't try to speak to her at all. I spent time instead with the people on my floor in my accommodation block. I cast aside my original judgements about them and made an effort to seem pleasant and kind. In return they let me into their circle. There was blonde Cathy who wore a variety of cardigans; curly haired Andy who liked to play chess; and, of course, self-appointed 'crazy' Irish Bob, who behaved rather tamely, but always embellished stories about himself. They were, I supposed, less stereotypically glamorous than the group that I had been hanging out with until that point in term. But the difference was that they appreciated me. They listened to things I had to say, and I didn't feel as though I had to monitor what I wore, did or thought in their presence. I felt, in that week at least, valued for who I was.

On the 17th of December, the Christmas holidays came around, and in accordance with the rules of my accommodation block I had to move home for a few weeks. My mother came to help me pack up my room. It took about an hour to fold everything into boxes. Seeing it bare, I felt an unexpected desire to talk to Marina. I wondered what she was doing. I wondered where she was going for Christmas. I knew that her father had a house in England but usually lived in the US. Would she be going there?

'I have to say,' my mother heaved a final box into the boot of the car, 'your room is a *vast* improvement since your father and I were at university. There is *so* much space!'

I grunted in response and got into the passenger seat. I wondered whether Marina would have to clear out her room too.

My mother hopped into the front seat, and as she did so her bob flopped up and down.

'Charming campus too,' she said. 'Just *charming*.'

I nodded absent-mindedly and reached into my pocket. I drew out my phone. I typed in Marina's name, and began to look at her Facebook profile, looking for evidence of what she'd been doing. There was nothing new. Nothing had been posted since a week earlier – when someone called Elena had posted a photo of her and Henry.

I looked closely at the photo, curving my hand over the top of the phone to shade the glare of sunlight from the window. It was a candid shot, taken in the middle of conversation. Henry had his eyes fixed on her, a cigarette raised in the air. She stood nearly a foot below him. Her face was tilted up, and it bore a strange expression. There was a glow in her eyes, something between amusement and … what was it? Fear.

I pinched the screen to zoom in closer. I realized I had never seen a photo of Marina with Henry, and the way that they looked at each other disturbed me. I held my finger against the glass and saved the picture to my photo folder.

Outside the campus began to diminish in the rear-view mirror. Branches brushed against the back window. My mother carried on talking.

'When we get home you must be cautious of your father. I don't know what's wrong with him at the moment. He's just in a bad mood *all* the time.'

And: 'Malcolm Chinn is taking a horticulture course. He's having to take his exams in a few weeks' time. You know Malcolm, Malcolm who lives up the road. Erica's father. You know, Erica from school.'

'What a time to be alive,' I said.

'Speaking of ex-bankers, the *seriously* hot goss is that Timothy Graham is running for the Lib Dems – I mean, what a surprise. *Not*. I can't understand why everyone is so shocked. He's been gunning for it for … Oh blast. *Blast*. Hang on I forgot the … Can you hold this for a second? *Bugger*. Anyway, yes, what they're saying now is that Bunny Carbuncle is going to clinch it for the Tories anyway. Fox hunting is seriously big around here. Don't give me that look. *Don't* give me that look. Is your seatbelt on?'

I wasn't giving her a look. I wasn't even listening to her. I was thinking about Marina. I had started to feel a pang of something – not remorse, exactly, but something close to it, perhaps the recognition of an absence. I missed her. Perhaps I should message her, I thought. I should be the bigger person. I clicked on her profile, and swiped into private messages. I wrote in the box:

Hi, I'm sorry about the other week.
Hope you have a good Christmas.

I looked out the window, vaguely aware of the fact that my mother was still talking. I clutched my phone tightly inside my pocket and waited for a reply.

PART II

CHAPTER FIVE

Late December 2013

i.

If time went slowly during the term, then during the holidays it seemed to stop completely. This was not a relaxing pause but one of boredom and stress. Though I had only been away for a few months, now that I was back in a controlled environment – with the chirpy mother who never stopped talking, the melancholy father who said nothing at all – the idea that I would have to be there for an entire month was intolerable. As a coping strategy I retreated to an early version of my teenage self: one with a short fuse and a flippant, snarky manner. When my parents asked questions, I would either answer snappishly or avoid giving any response. I stared at my phone and scrolled through pictures of Marina. I checked my emails incessantly. And now and again, I made contrived virtual small talk with my old school friends – friends with whom I now discovered I had almost nothing in common.

One such friend, Caroline, decided to organize a 'girly drinks' on the twentieth, so that we could 'catch up about our university experiences'. She had sent the invite to seven or eight other girls, whom I had also been at school with, and to whom I had hardly spoken since I'd started university three months earlier. It was strange, being part of that set. Even during our A levels there had been little to knit us together, except the subjects we chose and the teachers we hated. Now we weren't even in the same environment anymore, we only really had memories to bond over. Did that constitute a friendship, or a memory of a friendship?

The bar Caroline had selected was Le Bistrotheque, a small, cutesy affair in the centre of Walford. During the day, 'the BT' (as it was known by our mothers) was the favourite haunt of older women, but in recent years, we had started to occupy it for nights out. Such is the pattern in the countryside: the younger generation begin to emulate their parents the moment they're given an opportunity for freedom.

For a country bar, the BT thought of itself as rather upmarket and cosmopolitan. There was wood panelling along the wall; large, plushy sofas in a cordoned-off area, bunting around the bar, and several elaborate candelabras plonked on the middle of each table. It sold things like whisky sours with actual raw egg, which to us as schoolgirls had seemed terribly sophisticated.

Now, as I entered the lobby, I realized that there was nothing remotely sophisticated about it. It was fake and cheap. The drinks were overpriced and the decor was dated. Caroline and the other girls were sat in our usual spot behind the door. They clutched dinky cocktails in their manicured hands.

When Caroline saw me she sprang from her chair and moved in my direction with alarming enthusiasm.

'Evie!' she squealed. 'Wow, you've really changed?'

I hugged her, murmuring something self-deprecating. Her hair brushed past my nose. It was silky and smelled faintly of oranges.

'I mean wow,' she continued, stepping back to look at my outfit. 'What is this dress? You look so ... *edgy*?'

I should have seen this coming. Almost from the moment I had started spending time with Marina, I had changed the way I dressed. Seeing her move so easily, in pleasingly simple clothing, had made me think that my patterned, tight cotton outfits looked embarrassing and unfashionable. It didn't matter if they were new – some of them were even pre-ordered and quite expensive. There was just something about the way they hung off me which made them seem ugly.

I had sold my designer jackets on eBay. I gave away the clingy dresses and smart jeans that had been my uniform before Northam. Instead, I bought the loose style of dresses that Marina wore. I had a large, long overcoat that rippled over my ankles when I walked. I didn't quite have the grace to carry off some of the heavy materials, and a lot of my clothes were awkwardly big because I bought them from charity shops, but at the time I thought I looked better like that. I did at least feel more comfortable.

To my friends I looked weird.

Caroline moved back, trying to keep the smirk off her face. She raised her eyebrows at Suki, who was now moving in for a kiss on each cheek. I choked on a whiff of her perfume, and instinctively drew back as she drew me forward.

'Eeeeeevie!' Suki shrieked, crushing me into her huge bosom. 'Ohmygodohmygodohmygod!'

Suki had been the star of every drama show when we were at school together. Now, having failed to get into drama school, her need for attention and the dramatic cranked up to an unbearable pitch. Whenever she saw someone who had seen her act, she swept them graciously into her bosom and showered them with affection.

I stood there mutely with my shoulder wedged into her breasts. Her 'Ohmygods' carried on for an eternity. 'Ohmygodohmygod!

Oh my god you look so glam! I can't believe this dress you look amazing! Amazing! Ohmygod!'

I tried my best to look equally enthused and not think about the fact that Suki and I had never engaged in a conversation beyond these greetings.

As I wandered around the group kissing each of my other friends on the cheek – Oleana, Jade, Victoria, Abigail – I heard Suki begin unprompted to talk about her 'university experiences'. This was to say, her sexual experiences.

'Anyway. I've actually found this *great guy* – as in, he's kind of great? I met him through drama and we're literally getting on so well. Like *actually* though. We're getting on so well.'

I pretended to be interested for a few minutes, then I went to the bar and ordered a drink. On my way back to the table I saw Suki sweep past me towards the toilet. She winked in a knowing way and made flourishing hand gestures that signified nothing. Something about the combination of that look and those gesticulations made me feel dizzy with exhaustion.

I quickly sat down in a space next to Oleana.

'Hello,' Oleana said. She gave me a knowing grin. I gave a knowing grin back. Knowing grins were a currency in this group. You exchanged them in return for a bond.

I asked her how she was, and she gave the usual catch-up chat: a polite, succinct round up of the pros and cons of university.

After a few minutes of stilted conversation, a silence fell. This often happened with Oleana. She was the kind of person I always thought I should be better friends with, but we never seemed to have any common subject to latch onto however much we tried. For that reason, we bonded by bitching about our other friends.

Now Oleana took a sip from her drink, and then leaned in conspiratorially.

'You know what the weird thing is about Suki's new boyfriend?' she said. 'She didn't meet him through her *drama* society.'

'What do you mean?'

'She met him on Tinder.'

'You're joking.'

'I'm not.' She took a delicate sip from her glass, raising her eyebrows over the rim.

Tinder was relatively new at this point, but I was aware of it. It was the kind of thing that was often advertised on trains or buses or down my Facebook newsfeed, and it had always struck me as something used by those starved of attention in the real world. It didn't surprise me that Suki, of all people, had used it to ensnare someone.

'How do you know?'

'She told me a while ago,' Oleana said. Her tone changed suddenly. 'Anyway, I suppose it's not that big a deal. It's just funny that she feels the need to lie about it.'

I tried to maintain a neutral expression, but I couldn't help myself – I smirked. To hide it I began chewing the end of my straw.

'Do you have Tinder?' I asked, after a pause.

'Yeah, obviously.'

I stared at her.

'What? Everyone does. And the other apps, like Swipe. Most people have moved onto Swipe now actually.'

'What the hell is Swipe?'

'It's like Tinder, but it's different. Better in some ways.'

I snorted. 'Sure.'

'I mean for a start,' she continued, 'there's a feature where you can choose to see someone's exact location when you match them.'

I pushed my straw through needles of crushed ice.

'That's insane.'

'Is it?' She shrugged. 'You can unmatch them any time. I mean – it doesn't take that much to hack into software and trace your location anyway. If they were really creeps, if they were *really*

103

going to stalk and murder you, they could just do that on Tinder or Facebook or whatever. It wouldn't be as heavily monitored as it is on Swipe.'

The thought crossed my mind to say something then but I let it go.

'It also doesn't link you to Facebook as closely.' She paused to look at me meaningfully. 'It's just a game,' she added. 'All these apps: they're just games.'

I shook my head.

'This whole thing has gone too far,' I said. 'The Internet. Millennials. Humans.'

I downed the rest of my drink.

Later that evening I sat in front of my computer. I felt numbed by cocktails and the hours of mundane conversation. The room swirled around me, sounds and images and smells of the evening lurching past in swift, ugly fragments. Only my grip on the keyboard kept me upright in my chair. I dug the heels of my hands into the desk and dragged my fingers along the mouse board. I drew up the Safari page. I typed in the letters. I drummed my fingers against the mouse.

I needed to see Marina. I needed to see what she was doing, who she had been talking to, where she had been. I suspected – or convinced myself – that she wouldn't have replied to my message, but it didn't matter. My encounter with my friends from home had made me realize how valuable to me she was as a companion. I needed to just *see* her in order to feel less alone.

Her profile emerged. It looked the same as it always did: the picture of a dark silhouette leaning against a car, her face hidden behind a curtain of wavy blonde hair. One steely green eye shimmered behind it – just about visible, if you looked closely – and a slim, indecipherable curl of mouth, almost a smile, crept along the bottom of her face. I felt happy. She was beautiful and understated and clever. We were friends.

I clicked through her other photos, noting how the angle of her body shifted in each image, admiring how natural she was in front of the camera. She appeared unaware of the camera when her face was obscured, quietly irritated when her face was visible. Irrespective of her expression, however, she always managed to portray a sense of calm in each of her photos. Perhaps it was because she was symmetrical.

Looking at Marina's photographs soothed me then, at least for a while. But when I clicked back on her main profile to see what she'd been doing, I saw that it was the same as it had been nearly a month earlier. There were no updates. No one had tagged photos of her. No one had written on her wall. No one had recently friended her. I felt a strange mix of emotions: disappointment at first, and then – for no reason – fear.

Before I could stop myself I clicked onto Henry's profile. Blurrily I sent him a message.

I know this is out of the blue
But have you heard from Marina?

Having hit send, I looked at the words on the screen, frozen in that tiny box, waiting to be seen, impossible to erase or edit. I sounded pathetic.

I clicked off and walked around my room. I looked at my own childhood paintings on the wall. I looked at the bookshelf and thought about starting next term's reading list. Then my thoughts turned, again, to the relationship between Marina and Henry.

Once, at a party early in the term, Marina had left her phone on the chair before she had disappeared to meet a dealer. It had vibrated – once, twice, and I had bent over to pick it up. I looked at the screen and saw that there were two messages from Henry:

oi come back ill delete it
it was a joke

I remembered looking at those words on the screen, feeling Marina's phone in my hand, and consciously resisting the temptation to read their other messages. I'd rolled the thought over in my mind a few times before eventually putting the phone back on the chair. Now I regretted not choosing to take that opportunity to read that conversation, to see what their relationship was really like. Marina and Henry were so secretive.

My eyes tracked back to the Facebook icon on my screen. There were a few times I had seen Marina type in her password. I tried to think about what it was – something Latinate with numbers after it, like 'ancilla1930'.

Login attempt failed. Did you forget your password?

I realized what I was doing. I saw the words on the screen; I saw Marina's email address in the login box. My fingers started typing again. I tried the same password, but with different capitalization and the numbers in a different order: Anc1lla1930.

2/4 login attempts failed. Click here to reset your password.

Suddenly I felt dirty, and panicked, like I'd committed a crime. I clicked off the tab, then off the whole browser. My hands flew to the loose skin at the front of my throat and pinched hard. I stared at the wall, feeling the short sharp breaths tighten as the seconds ticked by.

Finally I opened up my laptop again. I logged out of all my social media accounts in the normal browser window. I opened an incognito window and made random Wikipedia searches. I pushed a few words into Google and then closed the browser again.

It was as though I were attempting to eradicate what I had just done; to cover my tracks with other items in my history.

CHAPTER SIX

Late December 2013

i.

Christmas and Boxing Day passed. I received no word from Henry. To distract myself I went on Marina's profile. I went on it again and again. Having deleted her number in a drunken fit of spite I had no way to follow up by texting or calling her: Facebook was my only available method of contact. I typed messages and then deleted them. I watched and waited.

Looking back it seems crazy to me how many hours of my life I voluntarily wasted processing the same information. Each morning I would wake up, pull my laptop onto my lap, whip up the lid, click on the Safari bar, type www.facebook.com, and watch her profile roll up. I would scroll through her photos one by one, photos I had seen a hundred times before. I pored over details that I had seen before too: the way her mouth arched in one photo, who she was looking at in another – and clicked on the profiles of the people who had commented. Once I felt sated, I would then pick up my phone and go through the exact same process on there, sometimes with the laptop still balanced on my chest displaying exactly the same screen.

Before long, it was only three days before New Year's Eve: 28th December. Outside the rain fell. I heard it thudding against the windowpanes. I heard the radio on in the room next door. My parents were arguing downstairs: some fracas about preparing for a New Year's party they were supposed to be hosting. Stress levels had evidently reached fever pitch.

I shut out their voices by concentrating on specific sounds. Rain against the windowpane. The buzz of lightbulbs. The soar of an aeroplane overhead. But try as I might, I was soon distracted by the thump of large, heavy footsteps. I shut my eyes tightly. I heard them coming up the stairs and I silently prayed that whoever it was would not come in. The footsteps clumped past, and my hunched shoulders loosened. I detached my fingers from the keyboard. I reached across to the bedside table and grabbed my phone.

There was a notification on Messenger. From Henry. I saw it flash across the screen and I sat bolt upright.

> Sorry for the late reply
> i don't use Facebook very often

I scrolled down. My fingers felt sticky against the glass.

> Have you heard from Mari over the last few days?
> Did she mention anything weird to you at the end of last term?
> Specifically to do with her email address

I wrote back quickly:

> No I haven't
> And no, nothing that I can remember
> What email address?
> Is everything ok?
> How is she?

I stared at the glass, willing Henry to reply. The more I stared at it, the more the individual pixels on the screen seemed to separate: I could see in the blue of the Facebook logo a light yellow, a dark gold, flecks of green. It reminded me of the time my mother had once come back from an art class and said that I had different colours in the skin on my face: 'You have a lot of blue underneath all that red.' I looked briefly at the veins over my hand, then back at the screen. The three little dots in the corner indicated that he was replying. Then they stopped. Then they started again.

I found my fingers drumming impatiently, of their own accord.

...
...
...
...

There is something odd about the medium of online messaging. It is simultaneously instant and stationary. You have the opportunity to say something immediately – but if the recipient isn't available, you are stuck in a state of paralysis. You are stuck behind the screen, just looking at it. Constant connectivity is contingent on other people interacting with you. This can be incredibly frustrating. And it was for me, sat there as I was, waiting for urgent information.

When I looked back at the screen I saw that the dots had stopped moving again, so I gave up. I reached across to my phone, and furiously scrolled through my contacts for Marina's number. It still wasn't there. Seeing the empty contact space reminded me about having deleted it. I paused.

I clicked back onto Henry's message. I saw he had still not replied. The dots had stopped moving. I wrote to him again:

Hey, what do you mean an email address?
Has she been locked out of her facebook account?
I see she hasn't posted for ages

A few minutes went by and still nothing. I picked up my phone and scrolled down to Henry's contact name. My finger hovered above the green call button, then retracted. I told myself to be calm.

I tossed my phone down onto the mattress and it bounced up and down briefly. Then I got up, out of bed. I needed to get out, to clear my head. I needed to think about doing something.

Just before I left I quickly opened up my computer and went into an incognito window. I put Facebook in the search bar. Then I typed Marina's email into the box and tried a new password variation: AncillA1930

Incorrect password: 3/4. One attempt remains.

I shut the laptop. I went on a walk and forced myself not to think about Marina.

I managed to stave it off for a few days. I didn't look at any form of social media, and I hardly touched my phone except to check the time. I distracted myself with various selfimposed tasks: painting my nails, watching TV, drinking with Oleana and Caroline. I checked my email a lot. I had lots of baths, read lots of books. I went out driving in my parents' car.

Some of my behaviour was a bit strange – too spontaneous maybe, maybe worryingly so. You could say that without my phone my life had less order. On New Year's Eve, for example, I was supposed to go to a party that Oleana was hosting. But while driving there I found my hands sliding over the wheel, gripping it tightly, swerving it sideways, and then before I knew it the wheels were twisting off the country road towards the motorway. Sometime later I was standing on the beach. I looked out over the sand. The sea swilled underneath the cliffs. It looked grey in the moonlight. At midnight, a series of hot bright fireworks fizzed into the sky. They exploded, spread out into a star shape and then dissipated into nothingness. In the distance I heard someone shrieking with laughter at the top of the cliff. I thought about Marina running into the waves that day we went to the beach. I wondered what she was doing for New Year. I wondered if she was high or drunk; alone or with Henry.

It was on the evening of the second of January that I cracked. I had been out driving again that day, with the windows down, with the air on my face. I had driven to another nearby town, walked around the buildings there, returned very quickly after a miserable encounter in the rain. I had drunk too much at lunch. I had made myself sick and depressed. I returned home, with my favourite clothes all soaked through, feeling horribly alone. There was nothing for it: I had to see Marina.

I logged into Facebook and drew up her profile. Inevitably it was the same. There was still nothing there; there was also no message from Henry. I wondered whether Facebook had sent her a login alert via email. I felt a shiver of anxiety at the possibility. I thought about sending her an explanation, so that if she did somehow track it to me then she would understand. But I couldn't face sending her anymore messages.

I went through my old messages – a sadomasochistic reminder of my loneliness – and it was then I saw that I had one from Oleana. She had sent it days ago – indeed, a few days before I had implemented my social media ban. I must have been so distracted that I missed it. Now I opened it and read what it said.

This is Suki's boyfriend
Literally lol

There was a link attached to the message which – when I clicked on it – sent me directly to the Facebook profile of someone called Richard 'The Legend' Joseph. His was a very public profile: you could see all the likes, friend lists, statuses, plus most of his photos dating back to 2009. I scrolled through these photos with a passive curiosity. Most of them were selfies. They showed him reflected in a bathroom mirror, or a gym mirror, or a bedroom mirror, each time curling his arm into a bulge.

'You can't improve on perfection ;P,' he had written under one; 'Unilad #noparents,' under another.

Several night-club photos showed him stood next to girls with drawn-on eyebrows and dark puckered lips. 'Schlags!!!' was the caption.

I picked a photo of The Legend in a bathrobe – the caption: 'Don't touch what you can't afford' – and pasted the link into the message box. 'I didn't know dickheads were a commodity,' I wrote.

Oleana replied instantly:

Haha

We had a short, derogatory conversation about The Legend, before Oleana said:

Btw have u set up your Swipe account yet? ;)

I stared at the words, blinked, then read them again. I let the idea sink into my brain. Then I clicked off the message and went onto another tab. I saw the option to set up a 'Swipe' account. I thought about it for a second, letting the reasoning cloud over my judgements. If I set one up quickly, then I could just *peruse*, I could just sample it – try it once to see what it was like. There was no need to be self-conscious. No one would have to even know that it was me. I didn't even have to put up a photo of myself. I didn't have to use my real name.

Before I had time to understand why, I sensed that my fingers were typing. I was putting in an email address. I dragged several photos into the boxes, and typed a very succinct bio:

18 years old, Northam University student.

I didn't think it needed more than that.

When I was finished a short while later, I looked at my profile to see what others would see. I looked at the photo. It was faded, but you could just about make out the curve of my eyelids, my little nose and the seductive, slim shape of my mouth. I admired the slight silhouette of my figure. I liked the way that my fringe curled over my eyes. I liked the sound of my name. I mouthed it to myself:

Marina.

Then I set my location, my age range, and I began to swipe.

***

It is hard for me to think about that evening now. It is harder for me to write about it, to capture my thoughts and emotions without imposing a retrospective judgement. All the events that followed: the way that I embroiled myself with Marina's family – the Bedes – the media attention, the death threats, the weeks of isolation … none of it would have happened had I not created that account. When I think back to my behaviour on that evening, I am physically repulsed by what I did. It was so invasive – so unnatural.

But at the time I couldn't see it that way, because it didn't seem to be anything but an inconsequential experiment. It was a silly distraction; almost a joke with myself. I recalled the way Oleana had used that concept of a 'game' to describe dating apps, and that seemed to me to be accurate. I was only doing this as a way to experience Swipe, without committing to it as me. It was a temporary window in, a way of looking without having to partake. It was just like being on social media, but through the eyes of someone else.

114

Is that true? I'm not sure. When I started actually using Swipe, Marina completely disappeared from my mind. Sliding my fingers over the screen, feeling the smooth glass against my skin – the movement and the sensation of it were like wiping away the physical barriers between us. It wasn't that I was simply hiding behind Marina, using her as a mask. I was her.

We morphed into one.

ii.

I spent that entire evening looking at profiles, browsing through boys. I scrunched my nose at their filtered photos and laughed at their tag lines. It surprised me how many of them there were. I set my location to just a 10 km radius and a very particular age range – yet there they were, zooming towards me for hours and hours. Many of them were boys that I recognized. A few of them I had secretly pined for at school, but now – posing as Marina, as someone both beautiful and intelligent – I could firmly reject them. It felt good to swipe left and see them disappear.

Several hours passed before I spoke to someone. Joe. Joe seemed different from the other boys, simply due to the fact that his profile demonstrated restraint. Admirable restraint. He had a few casual photographs of himself. He mentioned that he was six foot three, and studying at Moreland, another university in the area. That was it. There wasn't any crap about his favourite restaurants, how many countries he'd been to or whether he enjoyed 'a snuggle'.

Still, it made it harder to talk to him. What could I say? The weird thing about dating apps is that they have a sleazy reputation, but there's no eroticism whatsoever. The fact you've matched means that you both know that you like the look of each other, so the frisson vanishes. With that out the way, how do you start a conversation? How do you seem natural?

I had never had much experience of chatting up boys. It wasn't that I was afraid of what might happen – I wasn't a virgin – but I was never sufficiently sure of myself to know if I was reacting in the right way, saying the right things, *making them feel at ease*. I always seemed either too forward or too reticent. Maybe I didn't care enough. That was one plus about social media, I thought, as I eventually went to type a safe 'hey'. I could control how they saw me; everything was so one-dimensional.

Joe took a while to respond, so in the meantime I flicked through the profiles of my other matches and thought about talking to them. Ultimately I didn't. I stood up and went to the mirror to squeeze the blackheads on my nose. I had a very particular routine when it came to squeezing nose spots. I would start by pinching the ones on the top first, digging my fingernails so hard into the skin that they left a smattering of crescent-shaped indents. Then I would move to the side of my nose, squeeze the flesh between my thumb and forefinger, forming a pressurized, concave arc that hardened until tiny trails of pus oozed out of the tiny pores. It was satisfying to watch. I thought it looked like maggots crawling out of my skin.

A vibration in my pocket alerted me back to the Swipe conversation. I wiped the remnants of pus on the mirror – my trophies – and looked at the message.

Joe: *You're at Northam Is it as bad as everyone says?*

I wrote back:

Almost. Full of pseudo-intellectuals and anoraks
Joe: *Yikes*
Me: *Still not as bad as Moreland.*

It's not exactly *unembarrassing* for me to recall all this, but it's a realistic representation of how it began. I remember feeling surprised at how easy it was to talk to Joe, having never previously

116

spoken to a stranger online. From behind a screen, it was easy to strike up a conversation. Everything was pretty much taken on face value. They weren't looking to see whether you were telling the truth. They couldn't look at the way your eyes slid sideways as you spoke about yourself. They couldn't analyse the way your hands gripped your chin or the way your mouth wavered. There were still some conversational boundaries, obviously, but even if I embarrassed myself, even if I made a remark that was off-key or badly timed, I could leave at any time.

Besides, I was Marina. I had nothing to lose.

Joe continued:

How come you're down here? are you local?

I paused. There was a 'mutual friends' feature at the bottom which unnerved me, despite the fact it showed no matches. Obviously.

I said:

I'm visiting someone
Over the holidays

It wasn't exactly a lie. Since I had come back from university, my room had basically become a store cupboard. I was a guest in my own home. Still, I felt a need to divert the conversation away from myself, so I followed up with:

How come you're down here?
Joe: I'm also visiting someone
It's my cousin's birthday. We always stay for a few
weeks after the Christmas period
Me: Weeks???
Sorry to hear that
Joe: No, it's fun. Nice big house.

> *This is a beautiful part of the world*
> **Me:** *Sure*
> **Joe:** *well it's nice to see my cousin*
> **Me:** *When are you heading back to Moreland?*
> **Joe:** *Tuesday 20th*
> *I'm getting the train*

We spoke about our families, about our relative experiences at university. It was comforting talking to him, even a bit exciting. I had to keep reminding myself that it was not really me that he was interested in. I was speaking as Marina.

PART III

PART III

CHAPTER SEVEN

Early January

i.

That first night of my Swipe initiation, I slept well. It was a deep, suffocating sleep – the kind of sleep from which you wake with bright wet eyes and clear air passages. That brief experience of being Marina, of inhabiting her virtual skin, had invigorated me.

On the morning of the 3rd of January, I woke up with a vague awareness that something was vibrating in the room: my phone. When I looked at the screen I saw to my astonishment that it was Henry. He was calling me.

I picked up. 'Henry?'

'Hey,' he sounded breathless, unnatural. 'Eva, have you heard from Marina at all today?'

I wavered.

'No,' I said. 'Is everything OK?'

'I'm not sure.' There was a rattling sound in the background: it sounded like he was on a train. 'She's done this weird running away thing. Are you in Northam?'

'What do you mean running away?'

'Are you in Northam?'

'What – no, I'm back in like two weeks. What's happened?'

'Fuck, OK, look I'm not sure yet. Sorry I've got to go it's …'

His voice was muffling. I couldn't hear the rest of what he said, and then the signal cut out. I jabbed at the buttons, tried ringing again but after the second ring it continually went straight to voicemail. Frantically I sent him a message. I felt ridiculous explaining my situation:

Henry, I'm at my parents'
The signal is bad here
Are you on a train?
Or free to Facetime?

There was a pause. I saw that he'd seen it, but hadn't replied. I typed again:

Henry
???
I can drive to Northam if necessary
Just let me know what's happening

Ten minutes passed. I flicked frantically between Henry's and Marina's profiles; I googled her name and arrests in her area. I looked up the local hospitals, the local police station, and thought about ringing them. What could be happening to her? Why wouldn't Henry tell me? It infuriated me that he'd had the nerve to alarm me like that, that he'd ignored my messages and called me only to keep me on tenterhooks. If something had happened to Marina, then I had the right to know. I sent him a message again:

Tell me Henry

I typed with a furious speed and intensity. I felt the words flowing out from my head into my fingertips and I couldn't control myself – they kept on coming and the less he replied the more I typed. It was unrestrained, pathetic, and I knew that I was embarrassing myself but I couldn't stop. Then I noticed he was typing. I felt slightly calmer. I watched with growing anticipation as three little dots wiggled in the corner of the screen. Then, he wrote:

So I think it's sorted now
Sorry
I didn't mean to alarm you
We've traced location through her iPhone which says shes
in Northam
I'm going to go up and see if I can talk to her

My fingers lifted from the keyboard. I felt a mixture of intense disappointment and burning curiosity. I began typing again, but every time I saw the three little dots in the corner something made my fingers stop and erase what I had written. There was a pause, a kind of tentative rephrasing from his side, and then I saw the words:

Shes prone to these running away acts
Theres something not right with her
You know she's probably not coming back for the new term
right?

I stopped.
The words seemed thick and black on the screen.
I wrote back:

No

The dots began to wiggle again and then, suddenly, they stopped. I felt intensely frustrated. I decided that it was the *text* which was the problem – if I could speak to him on the phone, hear his voice, then I might be able to get more information out of him. I picked it up and jabbed my fingers against it. Voicemail again. I returned to my laptop, my fingers tapped against the keyboard.

No I didn't know Why?
Henry
Why isn't she coming back?
Calm down it's not decided yet
Not for sure
But she's definitely not going to be back for next term

'Henry missed a call from you'
'Henry missed a call from you [x 2]'

Chill out!
Look
she's been acting weird
taking loads of drugs
running away
lying
her dad found her drugs too
???
What kind of drugs?
party drugs i guess
look I have to go

He went offline.

I sat on the bed. I stared numbly at the screen. The hard black frame of the laptop grew thicker, blacker. I felt my eyes blur, my vision dim and I started to think about my situation as the abyss

124

grew deeper. My situation was this: Marina had a life that I knew nothing about. She kept me out of it and confided in Henry. She hadn't told me anything about it then – she had told him. And Henry wouldn't tell me now. I was worthless to him. I was disposable to her.

Marina was troubled, yes, but it was hard to feel sorry for her because she was so selfish and superficial and attention-seeking. She was a tortured artist without the art. I decided I was better off without her.

I went downstairs into the kitchen and looked in the fridge. A good distraction, usually – but I couldn't help looking when I felt my phone vibrate again. Another message popped up in the corner of the screen. It was a Swipe notification.

I had told myself that I would only use Swipe once. Being Marina had been exhilarating, but it had been a one-time experiment. If I wanted to use Swipe, I reasoned, then now I could set up my own account. I knew how to use it, and it shouldn't intimidate me anymore.

Had the circumstances leading up to that moment been different, perhaps I would have stuck to this mandate. Perhaps I would have set up my own account, and matched Joe as Eva. Perhaps we would have gone on a few dates and slept together and found each other disappointing and then it would have fizzled out. I would have saved myself the trouble that came after. But instead, feeling deserted and lonely, I clicked on Joe's message. I wanted to creep back into that distraction. I wanted to entertain the possibility that I could be a better version of myself.

Joe: Hey how's it going?
Me: yeah fine
How are you?
Joe: Well couldn't be much worse actually
Liverpool lost last night
my dad got really drunk in the pub

started shouting at this arsenal supporter so I had to
restrain him
Me: *Sounds like a character*
Joe: *he's definitely got a problem*
Me: *At least he actually speaks You should meet my*
dad
Joe: *steady on*
Me: *Well you'd have to take me to dinner first*
Joe: *or a drink? When you free?*
Me: *haha that would be nice*
a bit difficult while I'm down here though
Joe: *maybe when you're back at Northam?*
Me: *Yeah perhaps*

Over the remainder of the Christmas holidays, we spent a few hours talking to each other every day. The conversation was light and easy and relatively superficial, yet there was an energy to it which I hadn't really experienced since my conversations with Marina. There was something about Joe. It wasn't just that he was handsome. It was also that he was witty, and confident without being overbearing or forward. He seemed as though he understood what I was talking about and was actually interested in what I had to say.

Another reason that it was easy to talk to Joe was undoubtedly because I didn't have to interact with him face-to-face. It was a relief to be able to let my words do their own work – I could stop worrying about my physicality, my outfit, mannerisms or tone of voice.

Still, even as I knew this, I was also aware that talking to him online was a strange compromise. I felt like I was getting to know him on some level – about his family; about his education; about his opinions and tastes – but there were glaring gaps in my knowledge which made me feel simultaneously that I didn't know him at all. I didn't know how he sounded; I didn't know what his mannerisms were; I didn't know what he smelled like. I only knew enough of him to be able to pin expectations onto him.

The more I spoke to Joe, the more I felt a kind of gap opening up between the physical and the digital versions of myself. As 'Marina', I wanted to remain as elusive and detached as possible. But as Eva, I wanted to know Joe properly. Increasingly when we spoke, I found that my mask was slipping. I started saying things, private things, things that I genuinely felt. And it was frustrating to me that I was revealing myself when I didn't know other things about him.

An idea began to take shape in my mind.

The term at Northam started a week later than Moreland – on the 27th of January. Technically the accommodation was available a week before then, but since we had a 'reading week' and classes wouldn't start until early February, I figured no one else would be until around the 27th. So it was agreed with my parents that I would drive back on the 26th. Taking the car made sense: there were a few large items that I needed to take back with me, such as a heavy winter coat – the Northam weather was notoriously freezing from February to April – and having a car in the city would afford me some freedom.

This was out in the open. But secretly I was less preoccupied by the date of my own departure than that of Joe's – the 20th of January. The fact that he was going to be at the station on that day stimulated an indescribable urge to see him. I wanted to be at the train station. I had to see him in the flesh in order to discover what he was really about.

On the nineteenth, I asked him, trying to affect a wry, flirtatious tone:

Me: When did you say you were going back to Moreland?
Joe: Tomorrow, as it happens

I hesitated for a moment, wondering how to put my question to him. I didn't want to just come out with it and say 'what time is your train?' I didn't even really believe, at this stage, that I was going to go through with it. I just wanted to indulge the fantasy. And so I persisted:

> *Trains from this part of the world are a nightmare*
> *I'm not going back until 27th*
> **Joe:** *Yeah shame*
> *Still up for that drink once we're up next term?*
> **Me:** *Sure*

I looked at the clock. It was now two thirty. I wondered about whether I needed an alibi. Would my parents ask where I was going? I wondered if there was someone I could bring along with me; if Caroline or Suki might be free tomorrow – then I dismissed that suggestion as ridiculous. Someone like Caroline or Suki would spend the whole time talking at me, distracting me, and if Joe happened to walk past would ask why I was gawping. Just the thought of this made me feel annoyed at them, as though it had already happened.

In that case I would go alone. Since I could drive, I would just tell my parents that I had some errands to run in town. I would say that I needed to go to the post office, to post a letter, or to visit the doctors. Then I would sneak to the train station, see the ten o'clock train heading towards Scotland. I would get a cup of coffee, a paper, and sit on the platform until ten to catch a glimpse of Joe. That was the plan. Or, more accurately, that was the fantasy plan.

The next morning I came down the stairs and saw that my mother was sat at the table. She gave me a suspicious glance. Her narrowed eyes slid towards the car keys in my hand.

'Where do you think you're going?' she said.

'Just to pick up some things from town.'

'What sort of things?'

'*Things.* I have to grab some stamps ... and go to the post office and stuff.'

'Stamps?'

'Among other things.'

'I have some stamps here. Can't your other things wait?'

I shook my head. 'I won't be long.'

'Right.' She rolled her eyes, and ruffled out the newspaper. 'Well make sure you stick to that promise. We have things to do today. I need your help sorting the boxes upstairs.'

'Fine.'

I walked outside and unlocked the car.

As I sat in the driver's seat and shifted the gears, I caught sight of myself momentarily in the windscreen mirror. The realization of what I was doing hit me – the absurdity of it. It was both pointless and insane.

I thought about wandering back but then my hand, almost of its own accord, twisted the key in the ignition. The car surged into motion; I felt the thrum of the engine underneath my feet; I felt them pushing against the pedals. I felt the familiar pangs of self-belief that came with fanatical detachment and my doubts disappeared. I began to drive.

ii.

20th January 2014

Walford town train station was very small and, as usual, very empty. I had visited this station many times, from early childhood through to my teenage years, and it seemed to me to have never changed at all. The interior was grey and steely. The floors were tiled; the walls bare, rippling with a crusty layer of old white paint. The corners of the ceiling curled at the edges and when a train went past – shaking the room, making the floor and the walls vibrate – I saw little flakes of paint break off, and flutter down to the floor. The same two sour-faced workers – who had always seemed to work there – sat behind a smear of glass. Next to that were four old screens, with a number of yellow words sprawling down them.

I looked at the board that said 'DEPARTURES':

Time.	Exp.	Destin.	Platform
09.50	10.19	Glasgow	4
10.09	10.09	Edinburgh	6

My heart sank. Either could be the train that Joe was catching, on different platforms at opposite sides of the station. I didn't want to take my chances. With clammy hands, I took my phone out of my pocket and I noticed that the time now was 09.48.

There was a message from Joe:

Well what do you know
My train is delayed
Now I've got to hang out in this shithole with my
cousin
God knows for how long

I slowly stepped up the stairs towards platform four, my knuckles whitening around the chromium bannister. I felt out of breath, a little dizzy, but I kept my eyes focused on the stones ahead of me. I lingered finally on the last step, then looked up.

The platform was empty.

I didn't get it. Had he gone to another platform? Was he lying? Was I – this was exceptionally hard to believe – being catfished as well? I walked along the platform and pushed open the door to the waiting room.

That was when I saw him. He was sat on the far side of the room, his legs outstretched, crossed at the ankles, a copy of *The*

Economist in his hand. He was a little thinner than I'd expected, and bonier along the shoulders than he looked in his photographs. But otherwise his features were exactly the same. He had soft grey eyes and thick black lashes, a sharp jagged nose, and a full mouth that twitched slightly as he spoke. His mannerisms were refined – long fingers pulled at his hair, he leaned his neck gently sideways. I felt a tingle of terrified excitement as I slunk in through the door. I began to move closer, to sit near him.

'It's a close call,' he said to the boy sat next to him, 'but I think I should wait for this train.'

'But the one arriving is quicker.'

'Yeah, but I have a seat on this one. I don't want to take the risk.'

His voice was interesting. It was softer than I had expected, not quite as animated as his conversation suggested. There was a calmness to it, a peculiar quietness, with a sort of London lilt.

Suddenly I realized that Joe had stopped talking. He was looking at the boy next to him, who was looking at me. The boy's mouth opened into a broad smile.

'Evie,' the boy said. 'Eva.'

Before I could react, he had stood up from his seat and was moving towards me. His arms were outstretched. He approached, drew me into him, and as he did so his face came close to mine.

'Evie Hutchings?' he said. 'I can't believe it!'

'I ... well,' I stammered. 'Hello!'

His bulky arms squeezed around me, and I gathered myself for a moment to place his face in my mind. He was a rugby-looking type, with bulbous eyes, a red, dry-skinned complexion and an oddly aggressive manner which didn't match his voice.

I didn't recognize him.

It was clear, however, that he knew who I was. As he drew back he seemed to register my look of alarm and confusion and smiled bashfully, drawing his huge chin down into his neck. His pale eyelashes fluttered, then opened wide.

'It's Jonny, remember?' he said, and stared into my face with desperate eyes.

'Jonny Wilcox?' I said in disbelief.

'Yeah!'

Jonny Wilcox. I blinked at him, beads of sweat forming around my hairline. Of course. God, how different he looked. He had been extremely slim at school – scrawny-necked and chinless. Now he was huge in every way. He had an extraordinarily wide jaw, a girthy neck, hulking great shoulders and an enormous chest. The only feature that made him recognizable was his strained, bulging eyes. Everything else looked supersize.

'You look so different,' I managed.

At school, in year nine, Jonny and I had been in the same philosophy class. Forced to sit together, we had formed a contextual friendship. He had always seemed a gentle boy during those lessons: kind and inoffensive, albeit without much going on between the ears. After our exams, however, when our class had gone for an illicit drink in the park, he had pulled me into the shadows and pushed me up against a tree. I had told him to stop. He had put his hands under my shirt. I had told him to stop again, several times. But he had continued, sliding them under my bra, burrowing his face into my neck. Eventually I gave him a swift knee in the groin, which caused him to leave me alone. But it was after that that I'd had to quit school for a while. When I returned for sixth form, Jonny had moved away.

It seemed pointless to tell anyone about what had happened. No one would have believed me, they hardly knew who Jonny was, and I had been instructed – by my friends and teachers – that good girls kept quiet. But now, looking at his eyes popping out at me with the same aggressive neediness – the same idiotic sense of possession – now I wish I had. It repulsed me. The whole episode was grotesque. *He* was grotesque.

In the event, I forced myself to make polite conversation. I forced myself to stay focused on Jonny's face, to smile and breathe and to not – under any circumstances – look at Joe. I cleared my throat.

'You look – really, so different,' I spluttered again. 'Sorry. It took me a moment to recognize you.'

'Oh it's fine, it's fine.' A long smile stretched across his chin. 'It happens a lot these days.' Then he leaned in; murmured in earnest: 'It's *so* great to see you!'

I tried to suppress a shudder.

'Yes you too. Did you – ah—' I could feel my cheeks flaming up.

'I'm a bodybuilder now,' he interrupted.

'Right.'

There was an excruciating pause. Jonny cleared his throat. Then he affected a dismissive, laddish wave – something about it was out of joint – and said: 'Oh, I'm sorry! This is my cousin Joe.'

I looked over. Joe looked up from his copy of *The Economist*, and we stared at each other for a moment. His grey, almond-shaped eyes seemed to soften and register interest. His brow relaxed a little. He gave me a polite smile.

'Hi,' I said, in a strained voice.

'Hello,' he said.

'Hello,' I said again, idiotically. 'I'm Eva.'

'Joe.'

He nodded. It was difficult to stop looking at him and I was conscious of my face doing that eager, intense thing that it some-times did when I was impressed by someone. With considerable effort I looked back at Jonny, who was frowning.

'Eve was in my philosophy class,' he cut in. 'We were at school together. Really close back in the day.'

Joe smiled indulgently. His eyes wandered back to *The Economist*.

A knot of childish disappointment tightened in my stomach. I tried to dismiss it. It wasn't rational, I reminded myself, to think that he would like me. He had only swiped on me because he liked the look of Marina. But I couldn't help feel anyway that he *should* have been more actively interested. He should have intuited that I was I, that Marina was me.

Jonny cut into my thoughts again. This time his hand was on my shoulder. I felt his broad fingers over my bra strap and thought about them squirming under my shirt.

'What did you say you were doing now?' he asked. 'Hiding from real life?'

'I-I'm ...' I trailed off.

Joe had begun to flick through *The Economist*.

'You're ...?' Jonny prompted. He had this stupid face on, like he was flirting with a puppy.

'At university.'

'Oh yeah, where? Joe's at university too.'

I swallowed before answering: 'Northam.'

Joe's eyes, which had been skimming down the page of the magazine, suddenly stopped. I watched him in the corner of my vision. His mouth twitched; his finger slowly scratched his jaw. Then his eyes raised. He watched me with a new curiosity.

Jonny clapped his hands and made some impressed-sounding noises, though there was also an edge to his tone, as though I had somehow offended him.

'Wahey,' he said, putting his hands on his hips, rolling his shoulders back. 'Check you out.'

I tried to change the subject: 'You weren't tempted by university?'

Joe cleared his throat. 'Did you say Northam?' he asked.

'Yeah.'

He nodded thoughtfully.

'Funny,' he said. 'I'm at Moreland.'

I affected a look of surprise. 'Oh. That's not too far from here either.'

'No,' he said. 'How is Northam? I hear mixed things.'

'It's – oh it's fine,' I said, at a loss for something new to say.

'Not too stuffy?'

'No, I mean – yes, it can be heavy going, and there are some lecturers who are irritating, but overall …' My eyes jittered around. My mouth spasmed in a weird, comical gesture of self-deprecation. I knew I was behaving strangely.

'Right,' said Joe. 'Yeah.'

He stared at me sceptically. In a way that made me uncomfortable. Small beads of sweat started to form under my collar.

I tried to convince myself that it wasn't really possible for Joe to join the dots. How could he? Even considering the size of the town, the idea was surely too far-fetched to cross his mind. But even so …

'So is that where you're off to today?' Jonny interrupted.

'Today?'

'Yeah, as in where are you headed? To Northam?'

'No!' I burst out. I gave a superficial laugh in an attempt to lighten the atmosphere. No dice. 'I'm … just going to Chipwell. The shops around here are literally empty. There's some stuff I need to get before going back to university.'

'Aren't you on the wrong platform?'

Directly confronted, I found myself able to lie in an instant: 'No, it's actually often quicker to go via Durham. The connections are easier there.'

Jonny looked at me suspiciously. 'OK …' he said. Then, after appearing to mull the possibility over in his mind, his features relaxed, and he added a satisfied: 'Hmm.'

There was another silence. Both of us looked around the room.

'So you're at Northam,' Joe said, again. 'What do you study?'

'Ah – sorry?' I said, my fists clenching at my sides.

I heard the screech of the train wheels outside.

'What do you study?' he asked again.

'Do you do philosophy? You were so good at it,' Jonny interjected.

'I-I do English,' I stammered.

'English?' said Joe. Again, his mouth twitched. 'Cool.'

I stared at him, squinting into his eyes to see whether he had registered anything. I tried to focus on making my own eyes seem less panicked. I needed to gain composure. Had he cottoned on? Why hadn't I just lied?

'So that's my train,' said Joe. 'I'd better be off.'

I made as if to move too, but then realized I had told Jonny I was going to Chipwell. Joe grasped Jonny's hand and they leaned in for a short, punchy hug. They broke apart.

Joe tapped me with *The Economist*.

'Nice to meet you,' he said, opening the waiting room door. He paused for a moment, looked as though he were about to say something else, but just as he opened his mouth, he shut it again. He walked through the door.

I listened to the sound of his footsteps echoing along the tarmac. I tried not to turn my head after him.

iii.

Small-town trains crawl around the countryside. They aren't like city trains: flying over the skyline, swerving under bridges, always juddering frantically so their passengers know that they're moving forward, moving towards something. Sat on a country train you can hardly believe you're moving at all. It feels as though you're never going to be anywhere but there, on an uncomfortable seat with no legroom, neck stiff against the plastic headrest, watching an endless expanse of grass outside stretching into the foreseeable horizon. I leaned my forehead against the windowpane. I wondered how I'd got myself into that position: on that seat, on that train, staring out at the endless grass.

After Joe left, Jonny hadn't gone home like I'd thought he would. Instead he'd stuck around. He'd offered to buy me a coffee while I waited for my 'train' to arrive. I rejected the offer – I'd insisted, actually, that I had things to do and politely asked him to leave – but he still lingered. He gave long monologues, to which I gave monosyllabic answers. It was impossible to think of a further excuse that would permit me to get out of there.

I glanced at the departures board anxiously, panic mounting and then – when the train finally arrived and I heard the gears – I'd felt my feet moving forward towards it, entirely of their own accord, one leg in front of the other along the platform. Then I was hugging Jonny goodbye, I was making my way onto the train, through the carriage, and sitting down in a window seat.

In real life, things never happened in the way that I had become accustomed to thinking they would. When I was on Facebook or Instagram or Swipe, I seemed to have a level of control over my life. I felt confident that if I structured events to happen in a certain way, then they would unravel as part of the sequence I had predicted, as part of *my* narrative. I suspect that this level of control was down to the way I could edit my identity; the way I could look at and interact with only those who interested me and shut out opinions that seemed inconvenient. If I ever felt that my concentration might be slipping, or that the boundaries of the hardened world of which I had put myself at the centre were dissolving – then on the Internet I could look at something completely different that would take my mind off it, and I would relax again.

The distractions of the internet were only a mirage, however. When it came to real life situations – awkward social interactions, inconveniences such as Jonny – I was the opposite of 'in control'. I couldn't pull myself out of the current that other people pushed me into. I just went along with the flow, knowing it was a bad idea, knowing that I didn't want to be there, yet being unable to protest in any way.

The back of my neck was beginning to sweat against the headrest. My phone vibrated in my pocket. I glanced at it – a series of texts from my mother. She used all capitals and a dated text language, always pointlessly signing off with 'MUM'.

WHERE RU!!! MUM

I flicked the lock button quickly off with my index finger, then flicked it back on again out of habit. It buzzed again – another text. I looked down:

IT'S BEEN OVER AN HOUR. R U COMING HOME FOR LUNCH? MUM
HOW LONG DOES IT TAKE 2 BUY STAMPS!!!!!! MUM

I pressed down hard on the lock button and slid my finger across the screen. It was fine, I told myself. It was fine. I was going away for the day and they would have to deal with it. I'd get off at the next stop. While there I'd think of an excuse, calm down and then go back home to face my parents. In the meantime I would try not to look at my phone.

I looked out of the window. I thought about Joe and how he had seemed at the station. I dug my fingernails hard into my thigh.

It is surprising how little you notice when you're not on your phone.

You often hear the opposite – that by 'switching off' or 'detoxing' from technology, you're suddenly able to recognize the details around you. *Everything you usually miss suddenly becomes available – it's like seeing the world shift from greyscale into colour.* But whatever they tell you on your meditation apps, that's not what happens. At least, it definitely doesn't happen to me.

When I was walking around that country town, with the weight of my phone heavy in my pocket, I didn't pause to reflect on the scenery. I didn't notice the details on the friezes, marinate in the heady scent of the city and generally feel clear-headed and meditative. Instead I rushed around pointlessly, distracted, antsy, glancing from street sign to billboard to film poster without thinking about what any of it meant.

Like many small cities near the countryside, this one was large enough to get lost in but small enough not to warrant proper sign-posting. The town centre was full of high street shops and café chains. There was nothing new or exciting about it. Nothing notably quaint either. After ten minutes of charging around, the icy sting of the January wind in my neck and ears, I went back inside, back into the station. I looked to see when the next train was. Twenty minutes.

It was now eleven fifteen. I'd been away from my house for close to two hours. Taking the train journey back into account, it would be around three hours in all. This was not long enough, really, for it to be worth the punishment I'd suffer when I got home. I sauntered into a bookshop near the concourse and wondered whether a present would work as a bribe.

The shop was surprisingly busy – people taking advantage of the post-Christmas sales, I guess. There was a thin-boned lady with a crooked nose, grimacing at a paperback on the crime table; a man with a broad brow and a smirk, using an umbrella as a cane … my eyes scanned across them indiscriminately before they stopped, alarmed, on a face I recognized. It was the jowls that I noticed first, puffing over his collar, slightly damp. My eyes followed up to his pink cheeks, gripped by a set of pudgy fingers. He was smiling slightly, though his brow fell down over his eyelids.

My eyes followed the direction of his and I noticed what he was looking at: a bright blue paperback, the cover of which was embellished with waxy bold font. I saw the title:

HOW TO GET THE MOST OUT OF YOUR SMARTPHONE: A GUIDE

Includes tips on apps, camera features and privacy settings. PLUS:

What is the difference between iOS and Android?

At that moment the professor turned his head, and his eyes met mine. I noticed the surprise and fear, mixed with a strange glinting recognition – that unique expression that only appears when you recognize someone out of context. Perhaps the look was reflected from my face. There was nothing either of us could do.

'Odd coincidence!' he spluttered.

'Yes.'

'I'm just doing some very late Christmas shopping,' he said, gesturing at the bookshelves. He went on to give a lengthy explanation about buying a book for his 16-year-old niece. His relatives lived in the next town, he said, where they were hosting a party, and he had, *of course*, forgotten to get a Christmas present until the final hour.

I smiled patiently and nodded as he told me all this. I looked at his face, noted the strained skin around the eyes, the pronged wrinkle in the middle of his forehead. I made a point of telling myself to remember these details so that I could tell Marina later. It seemed to me typical that the professor should buy something so tragic and dated as a 'Smartphone manual' and then attempt to cover it up. Such was his vanity. I thought about exact ways to recount it, ways that would make Marina laugh. Then I remembered, with a thud, that she wasn't coming back to Northam.

'So, yes …' Montgomery reached forward towards the bookshelf, selected a pink-spined hardback apparently at random, and pretended to inspect the back. 'Ah, yes, here we are.' He gave a satisfied nod.

'Oh good,' I said.

'Yes … good.'

A few seconds of stilted silence ensued, and then he looked up, cleared his throat and smiled.

'Anyway, I trust all is well with Marina?' he said, with unnatural lightness. 'You two, thick as thieves.'

'Yes, yes I – guess so.' For some reason I didn't feel as though I could bring up the fact Marina was not coming back to Northam. His eyes flickered.

'I mean,' I continued, looking slightly past him, 'I haven't spoken to her very much recently, it being the holidays. We've both been busy I think. Have you seen her?'

'Er, no,' he said. 'It no longer being term time that would be …'

'I guess I meant that you might have seen her family.' My palms felt slightly sweaty. 'You know, because of her father.'

He looked at me quizzically. 'I'm sorry?'

'Because you're a family friend,' I said breathlessly. 'That's what she told me.'

'She did?'

'Yes.'

The professor wrinkled his brow.

'I must say that's a little bit odd,' he said. 'I wouldn't say that we know each other particularly well. I was at university with her father who is, as you probably know, Professor Marcus Bede, but we …' he trailed off. 'We haven't spoken in years. Really, years. I only ever see him in professional circles. Very intelligent man, however. Brilliant speaker.'

Silence fell. I looked at my shoes, not knowing what to say.

'Well,' the professor cleared his throat again. 'I'd better be off. Lovely bumping into you, Emma. Good luck in the new term.'

He made a frantic gesture with his hands – not quite a wave, not quite a handshake – and then he barrelled off towards the counter, where he paid for the book.

I watched him hand the money to the cashier. There was definitely something artificial in his manner, I thought. Something rushed. His coat flapped behind him, splaying out at spiky angles above his thighs, and as he put the book in his bag, I briefly wondered what his family was like … how he behaved at home.

There was something off about him. Something I couldn't put my finger on ... I couldn't entirely understand why, but the thought of touching his hand had made me feel unclean.

On the train, I dug my phone out of my pocket and switched it on. It had been two hours since I'd looked at it and I wanted to check on Marina.

I had to know what she was doing, whether she was at home again, whether she was really not coming back to Northam. I wanted to know why she had lied to me about her family's relationship with the professor. I wanted to tell her about that ridiculous coincidence, catching Montgomery unawares in the teenage section of a train station bookshop, about his pathetic present for his teenage niece. I wanted to tell her about my Christmas holiday and hear her sarcastic jokes about Caroline and Suki. I would message her again, I decided. I would go onto Facebook now.

I tapped along the screen. I ignored the little Swipe symbol in the corner, and went straight to Facebook Messenger.

Her name was frozen out: not blue, like the text of the other names, but a light grey. I tried to press the button to contact her, and hit a hard grey wall.

Instinct told me that something was very wrong.

I went onto the main Facebook app. I typed her name in the search bar, waiting for her profile to emerge. But nothing came up.

There was nothing to click on, not even a frozen-out grey screen. Everything had vanished.

The words rolled through my head. *She has blocked me. She has blocked me.* I felt something fierce in my chest. Why would she do that? Why would she do that *now*? Perhaps it meant that she had been thinking about me. Perhaps she had realized that I had tried to hack into her account. I shuffled in my seat. The woman opposite eyed me warily. I typed a message to Henry, unable to help myself:

Has Marina deleted Facebook?
Or is it that there's something wrong with her account?

I sent several more messages, powerless to stop the flow of questions once I had started asking after her. I wasn't even conscious of what I was writing, I just sensed my fingers flickering against glass, waiting for the tick to confirm that he'd seen it, waiting for the dots to say that he was writing back.

I went back into the Messenger app and looked at her frozen name. The Swipe icon flickered in the corner of the screen. Wait. Could that be it? Could Joe have somehow found me out? Had he contacted Marina and told her? My fingers hovered over the Swipe icon for a moment. Then I opened it and read what it said.

Joe: God this train is long

That was all.
I felt a rush of relief, tinged with a kind of disappointment. I asked Joe how it had been getting the train from dead-end Walford station.

Joe: Delayed, actually
Was just talking to my cousin for a bit, hanging around

I felt another stab of disappointment. I wanted him to mention me. I typed back, trying to probe. I asked for more details about the station. I asked him what he had done while he waited for the train. I tried to sound as disinterested as possible but I figured I was still coming across as fairly intense.

Joe: I was reading an article actually
The Economist

I didn't reply, so he continued.

143

Joe: Basically there's a rift between two oil tycoons in India
Their biggest company has been owned by successive generations of one family since it was founded
And it's just been taken over by a new guy basically who is trying to shake things up

He went on like this for some time, unprompted, and my fingers began to itch. They hovered over the screen as the text kept pouring down.

Joe: So now the new guy has been ousted
And they're refusing to trade with the other company
It's affecting the rupee, which in turn is gonna be affecting the pound
Probably

I felt increasingly irritated, knowing that we were moving away from my target conversation. Clumsily I reintroduced the subject of the station.

Me: Sounds intense
So were you boring your cousin with this at the station or did he have an escape clause
Joe:
Weird you should say that
There was someone from Northam there actually
Me: Oh really?
Sorry to hear that
It's a problem down there
Joe: middle-class circles
Me: Northam infestation
Joe: exactly

There was a slight pause. I saw the three dots wiggling in the corner of the screen, then they stopped. I decided to take the plunge.

Me: *Well perhaps I know them – did you get a name?*
Joe: *Er*
Yes but I can't remember
She did your subject as well though
Which is pretty weird

My heart beat faster.

Me: *Weird*
I guess it's a big course
what did she look like?

Joe began typing and then stopped.

Me: *Blonde hair? All girls on the course are sloanes*
Joe: *Like yourself you mean*
Nah she's brunette I think
Brown eyes maybe
Me: *10/10?*
Joe: *Absolutely not*
Just average

I stared at the letters on the screen, processing the text prickling under the glass.

Joe began typing, then stopped, and then started again.

Joe: *lol that was a bit harsh*
I just meant that she seemed to fit your description
of the types at Northam

My fingers hovered over the glass. It is rare that you get the opportunity to see you as others see you – an unedited version of yourself, someone that neither matches your interpretation of who you are, nor a filtered reflection as told to you by your friends or family.

Until that point I had persuaded myself that being in Marina's presence had enabled me to become like her. I wasn't so delusional that I thought I was brilliant or beautiful, but I did think that in being around her, basking in her charisma, I had started to emit some of it too.

Now I saw that that wasn't the case. I didn't belong in her sphere, and I never would. It didn't matter how much time I spent around her. Whatever I wore, whatever I did, however much I tried – I was average.

I put my phone in my pocket as the train pulled into the station. I put my head against the black glass, and as the shadow of Walford rose up behind it, I felt the familiar pangs of dread. I was home.

***

Looking back, my reaction to Joe's message strikes me as laughably out of proportion. What had I expected him to do? Gush to Marina about how attractive he had found some random at the station? Clearly Joe had said those things not because he necessarily thought that they were true, but because he assumed that 'Marina' would appreciate them. Talking down other girls was a tactful ploy, like mentioning how he'd remembered my description of people at Northam. The irony of this tactic now makes me laugh. But at the time it got to me. It made me depressed and irritable.

iv.

I climbed out of my car and slammed the door behind me.

'Where the hell have you been?'

The familiar shrill voice of my mother. Echoing over the rose-bush, travelling up the road.

'You're grounded.'

'Oh wow.'

'You're *grounded*.'

I walked past her silently, put a key in the lock.

'I'm not joking this time,' she said. 'No car. *No ... car.*' Out of the corner of my eye I could see her little bob shaking from side to side. Her hands were on her hips.

'We're not American,' I said. 'You can't *ground* me.'

'What was that?'

I looked up. Her mouth was a tight white line.

I stabilized my features. 'I said you can't ground me, we're not American. Why are you talking like that? I thought we'd banned soaps in the house.'

'Wh— how dare you speak like that to me!' she thundered. 'How dare you march in without telling us where you've been!'

There was an awkward pause in the tirade, and my mother hiccupped slightly before adding: '*Where* have you been?'

I shrugged.

'Nowhere,' I said. Then I opened the door and closed it behind me.

'You left the keys in the door! I'm taking them! For your information madam, you are *absolutely* grounded!'

She was right: I had left the keys in the door.

The next day they were missing from the rack. It was obvious she had hidden them somewhere – neither she nor my father would tell me the location. They smirked when I asked them, and widened their eyes at each other like, '*Oooh.*'

There was a note on the fridge, scribbled in my mother's distinctive hand:

When you are ready to explain where you were yesterday we will tell you where the keys are. Mince in freezer can be defrosted.

147

That was it.

I paced around the house. I went on a long walk along the country lanes. I checked my messages: nothing from Henry, nothing from Marina. I messaged Joe and complained of my family's unreasonableness.

I couldn't stand being there.

When I got home after my walk I went straight to my room, bought a ticket to Northam online and packed up my things. I did not feel guilty about leaving my parents without saying goodbye. I texted them a quick explanation as the bus pulled up to the station. I ignored the buzzes as I heaved my bag up the steps towards the platform.

The train was full. Heaving. Men in grey suits were packed tight alongside each other, red faces, sweat oozing in dark ovals under lifted arms, gripping the rails above the seats they stood by. The train stopped, groaning to a halt with a stiff sigh that sounded like my own.

I elbowed my way onto the carriage, lugging my bag behind me, and waited for the train to start moving. My phone felt heavy in my pocket. The whistle blew and the wheels began rolling forward.

CHAPTER EIGHT

Late January 2014

i.

At Northam: no calls, no texts, no Facebook messages. Nothing from Marina. No response from Henry.

The reading week wasn't due to start for another few days, and the only people who seemed to be back already were those who had never left. A girl called Phyllis had been there for the duration of the holiday. She was planning to stay in Northam for her entire three years, since her parents lived in China and she couldn't afford to go home. She was pleasant enough but due to her limited English the conversation always petered out after three or four minutes.

I logged onto Facebook and sent Henry another message. He still hadn't 'seen' the last one that I had sent.

Hey, when are you coming back to Northam?
Also is Marina OK?
Can you tell her I'm sorry

149

Once again without friends, family or anything to do, I spent my days on Swipe. Joe launched into one of his monologues.

> **Joe:** *I read Atlas Shrugged when I was 15*
> *And I know it's bad I mean it contains nothing that I agree with now in the way of ethics or politics and it has no literary value*
> *But it had a really strong effect on me at the time*
> *And now when I hear about it I feel a kind of adrenaline rush*

I enjoyed responding to these rants with deflationary authority – in a way that I imagined Marina would respond. It was interesting to me how liberating it was to have confidence in my thoughts – the way that, if I voiced *something* with conviction, even if it was something I didn't believe in, then it would lift a mental block. Just feeling confident would allow me to travel down wider mental pathways, to flesh out thoughts, to see ideas from several different viewpoints.

> **Me:** *well I'm sorry to hear that*
> *Perhaps it's your subconscious telling you that you really think it's true*
> *You've probably just adopted left-wing ideas because it's what the people around you accept*
> *You like art, you like novels, you like theatre …*
> *You like trendy clothes so you can't be conservative*
> *You must like socialism too!*
> *This is a question of following fashion, not what you genuinely feel or think*

But Joe failed to notice my observations. He was unfazed by my dismissive tone – or didn't detect it – and never fully engaged with the things I said. Eventually I'd give up and make a joke – something that would link me back in to his side of the debate.

> **Joe:** *I wouldn't go that far*
> *all I'm saying is that I think it's had an effect on me*
> *psychologically*
> *Like*
> *Yeah*
> *I know it's not true*
> *But there's a part of me that has a strong reaction to*
> *it*
> *Not a negative reaction*
> **Me:** *And it's that part which is the real you*
> *you feel you can't admit to it, like it's a dirty secret,*
> *because you're scared of the reaction*
> *even from yourself*
> *but it's what you believe, deep down*
> **Joe:** *No*
> *It's more like Later in life, I'm worried that it will come*
> *back and haunt me*
> **Me:** *When you're a sell-out property investor you*
> *mean*
> **Joe:** *Ha exactly*
> **Me:** *Yeah I can't help you with that*

Joe and I never had productive debates. They never reached conclusions, and I can see why – when faced with the question of what we talked about later – he hadn't known what to say. But there was an openness there, and in speaking about nothing we could also speak about everything. Initially I'd thought that this was because we had a special connection of some kind – one that went beyond the digital. Now I was beginning to realize that it was because he loved to hear himself talk.

Since I was posing as Marina, I shouldn't have been bothered by this: the lack of opportunity to talk about myself was, practically speaking, a free ticket. But as time went by I began to notice how little my confessional musings were addressed, how they were either completely ignored, or treated as mere springboards to Joe's Genius Observations. His points were always discussed for at least five lines each, whereas mine were a conversational segue. He saw me as ignorable, I realized, like Marina had. My posing as her hadn't worked: I was a doormat.

After I noticed this, I found Joe increasingly grating. A mental block that deadened my ability to discover new ideas. I tired of our conversations.

Joe: *So when are we going for that drink?*

Even though I knew that it was impossible, the idea of meeting him in real life, of having to compose my face to look interested, of having to listen to him drone on without being able to punctuate the boring bits by looking at other things on my phone – it made me feel exhausted. It was easy to rebuff him.

Me: *We'll have to see*
Joe: *Again???*
Me: *I have exams coming up*

Yet perhaps that was not the overriding reason for my diminished interest. Put simply, I didn't find him as stimulating intellectually as I thought I would – as stimulating as I found *Marina*. And as much as I liked *being* Marina, I wanted to be around her more. I missed her conversation. I didn't have the patience to listen to anyone else.

I switched off Swipe and went back onto Facebook. I sent Henry another message – something I instantly regretted: it was not well thought through, it was excessively accusatory. I looked at the other messages in my inbox. Marina's name was still frozen out.

Out of habit, I tried to click on it. I tried again, but nothing happened. My phone vibrated. I had a message from Joe.

Joe: *You really are mysterious*
Still playing hard to get
Why can't you just make time for one drink? I'll come
to Northam?
Me: *No, look I have to work*
I'll let you know whenever it's convenient
Joe: *Convenient?*
Woah

The typed 'woah' – obviously not vocalized – tipped my patience from dwindling to zero. What did he expect? I flicked off Swipe and went back to my Facebook messages. Still nothing from Henry.

My phone pinged insistently: another Swipe notification.

Joe: *Look, all I want is to see you in person*
That's all I'm asking

Seeing the Swipe account beside Marina's frozen-out Facebook unnerved me. It felt weird to be continuing this when her social media presence was deactivated. I didn't like it. Being blocked out of her online life made it difficult for me to remember what she had been like at all – as though our friendship had been a fantasy, a dream.

It was time for it to stop.

I tapped onto Swipe, ignored Joe's latest string of messages, and scrolled to the account settings.

Profile. Edit. Location. Privacy. More.

I clicked on *More*. There was no deactivation option. A prickle of anxiety shot through me. To quell it I drew up the lid of my laptop. I typed into Google:

'Delete Swipe account'

Thousands of results rolled up: a string of forums, spam adverts, news comments, even a few Buzzfeed articles.

WATCH: This guy spends 40 minutes trying to delete his Swipe account

Why is it impossible to delete a Swipe profile? 10 humiliating stories

Swipe CEO explains what he's doing with your data.

I ignored the clickbait headlines and went onto a forum. Someone had written an answer:

It's under 'Privacy' on a tiny box. Sometimes you have to download the app on a desktop because for some reason it's extra tight on this sort of thing. Does anyone have a more detailed explanation?

I opened another tab, googled 'Swipe, and downloaded the app on my desktop. As I waited for it to download I skim read some of the comments on the thread.

The thing about Swipe is that you can't actually delete your profile. It circulates round the app for about a year afterwards, even if it's technically deactivated. I'm not sure what the algorithms are or if you can alter this?

Someone else:

I was looking into this too yeah. But you can just delete your pictures off it and whatever. It tracks

some of your location data but you can just alter that in settings.

The first commenter again:

What about name change though? Tracks through Facebook? I guess it's just the first name that appears on the Swipe account but I'm surprised there hasn't been more of a crackdown on this TBH. It's a massive privacy issue

No problem, I thought. I could just deactivate the fake Facebook account. I logged out of my own Facebook and then put in the new email; the new password.

Access denied.

I typed again, this time pressing each fingertip carefully on the keys, making sure the ridge of each plastic square was separate, that it was definitely the right code. Still the passive aggressive response:

I'm sorry! Did you forget your password?

Shit shit shit.

How could I have forgotten the password? There must be a record of it somewhere – in my personal email drafts? No. In the notes on my phone? No.

I tried the original attempt at the password one more time, making sure caps lock was off, monitoring the movements of my fingers so, so carefully, one digit at a time.

You have been locked out of your account. To retrieve password, please contact an administrator.

I gripped the keyboard with both hands.

I thought back to the time I had created the password. I thought harder. As I did so, getting increasingly frustrated, I felt the plastic keys begin to give under the wrench of my fingernails.

I thought back to the moment I had created the account, tried to picture everything about the evening: the alcohol I'd consumed, the conversations I'd conducted. I relaxed my grip on the keyboard, ran one hand across it, and then found a loose key. I curled the corner under my nail, began to pick. Then I pictured the screen that night – the night I'd created the account. I pictured dragging Marina's photo into the box; pictured typing the password. I thought about trying it again – then and there – and I was just preparing myself to start doing so when I felt a sharp snap, heard a ping and saw a piece of plastic fly upwards. It danced in the air and landed on the desk beside me.

I stared at it for a second.

Then I carefully picked it up between two fingers and attempted to push it back into the keyboard, into the space between U and O. But my fingers were too slippery with sweat, my vision too blurry. Finally I flicked it away.

I sat back. I told myself to think rationally.

If there were no pictures on the account, then there was nothing to worry about. After a year all evidence would disappear. It would be fine. There was no real reason to get angsty, to get worked up about the fake Facebook account. It didn't *matter*. If I deleted the pictures, blocked Joe, deleted the app off my laptop and my phone – then I would be free of it. It would be like I'd never used it at all.

Having got this far I wanted the app to be gone. I wanted it wiped out of existence. And I had to get rid of it *now*.

When Swipe-for-desktop had downloaded, I logged in and immediately deleted all the photos. I blocked everyone I had ever matched with; deleted my bio; disabled location services. Then I went to the privacy settings and pushed the big red button.

Account deactivated.

Marina was gone.

ii.

I didn't mind being on my own after that. I felt I had excised my creepier urges and, now of a clearer mind, I could return to a reclusive position without experiencing guilt or FOMO. I could do my washing every week. I could do my reading unencumbered by cigarette breaks with Marina. I could walk alone around the fields without worrying whether I'd make it back in time to pre-drink with the others. There were benefits to being lonely, I realized, and selfpreservation was one of them. University was not the end point, but a stop-gap: an opportunity to train myself to be fit for wherever I went next. After two more years I wouldn't have to be here anymore: I would be moving on to different places, different people. And by then, I was certain, I would have made myself so clever that no one from Northam would be able to keep up with me.

Even if the campus architecture was of an acquired taste, the surrounding town and countryside were pleasant enough. On afternoons I would go out to the moors without my headphones, raising my head up to feel drops of rain fall over my forehead and the end of my nose, strands of hair slicked down over my eyelashes.

Now the snow had stopped the winter in Northam was tolerable. I didn't mind the sting of the wind on my cheeks. I didn't mind even when sheets of rain slashed into my eyes. I shifted the wet sleeves of the anorak forward over my knuckles and ploughed on through long stalks of grass. It felt satisfying to have the water seep in through my socks, clotting in the corners of my shoes. It *felt*.

Those were the days I cherish now, when I look back on my university experience. I value them for the independence I felt. I loved being in an environment where I could go places and do things without being monitored – either by the voice of my mother or the interruptions of Marina or a phone insistently buzzing in my pocket. I could go to the shop and buy alcohol in the middle of the day. I could have a glass of wine or a spliff without feeling self-conscious. There were a few days still before classes started again, and I felt relaxed, on top of things.

Back in the libraries I buried myself in books, and in reading them I felt my face soften. My mind opened like a flower. The more distant I was from social media, the happier I became. It wasn't the university life I had envisioned for myself, not the glamorous cocktail of parties and witty conversations. But I was stimulated, and that was enough.

I was glad to be free of Marina.

iii.

On the 29th of January, I went for a walk in the afternoon. I got back in the early evening, at about six o'clock. By that time it was pitch-black. As I made my way unsteadily, up the cobbled path towards the angular silhouette of the accommodation block, I suddenly noticed a group of smokers milling outside. They all had their hoods up, faces obscured by shadow and plumes of silver cigarette smoke. They were crouched around something, and when I came closer I saw from the familiar rectangular glow that it was a phone.

Only one face was fully illuminated. The outline was round, and strings of blue-tinted hair dangled like wires over her forehead. Her expression was calm, smiling slightly. She shook her head and I heard her mutter something: 'I know you're fucking with me. Like this actually isn't funny but I still know it's a joke.'

I recognized that voice: it took a second, then I paired it with her blue-tinted features and I realized who it belonged to: Rebecca Barnes.

She bent closer into the phone. Then her features contorted. She let out a scream. It was a piercing scream, one that reverberated through the courtyard. The hooded heads swivelled around in panic. Someone snatched the phone.

'How?' the girl said.

'Shhh!'

I sensed the group draw back as I approached.

'How?' she said again.

'We don't know yet.'

'But – God that's terrible. That's literally …'

I drew closer again. The group fell silent. Several people brought out their phones and began tapping over them, their faces obscured by hoods. As I passed them I saw their eyes skitter up towards me, a row of blue electric whites – the pupils moving slowly sideways. I listened to the sound of thick raindrops bouncing off their screens. I thought I saw one of them smile slightly, though it may just have been the light.

I entered my room and took off my raincoat. The water ran down the plastic in thick black streams. It pooled on the carpet like blood, and as it sank into the brown, matted gauze I shivered again.

I thought of the scene I had just witnessed. The words. The screen. The light and their eyes in the darkness. I attempted to shake off my growing anxiety and reason with myself. Some piece of university gossip, I thought. But the dread persisted. I couldn't ignore it.

I started up my laptop and went onto the Internet homepage. I googled 'Swipe Eva Hutchings'. My fingers drummed impatiently as the page loaded. The eyes, the words, the screen.

Nothing.

Some old article from six months ago appeared instead:

WATCH: *Celeb hunter Eva May swipes eBay bargain from Jol Hutchings with under thirty seconds to go!*

A sheet of rain drilled against the windowpane.

I went onto Facebook to see if Henry had replied. I clicked on my messages. No response from Henry. No new messages — but wait: Marina had 'seen' my message. More than that: the name flashed bright blue. Her profile had been reactivated.

I clicked on the link and felt flooded, instantly, with a kind of euphoric nostalgia. Seeing her profile picture again was like seeing a close relative: that sylph-like silhouette provoking familiarity and wistfulness. Looking at it I felt that no time had passed since the first time I had seen it: that I was yet to meet Marina, I had all the drinking and the smoking and the laughter and the fights to come. I stared for a few more seconds, then clicked on the next photo and zoomed in. Loose swirls of hair framed sharp cheek-bones, her mouth seemed wry and full, freckles danced on the top of her nose. And her eyes! Gleaming with intellect and vitality, self-possession. My friend was back. She wasn't talking to me, but she was back! She was tangible again. I could access her.

I clicked off, scrolled down and the mouse stopped.

She had been tagged in something. A status:

Thank you all for the messages and the support. Marina was a kind, beautiful, caring girl whose smile lit up every room. We are still registering the shock of her passing, and truly appreciate everyone sharing their stories of how she affected their lives. Rest in peace sweetheart xx

The edges of the textbox were blurry. My throat was dry. I found a sliver of skin along my throat and dug my fingernails into it.

It had to be a hoax.

The cursor flickered against the screen.

Slowly, slowly, I let go of my neck and felt the burn tingle along the skin. I reasoned with myself: a hoax, yes – or maybe

160

some art thing that Marina had been involved in. It was a cultural awareness project probably – that was it – designed to show us how social media fabricates truth; how susceptible people are to personal news.

I told myself this again and again, with a firmness that almost made me believe it – but it was ultimately unconvincing. My vision was blurred and my face felt hot. There was an acrid taste in my mouth, like vomit. I went onto Messenger. I saw that Robin, Henry's housemate, was online. I clicked the 'video call' icon. It rang and rang. No answer.

Henry was offline, but I tried him anyway. I sent him messages – one after the other, an outpouring of questions. But nothing worked to solicit a response. Finally I picked up my phone.

Every ring in my ear was a reminder to breathe, a reminder that everything was OK. Then, when it went voicemail – and when I heard the automatic strains of '*Welcome to Orange Answerphone*' – I stopped breathing and let out a fierce sob.

I lay on the bed on my back and stared at the ceiling. My breathing was shallow. I could see a spider slowly making its way across the cracks in the paint. I watched the slow zigzag tracks of its black legs and focused on the tiny hairs sticking out at each angle.

Suddenly my phone buzzed.

I looked at the screen. It was a message from Henry:

Yes it's true clearly
Please stop messaging me

iv.

7th – 14th February 2014

In the following days I stayed in my room. I didn't see anyone, I didn't eat anything, and when I tried to rouse myself from bed

I found that I could hardly move. It was as though my entire body, up until that point fluid and mobile, had hardened into stiff wax. Only my fingers could move easily. I was dimly aware of them scuttling along the keyboard. They were brittle and achy.

I hunched over the screen and scrolled through her photos mechanically, trying to remember what she had been like, what she had sounded like. Messages began pouring onto her Facebook wall. I blinked, confused, trying to fit them with my own picture of her.

RIP Marina – the funniest, warmest person I ever met. A wonderful girl.

Wrong. She wasn't like that. She wasn't warm at all. She would have hated being described as a 'wonderful girl'.

My eyes fell to the next tribute:

Marina, my oldest and dearest friend. Words can't express how much I will miss you. Such a shock xxx

The words were accompanied by a photograph of the two girls together – Marina smiling, showing her teeth. They had their arms around each other's shoulders, each set of fingers locking into the other's hair. It had fifty-four likes.

This was not a photograph I had seen before. I clicked on the profile of the girl who had posted it. It was private, but I could see a tiny two-by-two-inch photo in the corner of the screen. Even from that tiny filtered glimpse I could tell what sort of music she listened to, what sort of make-up she used, to which social stratum she belonged. It annoyed me that she had known Marina before I had.

Facebook urged:

Post a message on Marina's wall.

I thought about what sort of tribute I could write. There were no photos of me with Marina. We had only known each other for a few months. She had not spoken to me at all over the holidays, and then the last time I had seen her had been awful. I also had the impression that she would have hated this sort of thing.

I imagined us looking at the tributes together. I imagined her talking me through each person – explaining what, if any, connection they had had to her in her short life. I imagined us laughing at the inaccurate posts. I imagined rolling my eyes at the grammar, Marina rolling her eyes at me.

I felt a hot trembling grief as the reality of it hit me.

She is dead.

She is dead.

She is dead.

The word 'dead' was so cold and hard – like a piece of concrete – and it seemed so unfair, so disgusting that she should be reduced to it. But she had been. She was. Now she was reduced to one repetitive syllable: dead. Dead body without air, dead lungs without function, dead brain without thoughts. Heat pressed into my eyelids. I felt breathless and sick. My heart curled up inside my chest. I thought of her laughing outside her accommodation block, of her singing in the car, of her shouting in seminars.

She is dead.

A bolt of electricity shot through me. But how? From a car accident? A heart attack or a stroke? Perhaps there had been an illness which she'd kept from me?

There was no information on her Facebook page or anywhere else on the internet.

I clicked left along her photos, tracing backwards to those comments I had found a few months earlier. I hovered my mouse over them:

Marina Bede likes this.
Marina Bede likes this.

It was strange to live in a world where people could leave traces of themselves like that, trapped in the present tense. I imagined her sitting behind her laptop, edging the mouse along the screen, pausing for a moment and then clicking. It was such a mundane but concrete gesture. I couldn't believe she was dead.

I picked up my phone then, and pressed on my images folder. I began scrolling through a private file called 'MB'. These were miscellaneous photos – photos I had saved from her Facebook profile. They were not only pictures she had been tagged in but ones which she had purposefully untagged too, which I'd found by scrolling through other people's albums. I went through, zooming in on each one, studying her face and posture, before stopping on a photo of Henry and Marina. This was the photo that I had seen in the car as my mother drove away from Northam. It was the photo I had looked at on the evening I had created the Swipe account.

The Swipe account.

I felt a dizzying, almost pleasurable panic. My hand flew over my mouth. I bit on it so hard that my teeth broke the skin.

A collage of flashbacks flicked through my mind – the pictures of Marina; the conversations with Joe; the bio:

Marina, 18, Northam.

I turned over, the heat spreading across my face. I pressed my cheeks into the pillow and screamed. I let it pour out, howling, feeling the air scrape the back of my throat. Then I rolled over onto my back. I looked back at the screen.

There was a new tribute on her Facebook page. It was more formal in tone, posted by someone who appeared to be from an older generation.

So sorry to have heard about the death of Marina in The *Homeshire Gazette*. She was a kind, thoughtful, funny and smart young lady who I had the pleasure of meeting with in the village many years ago. A lovely, sunny disposition. I am sure she will be missed.

Immediately I clicked on the Google search bar and entered: 'Homeshire Gazette Marina Bede'. Her name came up. It was an article:

TRAGIC DEATH OF LOCAL GIRL MARINA BEDE

My eyes skimmed through it. It was clumsily written, I thought irritably, trying and failing to be sensitive – and it gave away nothing about the details of her death. I went to the comments.

Ls822: It's so sad what happens to girls like this. Fault of the system

S093: @Ls822 are you saying it's a suicide?

Ls822: @S093 Certainly seems like it if they're not mentioning cause of death

S093: @Ls822 seems pretty insensitive 2 be speculating at a time like this. I think they shuld of disabled the comments? @moderator

FrezzaMoney: @S093 @Ls822 I was a few years below her at school and there are lots of rumours about her having committed suicide. A counsellor came in the other day. It's really sad. I didn't even know her very well but it is terrible.

I tried to take it all in, identifying different, conflicting emotions. They all arrived with such force, and yet so fleetingly, that it was impossible to focus on one before it rolled into another. Everything happened quickly after that. The news of Marina's death came out in the university press, the campus was abuzz with reports; suicide counsellors interrupted lectures to give us

talks. No one knew exactly how or when or why she had done it
– it was only clear that *she* had done it – and on campus, a few
weeks earlier. It seemed that the news had initially been suppressed
so as to avoid 'causing unnecessary stress' to both students and
family, but because it had leaked on social media, it was now
campus responsibility to follow protocol. We received an email
from the University Chancellor referencing an 'incident'. It said
that if anyone was struggling with similar 'feelings of depression'
that they should 'not hesitate to get in touch'.

The only person that I wanted to get in touch with was Henry.
He hadn't responded to my messages since confirming that
Marina was dead, and he wasn't picking up his phone or
Messenger calls. I neither understood nor accepted this rejection.
I had to have an answer. I continued calling him twice a day. I
waited outside his house. I tried to find where his classes were
and waited for him outside the lecture halls. But he wasn't
anywhere.

I fretted – as a result of this behaviour – that Henry had
somehow discovered the Swipe account. I spent the next few
mornings frantically Googling myself in incognito: 'Eva Swipe',
or 'Marina Bede Swipe impersonator'. I checked Marina's tribute
posts regularly, typing 'Joe' into the search bar at the top of the
RIP page. But it never returned any relevant results, and eventually it struck me that I was overreacting by being so anxious
about it. My impersonation game was juvenile and insubstantial,
the stuff of digital fantasy – not hard, physical reality like Marina's
death.

This left me, then, with a fairly bleak impression of Henry. I
couldn't put his rejection down to anything except the fact that he
didn't like me. I was worthless now that Marina no longer existed.
I had always just been her shadow. Now there was nothing to cast
that shadow anymore, he had just wiped me out of existence.

***

166

I select another paper from the pile. The one with his face on it. The one with the congratulatory headline.

I am almost surprised at how easy it is to look at him. He is very photogenic, very kindlooking; handsome in his own two-dimensional way. I look at his smiling eyes, his avuncular grin, his proud and confident posture. I trace my pen over the eyelids, along the brow, towards the side of his head. I place the nib over his temporal artery. I look at his expression closely, take several sharp breaths. Then I grip the pen tightly and push downwards, downwards, downwards, piercing the paper.

He does not move his eyelids, move his head, move his body. Not this time. He can't.

I grind the pen further into the paper.

A thin trickle of black ink oozes out. It blots out one side of his face.

I suppress a little smile.

V.

I found the details of the funeral online. The local news in her town had run a small advert about it, and one of Marina's school friends posted a photo of the snippet on Twitter.

'*Anyone is welcome who knew Marina personally,*' it said, with the link to an email address. I drafted a long message, then deleted it and penned a short message. A few hours later I received an email response from 'Elena Bede' containing the whereabouts and the timings. It was generally written in a formal tone, but signed off: '*PS – catch the 7A. It's just a short ride from the bus stop!*' I thought that exclamation mark was inappropriate.

Elena Bede. Marina's stepmother. I clicked off the message and put the name into Google. The computer stuttered into life and the Internet cut out, but when I rebooted it and tried again the search returned many results. I read them with interest, scanning her tweets; absorbing the information on her LinkedIn profile; on her Academia.edu; reading her Amazon reviews.

Marina had mentioned the women in her family very rarely, and usually only in relation to her father. She never seemed to speak sincerely about her mother – questions made her tetchy – and Elena's role in her life was never entirely clear.

In some versions of the story, Elena had been portrayed as a responsible background figure – picking up the pieces after her haphazard step-family – but Marina also referred to her as 'Dad's piece', or 'Marcus's floozy'. For some reason this initially made me think that she was significantly younger than Marcus, and probably a bit vapid.

In reality, Elena was an academic. She had taught at three different universities, was fluent in four languages and – as I discovered when I put her name into YouTube – had conducted a 2011 TED Talk on the evolution of consciousness. It had half a million views. She was much older than I'd imagined, too: Marcus's age, maybe, but probably with a few years on him. Her face was very thin, gaunt even, with skin pulled taut over the edges of her jaw. Why had Marina depicted her in such a different way?

My mind wandered to Marina's mother. What had she been like, really? I stared at the photo of Elena and tried to find a maternal expression in her face. I tried to mentally superimpose an image of Marina over the top of the picture, so that I could imagine what her mother may have looked like.

I couldn't see it.

I shuddered again and clicked off the link.

vi.

On the morning of the funeral I took a bus down from Northam to Marina's home town. I remember the journey there: seeing the raindrops slide across the windowpane, the grey brutalist concrete curve into Georgian houses and neat thatched cottages. The bus was full of nervous silver-headed tweedy jacket types. Someone was playing tinny Eighties music out of an old radio, someone else was talking loudly about their grandson's cat. It smelled of sour cream and vinegar. Every surface – from the carpet to the seats to the flip-out trays – seemed to be covered in cracker crumbs. The vehicle juddered so violently that by the time it finally stopped I felt travel sick. I could barely stand up. A tiny wadge of vomit had lodged itself at the back of my throat.

I got out and, using Google Maps on my phone to guide me, began to trudge through the fields towards the village church.

Marina's town wasn't like the one I had grown up in. It is sometimes difficult to distinguish between English country towns. On postcards and pop-culture they are often presented as unanimously quaint: a picturesque, nostalgic image of England, populated exactly half-and-half by ruddy-faced friendly farmers and betweeded gentry folk. But that's obviously not how it is, and if you're from the country yourself then the differences are easy to spot. The thatched cottages here weren't flimsy and authentic in the way they were in my hometown. Here they were groomed, manicured. The walls were white and flat and clean, edged with sharp ledges of timber. Through the windows I glimpsed women in neat jackets with combed hair, standing next to large bowls of fruit, making animated gestures as they talked into their phones.

The church came into view.

I made my way up the hill, trudging over the bumps of the bank and neat stalks of hay. I began to feel anxious and doubtful. With every step I started to question my actions. I wondered whether other people from university would be at the funeral. Presumably Henry would be there.

This thought caused another strong wave of nausea. The wadge at the back of my throat reappeared. For a moment I thought about turning back, but then Marina entered my mind. I wanted to say goodbye to her. I wanted to pay my respects and feel the reality of her death. I wanted closure. I forced myself to continue until I saw the group of people outside the church.

They were expensively dressed, in clean dark overcoats that flickered like the pages of a magazine. I scanned across their faces to see if there was anyone I recognized. They all seemed to have the same complexion – polished skin, slightly snub noses – and their chins all had the same up-tilt, the same proud posture. They looked like they were waiting for someone to take their picture.

Among the crowd, I noticed a swooping a coat. It was a longer coat than the sort that the others were wearing, and the way it moved, sweeping to the right at the front of the congregation, carried the unmistakable trace of someone I knew.

Henry looked even smarter than I had expected. He stood in a stoop, talking gravely to a woman with bright red hair. His own hair was combed to the side, a black scarf was knotted around his neck, and his sharp, hollow features looked almost frighteningly stark against his pale complexion.

I watched him for a moment in the misty grey light. He crossed and uncrossed his ankles as he spoke to the red-haired woman, and his posture suggested, unusually, that he was nervous. He looked as though he were part of the group, but in a peripheral sense. I felt a sad, irrational sort of affection towards him.

Suddenly – as though intuiting my pity – Henry glanced in my direction and caught eyes with me. He looked away quickly, then immediately looked back. His eyes narrowed, his mouth pulled tightly downwards. I watched him murmur something to the red-haired woman and then, reluctantly, approach me.

As he neared my hands instinctively clenched into fists. My body shifted backwards.

'Eva,' His voice was sharp and aggressive. 'Why are you here?'

'I – was invited,' I stuttered. 'Elena emailed me the details.'

He shook his head briskly. 'You shouldn't be here,' he said. 'It's inappropriate.'

My cheeks burned.

'What? How is it—?'

'How is it not inappropriate?'

I didn't know how to answer that. I stayed silent and stared at him.

'Eva, your messages to me since the holidays have been insane. I can't believe how insensitive you've been.'

I looked at him blankly.

'Don't you – *don't.*' He shook his head in frustration. 'You know what I'm referring to – the conspiracy theories, the crazy insinuation that Montgomery … It's *indecent.* You hardly even knew Marina.'

I said nothing.

'You should be ashamed of yourself,' he continued, his voice raising a little. 'Do you have any idea what the family are having to deal with? Do you have any idea what *I* am dealing with?'

I felt momentarily paralyzed with shock. I couldn't speak, couldn't move, I was so humiliated.

'You barely knew Marina,' he repeated, shaking his head. 'You barely knew her. This is pathetic.'

A silence fell, and his mouth crumpled at the side.

Something about that word, *pathetic*, galvanized me. It was as though I could hear Marina saying it to me – *you're pathetic, you're worthless, you shouldn't be here* – and that association made me want to defend myself. I bent my chin up towards him and looked him in the eye.

'I have no idea what you're talking about with Montgomery,' I said flatly. 'If someone has been spreading rumours it has nothing to do with me. But … if I barely knew Marina, then why did you call me to help find her?' I clenched my fingernails into my palm. 'You called *me*, Henry. You directly sought my advice, and now you're refusing to explain to me what happened. I'm sorry if my presence is making you uncomfortable, but it's not pathetic to want to come to a funeral.'

'Oh please—'

'And it's not decent of you to speak like this. It's not *fair.*' I had raised my voice.

Several people from the congregation were now looking in our direction. I could sense the judgement radiating from their faces, could hear their stunned pauses in conversation. Henry – perhaps sensing this too – ran his hand through his hair. He looked past me. There was a haunted, pained look on his face.

'You don't understand,' he said quietly. 'You don't fucking understand.'

Now I could hear people murmuring under their breath in the distance. My eyes flicked up and I saw a stream of coats huddled in a circle. They were looking straight at us with wide, anxious eyes. One of them I recognized as Matilda Duke.

When I looked back at Henry I was startled by his expression. I had expected him to be calmer: yet instead all of his features looked incredibly sharp, incredibly *angry*. He moved towards me quickly

'Eva you don't—'

I grabbed his arm, whether as a reflexive defence mechanism or as a comforting gesture, I couldn't tell. But Henry did not react either way. He did not flinch and he did not retaliate. His eyes fell to my fingers. Then they moved to my face.

'What are you doing?' he said tonelessly.

'Tell me.' I said. 'Tell me what happened to her.'

He was staring at me.

'Tell me why you got in contact with me at least,' I said.

There was a long silence.

When Henry started speaking, the words came out quickly, as though he had no control over them.

'Look,' he said. 'I basically thought you might know something. I saw Marina a few evenings before … before she went back to Northam. She had taken a lot of drugs on New Year's Eve. She told me some weird lies, and then she went missing. I thought you might know something about where she'd gone or whether there was truth in what she said. But as it was you didn't know anything. You knew less than nothing.'

'And you went back to Northam – on that morning? The morning she died?'

I heard someone calling to Henry then, and when I turned I saw the woman with red hair approaching. Instinctively my hands fell away from his arm.

'I just thought you might know something,' Henry muttered.

'Henry,' said the woman . Her skin was freckled and tanned. As she spoke her teeth jutted out over a thick bottom lip.

'Marcus was asking after you,' she said tartly. 'Is everything all right?'

A tense silence gave her an answer. I felt the adrenaline of the confrontation wash away. The shame of the conversation dawned on me.

'I'll come now,' Henry said.

The woman looped her arm through his and they turned to leave. I stayed where I was, and studied Henry's long, slow walk. The sun was burning red in the woman's hair.

My throat was dry with the effort of not crying.

I found a secluded spot at the edge of the church and stood there, watching the procession trail inside. I waited until the last person had gone in and took a deep breath.

Then I felt a broad, flat hand on my shoulder. It stayed there and squeezed.

'Are you all right over here?' A smooth voice. A man's voice.

I turned my head slowly to look at my shoulder. There were slight, golden hairs along the knuckles. The fingernails were immaculately polished, a pentagon of fine squares. I followed the line of his lean wrist – leather watch, gold cufflinks – to the cuff of his shirt. Then finally I looked at his face.

He must have been about fifty, with long eyelashes, a broad brow, and hollow circles under his eyes. As I peered at him closer I noticed that they were green, with little pieces of gold in them.

'I assume you're a friend of Marina's?' he asked.

173

I nodded, unsure of what to say exactly. But his face was reassuring: gentle, kind, fatherly. I felt relaxed all of a sudden: whatever answer I gave, it would be OK.

'Not from school,' he said questioningly. 'Perhaps from university?'

'Yes,' I said. 'We ... were on the same course.'

'Ah,' he nodded and smiled. As he did so his mouth curved upwards, tilting into a sort of trapezium. The odd shape of it looked unnervingly familiar. He lifted his other hand. I saw that it held an unlit cigarette.

'Well thank you for coming,' he said, lighting it and taking a drag. 'I'm Marcus, Marina's father.'

So he was. I studied his face then, thinking of all the anecdotes Marina had told me about him. I thought of the time that he had accidentally bought a pair of red and yellow tartan trousers, having thought (because of his colour blindness) that they were navy and green. I thought of the time he had attempted an all-you-can-eat buffet on the afternoon before an important meeting with the Italian ambassador, and then vomited over his shoes. I thought of his other business blunders; his religious phases; his favourite phrases and witty epithets. My mind rolled back to the essays I'd read of his online; the barbed comments he'd made against other academics – against Montgomery. An inappropriate smile flickered across my mouth. I did my best to suppress it.

'Eva,' I replied.

We continued talking for a few minutes. He asked me about my journey down from Northam, in what specific contexts I had known Marina, what my experience of university had been like. Speaking to him was easier than I could have imagined – easier than I found appropriate, even, considering the circumstances of our meeting. He led the conversation with an easy confidence, a certain brashness, and in such a way that I didn't feel as though I should tiptoe around the subject of Marina or her death. He told me that they were setting up a foundation in her name.

'When the first event comes up we'll be looking for volunteers,' he said brightly. 'If that's something you'd be interested in.'

'Definitely.'

As Marcus spoke I watched his mannerisms. The way that he tilted his head slightly to the right when listening, the way that he flicked his ash with a careless index, the way that his eyes curled at the sides as he smiled. That casual elegance – it all carried the ghost of Marina. I thought, impulsively, of asking him about what had happened to her on the night before her death.

Just as I opened my mouth Marcus began speaking again:

'Well, we'd better get inside, I think they're starting to sit down,' he said, glancing at his watch. He took a final drag of the cigarette and then flicked it on the ground. 'Please don't tell my wife about this, by the way.'

'No, of course not. I understand – it's a difficult time.'

'She hates me smoking,' he said.

I noted a small but detectable sting of resentment in his voice, and hearing it caused me to reflect again on the weirdness of the conversation. Here was a mourning father at the funeral of his daughter, only weeks, I assumed, after she had been found dead. After she had *committed suicide*. How was he so composed? How was he even able to *speak*, let alone with such effortless joviality? Where was the rest of the family?

Perhaps it was a coping mechanism, I thought, as we walked into the church. He hadn't yet had time to process the trauma. After the funeral he would fall apart.

I went through the doors and looked around the church interiors. It was taller, grander and more opulent than it looked from outside. There was a grand arch in front of the altar, and etched into the stone ceiling were a series of Latin quotes. A tapestry of religious scenes hung like a rectangular kaleidoscope along the wall. A huge stained-glass window at the end of the hall caused an explosion of colour when the sun passed through it.

Out of the corner of my eye, I saw Henry again. He walked

up to a brunette woman, took both of her hands in his, and kissed her cheeks. Then he did the same with a brown-haired girl and several other smartly dressed people. He bent forward to take his seat beside them.

I stared at him. Was that Marina's family?

Just as I thought this, the brunette woman's head swivelled towards me and she stared right into my eyes. Her eyes flashed – a gleam of steel. They tracked from me to Marcus. Then back again. I recognized her: it was Elena.

I felt my breath catch in my chest. I felt the same panic, the same anxiety, the same worthlessness that I had when I had first arrived at Henry's house on that day in October. I was out of place here.

She turned back to Henry, and made a very discreet pursing gesture with her lips. I slunk to the left into a seat near the back of the church. Somewhere I hoped no one would see me. Meanwhile Marcus strode ahead, nodded at Henry, and then sat down beside him. Once he was settled, Henry turned around again. His eyes studied me carefully. His mouth was pulled down in a tight, humourless frown.

How much did he know? What had he said to Elena?

As soon as the service was over, I thought, I would go home. I couldn't stay here. I needed to leave, to extract myself from her life entirely. If I didn't get out of there soon, someone would discover what I'd done.

The organ played. The congregation stood up. There was a low, rumbling sound from the back of the hall and then the sound of footsteps clacking on the concrete. The coffin came into view.

I turned my head to look at it as it passed the pew. I tried to take in the image, rest it in my mind, accept that she was in there. But I couldn't concentrate properly. I couldn't see the coffin even though I was looking directly at it. Even now, thinking back to that moment, I can only remember fragmented images: the wrists of the funeral bearers; the shape of their hats; the shadow of the white flower that lay still, calm and motionless, outstretched on the lid.

I felt entirely numb. My head swayed lazily, creating a weird sensation at the top of my nose. My hands gripped the wooden seat underneath me. The woman next to me turned, frowning and – upon catching my eye – then tried to disguise her distaste, offering a bland smile.

That smile caused me to remember something Marina had once said to me. We had been sat in my room one evening, watching a film, when a funeral scene came on screen. She'd rolled her eyes.

'The thing about funerals that I can't stand,' she'd said, 'is not the death element. It's not the sadness of saying goodbye to someone. It's how fake the whole thing is. Everyone's trying so hard to look depressed. It's so stiff and boring.' She lit a cigarette. 'When I die I just want to have a cardboard coffin, with the words 'OH WELL' painted on it in bright colours. Then I want someone to throw it into a fire, and dance around it. After that they can forget about me.'

That was the only time she ever spoke to me about death in a personal sense, as far as I remember. She'd made some general comments about it, in one of her virulent philosophical tirades – how she didn't believe in an afterlife, how she thought religion was nonsense. Once she'd even hinted at the 'interconnectedness' of things, some vague hippie riff which sounded like it was possibly plagiarized from Spinoza. But she never said to me how it affected her, or how the idea of death made her feel. However flippant that comment had been, it offered at least some kind of insight into her frustration with the way that people behaved towards death; how they attempted to sanitize it.

As the coffin reached the front of the church, I wondered if that conversation had been a way of her trying to tell me something else. I turned it over in my head, trying to place exactly when it had happened. I tried to remember the exact words she had used.

The priest stood up. He walked quietly to the front of the steps, smiled unctuously, and began to recite a prayer.

'We are here today,' he spoke in low, resonant tones, 'to celebrate. To celebrate the life of a girl who was known to, and loved by, all of us. Now she has been received into God's arms …'

I shifted uncomfortably. It was so severe, so formal and austere the whole thing – so contradictory to everything Marina had been, everything she had stood for. The pointlessness of her suicide overwhelmed me. Marina's atheist rants counted for nothing now. Marina's personality and vibrancy meant nothing. She was nothing but a limp, lifeless body, and her life 'story' was nothing but that – a *story*. A story other people could tell, listen to and tinker with. A story people could use to push their own agendas, tell their own stories. Where was she to contradict them now? It was such a waste. *She* had made such a waste of it.

The priest now spoke some words in Latin which I didn't understand. I felt a hot, numbing sensation at the back of my mouth. I tried hard not to cry.

Once the funeral was over I crept out of the church, careful not to make eye contact with anyone else, and especially careful to avoid Henry. I went back to my hiding place outside. Rain began to fall with increasing speed and density. I pulled my phone out of my pocket and jabbed at the screen. I googled taxi numbers.

'I hope you're not thinking about leaving.'

That voice again. Hoarser. I turned to look at where it was coming from.

'You must come to the wake.'

Marcus was standing very close to me, already holding a cigarette. Gone was the polish of the former father figure. Now he looked dishevelled. The rings around his eyes had darkened and deepened. They cut shadows into his skin. The lines along his brow were thick and deep. I thought that he looked old.

When he spoke again I detected a desperate strain. 'Surely you're not leaving us?'

I looked at him. Every flicker of his mouth, every slight movement of his hand around the cigarette – those were her mannerisms. That was *her*. I stared at him, trying to see her, really see her, to pin her down. But every time I thought I had fixed on something, suddenly it became smothered by the larger picture, and then his face would mould back into that of a wizened father. I couldn't see the resemblance anymore.

Suddenly I realized I was staring. I had to say something.

'I don't think I can make it,' I said quietly. 'I have to get back.'

He nodded politely, but still looked deflated.

'I'm sorry,' I said.

'Are you sure?'

I pursed my lips. 'Sorry.'

As I trudged back through the rain, a stinging feeling of guilt began to sink in. How I must have seemed to Marcus, to the Bede family, to Henry … A funeral crasher, a fraud, an impostor who hadn't even had the decency to stay behind and attend the wake. Why was I so selfish? How had I become like this, so narrow-minded, so socially incompetent? Maybe Henry was right.

I boarded the bus and flicked on my phone. No new messages. No new notifications. No new tagged posts.

I googled 'Marcus Bede' and found his email address on a university website. I sent a quick email, apologizing for my abrupt departure, and then explained, in a frenzy of emotion, how embarrassed I'd been at the funeral, not knowing anyone, not knowing how to talk to anyone and not understanding what had happened to Marina. I hadn't wanted to make it about me at all, but perhaps by disappearing I had inadvertently done that. I apologized again. I said it had been lovely to meet him. It had been a lovely service

and a privilege to have known Marina. I said that I would like
to be kept informed about the Foundation.

The rain slid down the window. I wondered what it would be
like being back at Northam. I wondered whether, having been to
the funeral, I would now feel the impact of her death there.
Perhaps it would haunt me.

vii.

18th February
Dear Eva,

*Thank you for your email. Of course it isn't necessary for
you to apologize. This is a difficult time for everyone – we
understand there are different ways of coping with trauma
and, irrespective, it was lovely to meet you, even in the circumstances.*

*On that note, I will be visiting Northam in the coming
weeks with Elena. There are a few things we need to do there
before returning to the US. Perhaps you will join us for lunch?
It would be lovely to speak to you for longer.*

*Thanks for your interest in the Marina Bede Foundation,
but we're not looking for volunteers at the moment. Once the
charity is up and running I will let you know.*

Marcus

In the days after Marina's funeral, the press got wind of her suicide
and ran with it. It still isn't clear to me why this happened: why,
out of the 130 university students who committed suicide in
2014, it was Marina who drew in the journalists. Her story was
tragic, yes – but it wasn't unusual. At Northam alone there were
several suicide attempts that *term*. I read somewhere subsequently
that in 2014, fifty per cent of ambulance services at the university
were responding to acts of self-harm. So what was it about Marina
that summoned the media? Perhaps it was because she was an

overachiever. Perhaps it was because her father was semi-famous. It's hard to say. Perhaps it was because her picture would look good beside the headlines. I still don't know.

Whatever it was, I didn't question it at the time – I just assumed, like so many other things, that she had attracted attention by virtue of *being herself*. I watched the news spread along my feed like a virus: first the tender messages from her close school friends, then the public photos of the wake, then the links to local news, the national news, the TV interviews with Marina's parents.

The 'RIP MARINA BEDE' page doubled in likes, then tripled, and soon it had hundreds of posts pouring onto it. Complete strangers began to write their own tributes, often as though they were addressing her directly. Some of them even had a reproachful tone.

'*Marina I didn't know you*,' one said, '*but you seem like someone so full of promise. I hope that other girls see this and realize what a waste it was to end your life like that.*'

I scrolled through, clicking on the profiles, judging them. There were hundreds of posts. Reading them often made me feel protective – and depressed. Sometimes I thought that I should write something to her. But I had nothing to say, or maybe I had too much.

When I went outside there were reporters swarming the campus. They approached some of the students to ask for quotes (but never me). We received an email instructing us not to speak to them. The news coverage continued anyway. Journalists wanted to why she had done it, when she had done it. The public wanted to know how. I watched in the shadows, waiting for answers. I went onto Reddit and checked the comments page there. I refreshed her Facebook profile over and over again.

One day, without warning, the headline emerged. It made me bristle when I saw it.

DEATH BY FALL: NORTHAM SOURCE REVEALS ALL

I clicked on the link and absorbed the details. A member of security had found her outside her window one morning in early January. The article revealed that she had died from 'trauma to the body and was pronounced dead at the scene'. *Trauma to the body*: what did that mean? Was her face smashed in? Was she a heap of blood and a smattering of bones? A cracked neck and a mashed skull? Or had most of her stayed intact – only one side of her skull broken open, a trickle of brain rolling out?

I read on further: she was thought to have opened the bedroom window and jumped down six storeys, falling on the hard stone of the path below. It was too vivid. I could see it happening so clearly: the determined look on her face as she drew up the window, her slim hands spread out over the ledge, the way her back arched and the wood dug into her knees as she hoisted herself onto it. She would not even think about what was coming – she would just do it, like she did everything.

I clicked off the link. I couldn't breathe properly. Small bands of light made everything distorted.

I went outside for a walk. I wanted to be away from the campus, so I went to a café on the outskirts of town. There was a huge screen towering over the chairs in the corner. It was showing a press conference on the news. Marcus was sat on a stool with his hands out in front of him. He looked tired and depressed. It was unnerving to see him in that two-dimensional format. He had lost a lot of weight since the funeral – his jaw was sharper, chin more pronounced, and his features, by comparison, were swollen and out of proportion. The lines around his eyes had deepened, making the green bulbs bulge out of their socket. The pointed face, which had often carried a calm expression before, now looked grotesquely animated, like a gargoyle.

The camera moved in towards him: his lips began to move. I snatched the remote from the top of the bar and turned up the volume.

'*I would like to address the death of our daughter,*' he said, in gravelly, measured tones. '*Over the last few weeks we have received a lot of attention – from the press, from our friends, from strangers. We would like to thank people for the kind messages.*'

The camera panned out to the rest of the room – the policemen, the journalists jotting down things on their notepads. Then it moved back in onto his face. He looked different this time. I noticed that there was a look behind his eye: the same glint that Marina's eyes had possessed when she was playing a prank or saying something rude to the professor. It unnerved me to identify it. It unnerved me that I was making that comparison.

'*We have, however, also found it overwhelming. Our intention today is to deflect the attention away from ourselves – and our daughter – by highlighting a cause.*'

As Marcus had explained to me previously, they were setting up a foundation in her name. The Marina Bede Foundation would raise awareness for depression and suicide among high-achieving students. Their focus was on teenage girls especially.

'*Marina was under an enormous amount of pressure, both socially and academically,*' he continued. '*We didn't realize how swept under she – I'm sorry,*' he swallowed, '*how overwhelmed she felt. We would like to increase support facilities for students within universities who are suffering. It is a huge problem in the UK and one that is not frequently enough addressed.*'

My fingers tightened on the remote. Was that the yarn that they were spinning now? That she was under *academic pressure*? It didn't make sense. From everything Marina had told me, from every impression she had given me from her behaviour, university was a lark. Marina had seen it only as a place to waste time. She hadn't even wanted to come to Northam in the first place – it was a last-minute decision engineered by a scholarship.

Marcus continued, his eyes doleful: '*Our lives have changed immeasurably since the second of January, the day of Marina's death.*'

The 2nd of January.

The number rattled through my brain and I felt a wave of panic begin at the centre of my chest, spreading up over my throat.

The 2nd of January.

Involuntarily my mind flashed back to the order of service at the funeral: 4th February 1994 – 2nd January 2014. A headline from a week before, the image of a newspaper printed on my mind: 2nd January. I brought out my phone and quickly googled it: 'Marina Bede January':

… student Marina Bede who was found dead on 3rd January, having committed suicide the previous evening …

I watched Marcus's mouth continue moving but now the words were silent. The 2nd of January was the day I had set up the Swipe account.

The phone fell from my grip. I stared at it, there on the floor, as tiny hairs in the carpet curled around the plastic edges. The 2nd of January. I had imitated Marina after she had died. I had imitated a dead girl.

Up until that point I'd told myself repeatedly that the Swipe imitation was just a game. I had convinced myself that if Marina ever found out about it, then she would understand. If Marina had known about it at the time, then – well, she was my friend, we would be able to laugh it off. My actions were always justified by the idea that she might have known about it at some point.

If she'd always been dead then this was a different story. The Dead Girl was not my friend. She was a completely different person. Dead Marina was the kindly do-gooder with the genial aura and the childhood friends, the overachiever who had succumbed to academic pressure, the nice friendly girl from a Catholic background. That was not the Marina I knew. I knew a series of contradictions. I knew the weird, twisted fragments. I knew a person volatile and argumentative, razor sharp and rude, funny but thoughtless … Many different adjectives which didn't seem compatible with the sweet narrative that had been written over her.

'*The Marina Bede Foundation will address not only university students,*' Marcus said, '*but also troubled teenage girls across the spectrum. Our aim is to help parents understand the root of the problem.*'

More than that, I thought suddenly, someone *must* have recognized the account. Maybe Joe had screenshotted our conversations, with the date, with the time …

Joe and I had been talking every day for nearly three weeks after Marina had died. Three whole weeks.

I went back to my room and pulled my duvet over my head. I let it lie there. I felt my breaths get longer, slower, as the cotton folded into my face, mouth, nostrils. I sucked it further into my air passages and allowed the realization to settle. I stopped breathing. I thought about what would happen if I stopped breathing completely. Then the pressure was too much: I ducked my head out and took a gasp of air. I rolled over and turned on my laptop.

My fingers manically tapped onto the Chrome bar. I put in cautiously: 'Joe Swipe Marina'. I waited. My fingers shook slightly above the keyboard.

The page loaded.

*No results. Did you mean Joe **swiped** Marina?*

I felt a swift whip of panic upon seeing those two words together in public: Joe and Marina. Then I felt relieved. I tried to sustain that feeling.

He had forgotten, perhaps. Or he had not put two and two together. Or he hadn't seen the news stories about her at all – maybe he would never see and never know. Still, a cloud of doubt hung over me. I felt wired by a violent, restless energy. I checked all other forms of social media. I rolled from the top of the feed

185

to the line where it juddered at the bottom, still loading, loading, still loading, still loading. Eventually I clicked onto my inbox instead.

1)RE: Marina's funeral; SENDER: marcus.bede@ charlton.edu

For a moment my blood ran cold. The possibilities of Marcus's response rolled through my mind and made me nauseous.

But then I read it. It was fine: he said once again that I didn't need to apologize. He gave a specific time and a date for the week after, when he and his wife were coming for lunch. I felt strangely elated at the prospect of seeing him again.

I replied, saying that I'd love to meet him. I added that if he were looking for volunteers in the Marina Bede Foundation, then I would still be very happy to help.

1)SENDER: marcus.bede@charlton.edu

Marvellous. We're getting to Northam around 1, so I propose a light lunch at Cassio's at 2 p.m.?

In case you missed it in the previous email: as it stands we aren't looking for volunteers yet, but I will keep you in the loop. We hugely appreciate your enthusiasm for the foundation.

See you then. M

viii.

We met in a small bistro near the campus, around the corner from the café where Marina and I had had our mid-afternoon brunch. It was in the expensive part of town, down a little alleyway strung with little fairy lights and signposted with swirly-chalked blackboards. I remember that it was snowing that day. A light white crunchy sheet had fallen over the campus, softening the edges of everything, making the city seem ghostly, ephemeral. Predictably, I had forgotten to wear sensible shoes, sacrificing comfort for a new pair of canvas plimsolls. As I walked up to the door I felt my socks dampening at the edges. The skin between my shoulders was wet. The ends of my hair were dripping with sleet. I wiped the make-up from under my eyes, opened the door with a red wet hand, and walked inside.

In the days leading up to my meeting, I had been following the news on Marina constantly. I had been tracking the Bedes' TV appearances; noting the money for the foundation steadily increasing on their crowdfunding page, refreshing the contact page to see if they'd uploaded the volunteer application form yet. I read each analysis of her death in every paper and scanned over every comment, every retweet. But after a peak in mid-February, two weeks after the news went viral, public curiosity was dwindling. Then the media had started to lose interest.

This pleased me: although I was obsessed with reading the coverage, fundamentally I didn't like the fact that Marina's life had been overwritten by a narrative which was incompatible with my own version of events. I felt that the less attention people paid to the tributes, the more likely it was that my story would prevail – and the less likely it was that the Swipe account would emerge.

Now, I walked into the restaurant and cautiously found my way to Marcus and Elena's table. From a distance they looked like a 1950s postcard: so serene, so graceful and poised. He was wearing a stiff white shirt, loosely undone at the collar. Rose-gold cufflinks complemented the pearly pastel of her dress.

But edging closer I noticed there was something off in the way that Elena was looking at him. It was an accusatory look, almost suspicious. Her thick-rimmed eyes were slightly bloodshot. When she saw me, however, her expression neutralised: she stood up and kissed me on both cheeks. Marcus smiled graciously and did the same. I seem to remember that they both smelled expensive – sweet walnut and honey, washing powder.

187

We spoke for a while about Marina. I teetered on the edge of the conversation, trying to make myself inconspicuous – but with little luck. Marcus constantly deflected, keeping me the centre of attention.

'So,' he said, tucking a napkin into his collar. 'Have *you* been well?'

I faltered, saying that I had spent a lot of time focusing on the course. When he asked about my social life I wasn't sure what to say. I stuttered that I had spent a lot of time online, then regretted diverting the conversation in that direction. I monitored Marcus's face closely but he didn't look suspicious. Elena stared at her plate.

While I was talking, Marcus looked past my shoulder, and soon enough he seemed to catch eyes with the waiter. His hand fell on the table. A finger crawled towards my menu and tapped impatiently. My sentence trailed off.

'What are you having?' he said. 'We've ordered already. Elena is having a salad, I'm having the steak. I'd really recommend the fish, or the salad.'

'Oh,' I said, reaching for the wine. I thought it strange that he had recommended those items, when he was having something else. 'Yes, I'll have one of those then.'

I looked up and, without meaning to, caught eyes with Elena. In the flesh she looked even older than she did in photographs: cracked veins, profound wrinkles, spirals of chestnut and light grey hair twisted into a bun at the nape of her neck. She was smiling then, but there was something about the way her mouth wavered that unsettled me. I thought back to that moment at the funeral: that mean, ugly look she had sent in my direction.

She took another sip of her wine.

Soon Marcus returned to the subject of my life – what I had been doing, what I had been reading.

'And how are your studies?'

'Fine, I think.'

How like a parent he was.

'Do you see Colin a lot?'

'Who?'

'Colin. Sorry, Professor Montgomery. He teaches you, does he not?'

Oh.

'Well not anymore actually. This term I'm taking modules with several … well, PhD students mostly. Montgomery taught me last term a little.'

'He and Marina had some issues.'

'Yes.'

'We were at university together, Colin and I.' He glanced at Elena, but she didn't seem to notice. She was busy looking at me. 'He's an odd fellow.'

I was surprised by this admission. 'In what way?'

'Oh, you know, how he is,' Marcus waved a hand – a little swat like Marina's – and topped up my glass.

I sipped the wine tentatively, self-consciously – careful not to slug it. I thought about mentioning the episode at the bookshop in the train station around New Year, how that had caused me to think weirdly about him … but I said nothing.

Marcus looked at me pointedly. 'I'm assuming you know about his past,' he said. 'Marina must have told you.'

I struggled to stifle a smirk.

'The women …?' I stumbled.

'Not to mention the students.'

I felt a short zing of something – resentment, perhaps.

'No.'

'No?'

'What happened?'

'Well he was … indiscreet with a student,' he said. 'It was years ago, and consensual of course. But it wasn't cricket, what with the regulations and so on.'

It was resentment that I felt, definitely. Here was another thing she had neglected to tell me.

Marcus continued: 'They gave him a slap on the wrist and sent him to Northam.'

'A slap on the wrist?' I sipped my wine cautiously.

'Well yes,' Marcus smiled. 'There was a tizzy about it, but at the end of the day it was two consenting adults.'

The wine began to take its effect: I could feel the alcohol pulsing along my synapses, making my face numb.

'Wait,' I said, 'what do you mean "they" sent him to Northam? Who sent him? How?'

Marcus looked at me. It was an intense expression: like he was trying to communicate something to me, while simultaneously trying to figure something out.

'He was working at Charlton in the US, the same university as me. And then it was ... revealed, among staff, so he had to leave. Northam had sister ties and they were looking for a new English professor, so I sent a strong recommendation. As did a few other professors. It worked.'

'I didn't know that academic circles worked like that.'

Marcus shrugged. 'Anything can work in whatever way you like, provided you're persuasive. Anyway, it's much harder to find competent lecturers than you think – they have to be willing to accept the pay packet, experienced enough to draw in students ...'

'Still ...'

'Well, in any case, it happened and everyone benefited from the move.'

I put down my fork. I had lost my appetite. Marcus laughed and tapped my plate.

'Come on,' he said. 'You've hardly touched the fish.'

'I'm sorry, I just – I didn't know that about him,' I said quietly. I wondered why he was telling me all of this.

'Good. There's no reason you should. He's a superb teacher. That's what matters.'

A question hovered on my tongue. I looked at my plate. I

breathed slowly, feeling the wine work itself around my brain. The room seemed very hot all of a sudden, full of gold leaf and garish bright lights. I couldn't feel my mouth, but I somehow knew that it was moving. It was emitting words beyond my control.

'He was a bit odd though,' I said. 'I mean towards Marina.'

Marcus looked startled then.

'What?' he said.

'I wonder if … you know …'

Elena coughed into her napkin. A silence descended. Waiters circled around other tables. I heard metal cutlery clink against china.

Eventually Marcus said: 'I'm not sure I've been clear. The Charlton business was a long time ago. Colin was a lot younger, and the boundaries were a little blurry in those days. He has known Marina for a long time, since childhood. There is … no, there is no way.'

We all avoided each other's eyes. There was another tense silence: this time longer. The waiter arrived and began to shell out our side courses. I stared at his hands, focused on the way he prised the silver dishes from the stack. One, two, three. As he walked away, I stared after him, noticing that his apron was undone at the back. My chest was still tight.

I mumbled: 'I'm sorry.'

'It's fine,' Marcus said quickly. 'Frankly I am relieved that you hadn't heard any of that before.' He gave a small, forced laugh. 'I mightn't have mentioned it to you if I had known that you were ignorant. Don't get bogged down in university gossip. It's not what first year is about.' He smiled again, too broadly. I caught a flash of his brilliant white teeth. 'First year is about having fun – which I know sounds strange now.' He poured some more wine into my glass. 'But you have to take your mind away from what's happened. We all do.'

At this point Elena cleared her throat. I realized she hadn't spoken in all that time, she hadn't even muttered an 'mm'.

'Darling,' she spoke in a smooth American accent. It sounded like coins in a velvet purse. 'Would now be a good time to ask Eva about the room?'

I glanced from her to him.

'Yes,' he said emphatically. 'But let's have a toast first.'

Our hands moved to the middle of the table and clinked the glasses against one another. There was a silence as we drank.

Marcus set his glass on the table in front of him.

'One of the reasons we're up here—'

'The main reason.'

'It's required of us to clear out Marina's university room.' His eyes were heavy with meaning. 'We had a look around earlier which was, as I'm sure you can understand, very difficult. But there is a lot to clear out and we were wondering—'

'We were hoping you would help us with the packing.'

My throat went dry. I felt a sudden impulse to escape.

'There's an awful lot of stuff in the room, Eva, and we could use an extra pair of hands. We did ask Henry but he … is finding things difficult.' There was a pause. Marcus looked to Elena again. She was staring at her napkin.

'That's putting it mildly,' she said. I watched her gently playing with the napkin. Sunlight flooded the room and a sharp golden rectangle glinted off her fingernails. 'We may as well tell her, Marcus.'

The waiter walked past again, still with his apron undone and I couldn't think about anything except the pieces loose pieces of thread dangling from the tie.

'It's not necessary to go into this now,' said Marcus.

'Oh come on, I'm sure she knows already,' said Elena.

I felt cold. 'Knows what?'

'Henry has transferred to another course,' she said bluntly. 'He's gone away for a while.'

At the same time, Marcus said: 'It's a brilliant opportunity.'

My throat felt dry. I couldn't concentrate on seeming natural, on making the conversation go smoothly.

'Where is he going?' I managed. 'I mean – what?'

'One of my historian friends wants him to work as a researcher. It'll be in London probably. Perhaps New York.'

'But … how long is he going for?' I said.

'Probably just the year,' said Marcus. 'He's had a very, very tough time of it at Northam.'

I thought back to my confrontation with Henry at the funeral: '*do you have any idea what I am dealing with?*' What had happened to him? Why exactly had he been suffering? Did he know something about Marina's death that I didn't? Just as I opened my mouth to ask this, Elena cut in impatiently:

'Will you help us with the room?' Her fingers gripped the silver cutlery. She bent her head forward, opened her small mouth and put a tiny piece of lettuce inside it. Her eyes slid up at me.

'Yes,' I said. 'Of course.'

Understandably I was nervous going – but, I have to say, I was also inappropriately excited. Oddly, I had only ever been in Marina's room a few times before. Back in those early days of our friendship, she had always asked to spend time in my room instead. The brief moments I had spent in there – waiting in the doorway while she picked up a lipstick; hovering on the bed while she drank the remnants of a vodka bottle and slipped on her shoes – they had always been a stop on the way to somewhere else. Her room was never the destination itself. And while I had been in there, standing or sitting, she had distracted me with some witty chatter so that now I couldn't clearly remember what it had looked like.

I shuffled up the stairs after Marcus and Elena, trying to stay calm, trying not to catch eyes with her floormates

From the moment I'd read about Marina's death, I'd spent hours imagining her doing it. In those early February days I had lain in my dark room at night, conscious of the smell of damp emanating from the walls and a nebulous flow of headlights, moving slowly over the ceiling. I imagined tracing my feet along the scratchy welcome mat, flicking the lock, slowly ascending the stairs, opening the door, and climbing onto the windowsill. What clothes had Marina been wearing when she had jumped? Had she been wearing shoes or barefoot? What had her feet felt like against the rug, against the carpet, against the stone? All these scenarios I had imagined vividly.

Yet now, actually embarking on that journey, I found myself thinking instead about how the room was going to look. I couldn't remember anything specific about it, and even in the hallway the walls seemed to me a different colour than they had been. The wallpaper was a light yellow rather than cool cream.

Marcus stepped up to the door and put the key in the lock. He glanced at his wife. In that moment I saw a brief look of sincerity pass across his face: there was a fragility, an uncertainty, an expectation, that disappeared as his eyes tracked to me. Then he smiled politely. His hand twisted the key and the door opened.

Seeing Marina's room was a shock. The walls were bare. The shelves were bare. No posters; no pictures. Only one bulb hung in the centre of the room, emitting a thin, ugly yellow beam over a bookshelf stuffed with heavy tomes. There were books of various sizes – heavy and thin, slanting and sturdy – and sat uncomfortably beside each other. Her bed lay in the corner, stretched over with a white paisley sheet, like a death shroud.

'Did it always look so …' Marcus paused. 'Empty?'

I dug my fingernails hard into my palm. I tried to formulate things to say.

What could I say? I wanted to provide him with some comfort, to say that I remembered it brighter, full of photos and memories which she must have taken down when she moved home for Christmas. But that wasn't what I remembered. Was it? I cast my mind back, and a memory surfaced: standing outside the door before Henry's party; knocking once, knocking again; hearing her feet shuffle around inside. I'd pushed open the door lightly, and it was then that she had sprung towards me, leaping and laughing, snapping a Polaroid camera in my face and dancing around with her long full ponytail swinging to the sides. I'd tried to just walk in past her, but she leapt in front of me again and the camera had kept on flashing.

Now I tried to think. I tried to see what the room had looked like behind her, whether there had been posters on the walls. No matter how hard I concentrated I could only see her. She lifted her face away from the camera and looked at me again. Her mouth was painted with a dark red lipstick and her eyes, curving upwards, were lined with smudgy black.

I shuddered.

'Yes. I mean, ah,' I said. 'I think there used to be some fairy lights.'

'Fairy lights?'

'Yes.'

Elena's head whipped around. 'That doesn't sound quite like Mari.'

'I know. I think it ... Well ... it used to look brighter. Somehow.'

'*Somehow*,' she repeated bitterly.

Marcus muttered: 'Elena stop it.'

'Stop what?' she said.

He paused. He drew in a long, deep breath, then shook his head.

'Stop *what* Marcus?' she said again. I could hear her voice steadily straining, ready to erupt. 'I said, stop what? Stop acting irrationally?' There was the eruption. 'Stop acting in a way that isn't *normal*? How can you possibly be standing there saying that to me? Your daughter is dead. By *choice*.'

Marcus's jaw clenched. His eyebrows furrowed, causing the skin of his tanned forehead to crumple, like a sheet of tea-stained paper.

'Please,' he said.

'That is a fact,' she continued, at the same volume. 'And rather than facing that fact – that she is *dead* – we're going on as though everything is fucking normal! She died in this *fucking* room.'

She looked me dead in the eye then, and in the yellow light of the room I saw how red the edges of her pupils were. I thought I could smell something: the hot waft of alcohol.

She breathed hard. 'I'm guessing you've been here a lot right? As Marina's best friend.'

'Well … sort of …'

She gave a low, bitter laugh, and shook her head.

'Sort of,' she said, imitating my whine.

'Elena,' Marcus said.

'Were you even *friends* with Marina?'

'*Elena.*'

'I know about what you said to her,' said Elena sharply. 'And I know that you pushed her.'

'What—?'

'She told me,' she continued, matter-of-factly. 'She told me about the time you had a fight. You said those awful things and then you … you got physical, you pushed her chair over.' She stepped towards me. 'That's not what close friends do. You should have been supportive. She needed *help.*'

'Elena, enough.'

Marcus stepped forward then. He put his arm around her shoulders, gently, and I watched as Elena – almost spellbound – hesitated before relaxing into it. She took Marcus's wrist in both her hands. Her nails looked fierce and indestructible, like a metal clamp.

Marcus's voice was child-like: 'Let's get some fresh air. OK?'

Elena nodded.

'Some nice fresh air?'

The question was directed at Elena, who nodded sulkily, but he was looking at me.

I felt awkward and out of place then. It wasn't clear where I was supposed to look, what I was supposed to stay.

'I'll just—' I stammered.

'Yes, you stay here. We'll be back in a moment.'

Alone in Marina's room, I felt even more uncomfortable than I had before. It felt like I was being watched. I looked at the window and tried not to imagine Marina climbing out of it. I thought about what Elena had said. I wondered what Marina had said about me. I wondered whether Elena had spoken to Henry.

Certain scenarios began to play out in my head. I thought of Marina on the night she died. I imaged her undoing the catch, digging her fingernails underneath the heavy wooden frame, pushing the fingertips in a little further, shunting it upwards, feeling the cold bite of the wind on her face. I thought of a foot on the windowsill, the knee bending up onto it, the palm lying flat and then the elbow crooking, arm straightening and flexing, other arm reaching up to steady herself, the shaky forward-bend of her body as she hoisted herself upwards. Then she would breathe in the last gulp of cold air. Maybe she would look at the stars briefly, see the moon behind the fog. And she would be leaning out, leaning out, leaning out, leaning out …

I started to feel a spinning nausea. Clearly I needed to distract myself. But there was little that I could do. I didn't feel I could start packing up Marina's things – I didn't feel as though I should be allowed to touch anything. I could hear people playing football on the grass outside. Geese squawking. Footsteps along the concrete.

In a panic I looked at Marina's bookshelf. That was better. There were many that I recognized. The copy of *Doctor Faustus*, with which she'd practically bludgeoned the professor. Virginia Woolf and Charlotte Brontë. Frederick Douglass. Her tiny copy of *Wide Sargasso Sea*, well thumbed. There were other books here too, I noticed – books that I had lent her.

I was fixated by these titles in particular. Being close to them was comforting. They made me feel that I wasn't crazy. They made me feel that my version of Marina was a reliable narrative: that she wasn't a eulogy or an obsequious Facebook post or someone who *needed help*. She was the Marina I had known, after all: someone who had the same interests that I had. She was someone who took my stuff and didn't give it back.

A shadow passed under the window. I heard Elena's sharp voice outside, the muffled crescendo of Marcus'. They were making their way back to the room.

Without being entirely conscious of doing so, I felt my fingers edging out of my pockets. My arms reached out towards the bookshelf. I grabbed a large stack of the books, some of them mine, some of them hers. I swept them off the shelf in one swift movement, and stuffed them in my bag.

ix.

The next day I thought about Marcus and Elena. I thought back to what they had said about Henry. I thought about Elena's warped impression of me, which filled me with anxiety, and that subsequently led to a desire to build bridges. I wanted to let Henry know that I cared about him, before he went to America. I tapped onto his Facebook profile and sent him a message. I apologized for my behaviour at the funeral. Then I wrote:

Marcus told me that you're leaving
don't worry, I'm not stalking Marina's family or anything
They asked me specifically to help clear out her room
I just wanted to check you're ok

Straight away – and unusually – Henry replied with an outpouring of messages:

its all right im sorry too
I shouldn't have involved you from the off
I was scared
and yeah I'm going to Charlton for a year at least
its impossible to be at northam

I started to type a reply – then my eyes flicked to the right and stopped dead. Marina was trending on Facebook news. I clicked off Henry's message, and hovered my mouse over the name. A headline emerged.

BREAKING: MARINA BEDE IMPERSONATOR SWARMS 'SWIPE' APP AFTER HER DEATH

I felt numb. I breathed slowly, then faster, then faster again… My entire body felt hot and wired. An electric jolt went plummeting to the pit of my stomach, and hairs spiked up on the back of my neck. I tapped on the link.

After the death of Marina Bede, the 19-year-old student who committed suicide at Northam earlier this year, it has been discovered that an impersonator created a fake Swipe account using her photographs. In an exclusive interview with one of the impersonator's victims …

I scrolled down until I came to the picture of Joe. Next to him – the picture of Marina, the one with her back to the camera, her head twisted sideways. The one I had stolen.

Joe Schwermann, a 19-year-old student at Northam, approached The Economist earlier this month with screenshots of their conversation. He had saved the conversations after screenshotting them to ask his friends for advice about asking her on a date. 'It wasn't like a normal Swipe interaction,' he said. 'I feel like an idiot saying it, but it was like an actual relationship. She was so convincing. We spoke for about a month and she told me loads about herself.'

My eyes tracked down the page, and I saw one of the conversation screenshots printed next to the article.

25/01/2014

Joe: *Why are you being so cagey? It's just one drink cmon*
Marina: *Like I said*
Bad time
Joe: *You might regret it if you push me away*
What if we're meant to get married?
What if we're predestined to match on Swipe, meet at university and rear four disappointing children?
Marina: *I don't want to get married*
Joe: *Well*
let's just grab a drink anyway?
Marina is offline

The article continued:

Schwermann believes that the suspected imitator was either close to Marina, or a fellow student at Northam University. 'I mean she was obviously smart, definitely a student. She spoke a lot about the course at Northam,' he said. 'I'd be very surprised if she wasn't also an English student there.'

If that is the case, the timing of the interaction has disturbing implications. Their first correspondence, which Schwermann dates to 2nd January, was the day Marina Bede committed suicide. Their final correspondence is dated 27th January. On that date, says Schwermann, 'Marina' went offline, and the next day she had 'unmatched' him.

It felt bizarre, horribly bizarre, seeing the conversation printed on the page like that. Those were my words. Those were things *I* had said. The text of the article described things I had done. Then why did I feel so indifferent, so detached from them?

I murmured to myself: 'Marina is me', and – I'm ashamed to admit it – an inappropriate glow of satisfaction suddenly flushed over me. I felt validated to be equated with Marina, even like that, and there was an odd thrill to being spoken about in the public press. But the feeling passed quickly, and I was left with an emptiness again, a detachment, an inability to relate to the situation. I couldn't remember typing the words, I couldn't remember where I'd been or what I'd done on those days. Even though I had been worried about this coming out, now that it was happening the crime felt entirely alien to me. The accusation seemed distant, irrelevant, like I was overhearing a stranger's conversation.

Schwermann says he was 'put out' by the rejection, but did not think it suspicious. 'What happened was, we'd been planning this drink since basically our first chat,' he said. 'But whenever I pushed for a specific date she kept coming up with excuses – saying that she was depressed, and there were problems in her family, her dad wasn't speaking to her or whatever. I just thought she was going off me. So when she deleted me ... I was bummed out but I got over it. I screenshotted the messages and sent them to my friends, asking for advice. When I logged back on she'd gone. Just disappeared. I guess that's the way of these dating apps.'

Two weeks later, he saw a news post about her death. He called a friend to express his horror and remorse.

'At first I was just, yeah, horrified. She'd told me that she was depressed ... I thought maybe I could have done something or said something to save her. It was so rough seeing those photos next to the headlines.' Then he noticed the date. 'I felt

sick to my stomach, honestly. I thought it must be a typo, but then I checked other sources it kept coming up everywhere. Gradually I sort of realised I had been talking to an impersonator.'

Schwermann immediately attempted to contact both Marina Bede's parents and the police about the fake account, but says that he was rebuffed as a hoax. 'The Bedes never replied,' he said. 'I suppose they get hundreds of emails, and some of them will be from weirdos. But I really have been trying hard to contact them.' And the police? 'The police said they'd look into it but I never heard back from them. I think they thought I was a time-waster.' Did he think about posting it on social media? 'I didn't feel it was respectful and, to be honest, I was reluctant to reveal personal details publicly. I felt kind of embarrassed. Even this is a last resort. I'm just trying to do the responsible thing.'

At the time this article went to press both the Bede family and the Northam police force were unavailable for comment. The University of Northam has confirmed that it is investigating the case.

I saw my reflection in the screen. My skin was a bluish pale. My eyes were hollow, dark, with thin strings of text swirling inside them: *imitator, hoax, time-waster, police.*

Over the next ten minutes, I watched as the headlines began to spread across Twitter, across Facebook, as sections of the article began leaking into other news sources. I forced myself to read it all: the retweets, the statuses, the comments underneath them.

It's depressing that people like this exist in the world. *62 upvoted*

You can blame social media all you want but it's probably the parents *31 upvoted*

They can track using location data. *86 upvoted*

Swipe account won't be deleted? It's probably just frozen out but u cant delete. Surely administrators can find her.
Where did Joe Schwermann match the account? That will help. *113 upvoted*

They were after me. They were all on my case, working together, working to expose me. What was going to happen to me?

This is beyond sick. This person deserves to be put in jail *77 upvoted*
Bring back the death sentence and have someone impersonate her, see how she likes it *86 upvoted*
Sick bitch *22 upvoted*

For a moment my entire body felt numb. Then it was energized again, restless, and the nerves along my arms were fizzing, and my eyes were growing to saucers, everything transparent, everything separating into tiny particles, bristling with an unknowable charge.

I felt my hands moving at lightning speed. The laptop snapped shut, went flying across the desk and knocked a glass onto the floor. I heard the glass smash into thin, light shards. I was aware of becoming vertical. A bag was wrenched from the top of the cupboard: clothes flew, shoes smacked against them; books followed. I watched the zip being pulled along straining material, catching, then rising, then the whole thing being heaved into the air, the strap scratching against my wrist, rucked up the inside of my elbow, the bulk weighing heavily over my shoulder. I didn't know where I was going. I left my phone on the bed. I left my laptop on the floor, the fragments of the glass around it. I saw my silhouette reflected in one of them, dark and lean. Then I pushed open the door and started walking.

Far behind me down the corridor, someone called my name.

I heard the dim echo as my footsteps quickened and I did not turn around.

Northam station was virtually empty by the time I got there. My fingers were numb and my teeth hurt. I felt a string of sickly phlegm rising in my throat.

My fingers moved clumsily towards the direction of my pocket. I dug in, and moved around. No. There was nothing in there. Panic – flash of panic – but I told myself to keep moving. Keep moving. I surged forward, past the barriers, all faces and bodies a blur, a cacophony of noises whirring around me. I climbed onto a random train. It didn't matter where it was going. I only had to be moving. I only had to be disappearing – disappearing forever, so they would never find me.

The whistle blew: a deafening screech, and I felt the stiff wheels of the vehicle grind forward. I crouched in a corner of the carriage. I kept my head low, shoulders bent over the zip of my bag. It strained with the bulk of the contents. What did I have with me?

Balancing the bag on the floor of the carriage, I edged the zip down slowly to the halfway point, and impatiently began to riffle through the contents.

I snatched past the clothes, grabbing the shoes, scraping my palms against the sharp teeth of the zip, and then came upon Marina's books. At that point the train spluttered over a joint in the rail. The bag split open, causing a loud *vrrrup*. The clothes and shoes and underwear spilled out onto the floor.

I panicked.

I leaned forward as the train juddered left and right, frantically grabbing at fistfuls of the spilled items. They sloped along the floor away from me. I leaned forward then sideways, snatched them up and hastily rolled them into the fabric of the bag. The broken zip snagged against the heel of my hand.

There came a noise from the next carriage. Footsteps. The whirr of an opening door.

I saw a visibility jacket – a ticket inspector was poking her head left and right over the seats. My breath shortened. I scrabbled to a standing position. I jumped into the opposite toilet cubicle. I jabbed at the button to close. The door slid slowly shut.

A voice over the tannoy:

Next stop: Drutherton. Alight for Moreland University.

The train was going south. If I stayed on for long enough then I might be able to find my way back to my parents. They would help me, surely. Maybe they would even be able to resolve the situation, find a way to defuse it before my identity was leaked. I breathed deeply, repeating the thought over and over again. I calmed down. I began to register my surroundings. I looked at the plastic walls of the toilet, the artificial buttons, the window and the spire of Moreland beyond it.

It was then that I noticed what was in my hands. A roll of snagged material, and a thick stack of pages clumsily fisted together. The train shuddered to a halt, my fingers lost grip, and the stack jolted about thirty centimetres before I caught it again.

Something had fallen. I watched it slalom along the linoleum, through a dark viscous patch of liquid, and skitter to a standstill in the corner of the cubicle.

It was a notebook. I squatted forward, and snatched it up. I dried it on my trousers. The leaves of paper were unfurling around the edges, and I saw how scrunched the pages were, that they were now beginning to mottle. I wiped it again on my trousers, careful not to blot the ink. Then, balancing against the corner of the cubicle, my face brushing against the used paper towels which overflowed from the bin, I carefully bent it open.

Marina Bede. September 2013

It was unmistakably her handwriting.

I turned the page and squinted at the faded hieroglyphics. I turned another page and did the same. It wasn't a notebook, exactly, but a kind of a calendar: a diary in the dullest sense. Each day was marked with a to-do list or a reminder of an event.

14th September Pack bag. 2 x t-shirts; 4 x trousers; 2 dresses
19th September Meeting with Prof CM. Buy: yoghurt, carrots, celery. Stretches.
30th September Dad back from US for 2 weeks.

My fingers paced through it, looking for a chunk of writing, any sort of personal reflection which might tell me who she really was – reveal her thoughts and secrets, her true motivations. But the entries were sparse. Only a few entries existed for every day, then after October they thinned out entirely. Some of them had even been scribbled out.

1st October (reread Woolf)
2nd October Meeting with Prof CM.*
27th October Get login details from prof
29th October Essay 2 due. Skype w dad*

Suddenly there was a whirring sound. I whipped my head up, and saw the door beginning to open in an automatic sliding motion. I stabbed at the close button frantically but a hand forced its way between the gap and shoved it aside. The ticket inspector stood there, bright yellow jacket billowing in the wind. Her grey hair stood spiked on the top of her head.

'Excuse me,' she eyed me warily. 'These your things?'

Her hands curled open, revealing other items from my bag. A few pieces of jewellery, a pen, a handkerchief.

I felt my head moving heavily – forwards and backwards in a nod. Our eyes met. Hers narrowed a little, and then fell towards the papers in front of me.

'What are you doing in here?' she said.

I sprang back into a sitting position, snatching the book towards me.

'Nothing,' I said.

'Can I see your ticket, please?'

I couldn't bring myself to answer. I huddled the papers closer into my chest. A window was open somewhere: the wind streamed in and stung the corners of my eyes.

'Look. It's not often I put up with types like you,' she said. 'I'll let you off this once. But clean up your things and make sure you're not here after the next stop. I'll be checking.'

She turned back to look at me once, and then with a lasting sigh went to leave. 'Take care tonight,' she muttered, as the door snapped shut.

The moment she was gone I opened the notebook again. I read through the dates, the notes. I looked at them carefully – and now, rather than disappointed by the lack of fleshedout information, I was gripped by the fact Marina had recorded any information at all. The few things she had put in there spoke volumes about her personality. Her capacity for organization astonished me. I couldn't believe that she had been so conscientious. It didn't fit with the image I had of her – it didn't fit with the way she had looked or spoken or moved or dressed or otherwise seemed to me.

1st November Meeting with Professor CM*
5th November Laundry, reading. Meeting with Prof CM*

Meetings with the professor, I noticed, came up more than any other item. Some were marked with asterisks – I wondered what that meant. I totted them up. There had been twenty meetings with the professor overall — only eight were marked with the asterisk.

The next station is York.

The voice over the tannoy. Footsteps shuffling outside. The

sound of a sliding door muffling open and slapping shut in the distance. I sensed the ticket inspector approaching.

10th November Meeting with Professor*
11th November Meeting with Professor.* Do washing. Elena
bday present – check cow-print hat?
12th November Buy pants. ~~Meeting w PCM~~
4th December Meeting with Professor*
5th December Essay due – Bergson
13th December Meeting w Professor CM.*

What did it mean – if it meant anything? Were those asterisks somehow linked to the professor, or was I simply trying to find meaning where there wasn't any? My fingers flicked towards the back. That was when I saw it.

In the corner of the penultimate page there was a tiny, barely legible scribble. It was in pencil, half-rubbed out, but I could just about decipher the letters.

ast3r1sk_12_2013@gmail.com
a5t3r1sk

An email address. I stared at it, squinting my eyes into fine points. It was not the email address Marina had habitually used. I'd always watched over her shoulder as she logged into Facebook, and during boring lectures we'd emailed each other from our university accounts. Neither of those accounts corresponded with the mishmash of letters and numbers written there.

There was a cold feeling on my face.

I looked up to see the ticket inspector standing in the doorway.

'Oi! I warned you!' she said. 'Get off!'

York station was cold and imposing. The ceilings were high, there was no insulation, and night-shift security guards patrolled the grounds. I had the realization that I was in an alien city – with nowhere to sleep.

I thought about catching another train in the opposite direction. If I went back to my room in Northam, I thought – where my phone and laptop were – then I might be able to log into the asterisk account. I might at least be able to test out the password, if nothing else.

It's hard now to think that this was an option. So much would be different if I had gone back – so many people would have avoided being hurt. But in the station, the thought of being back in Northam – the horror of it – struck me with the force of a lightning jolt. The dark damp walls, the jeering faces, the lowered hoods, the police … My breath began to quicken. My palms tensed. *No.* I couldn't go back there. I wasn't in a game anymore. The possibility of being discovered was a real, imminent threat.

An Internet café, then, if they still existed. There must be somewhere in a touristy city like this which offered access to the Internet. Yet as I exited the station, passing through the curled pillars and into the road, I saw that it was pitch-black. The air was freezing and dark. Nowhere was open except the odd kebab shop, and a dingy neon-lit bar.

Eleven chimes rang out. I became aware, again, of the situation in which I had placed myself; I became aware of the freezing temperature and with it, how underdressed I was.

I drew my bag onto my knees and dug through it for a jumper. There wasn't one in there, so I wrapped swaddles of clothing around my wrists and fiercely rubbed my knuckles together. The wind speared my cheeks, shoulders, ankles.

I found a nook in the corner of the station where I hoped the guards wouldn't see me. With my bag pulled in close to me, I bent down and burrowed face into my knees. It was still freezing. To distract myself, I took out the book and leafed through it. I squinted at the words. I crouched my head into my knees away from the wind so that I could read. But I couldn't focus on the sentences, and my fingers, when exposed, turned rigid from the cold. The book went limp in my hand. I put it into my coat pocket.

The wind picked up then, and the air felt sharper than before. A familiar feathery dread began to crawl up my spine. I pulled my cuffs over my knuckles and brought them to my mouth. I bent my head forwards. I bit them to make them warm. Then, in several long outbreaths I repeated the password to myself: slowly, so that I would never forget it. A-five-t-e-r-one-five-k. Asterisk, underscore, twelve, underscore, two thousand and twelve. Asterisk, underscore, twelve, underscore, two thousand and twelve.

I carried on like that, with my head bowed into my lap, until a slim line of bluish gold parted the clouds, and six chimes from the Minster told me that it was morning.

CHAPTER NINE

Early March 2014

i.

When the world discovers that you've done something terrible, the shock you experience isn't a quick jolt – not a knife in the chest or a plummeting stomach. No. Instead it is a slow prickling feeling – a sort of pervasive shiver, like a piece of cold metal is trying to escape from under your skin. It comes and goes in waves: *It's fine. It's not fine.*

Perhaps all that is easy enough to understand. Less comprehensible is the fact that, bound up with these feelings of anxiety, amidst those waves of fear and doubt and selfhatred, there's also an intense relief. It's a sense of freedom – a sense that you don't have to bother anymore because there's nothing else for you to prove to people. You've exposed your real, base self, precluded any chance of realizing what others once perceived as your potential, and now everyone finally knows that you are inherently evil, a waste of space, a failure. The realization of that fear inexplicably produces a rush of excitement. It feels *good*.

The nurses tried to break it to me gently. One of them held

my hand and placed a cool cloth over my head. I lay in the hospital bed with my eyes straining at the ceiling, trying to keep my breathing consistent, with the thick plastic tube scratching against the inside of my throat. I tried to concentrate on the words coming out of her mouth.

Freezing. Kind strangers. Here to safety.

She smoothed my hair and I sought to fit her words to a memory. I stared at the map tacked onto the ceiling, tracing its roads and buildings. It was York. My eyes tracked along the streets, and soon a memory emerged: a hand grabbing my shoulder. A visibility jacket. Arms lifted into the van. Lips chattering. Mind fogging over. Grey snowflakes dusting eyelashes. Everything opening up into a white, white mist.

I looked back at the nurse.

Hypothermia, she was saying. Lucky. Parents coming. Understand?

I winced then nodded.

On registering my response, her eyes darkened and her voice lowered. She began to speak more quickly. She said that there was a policeman outside who wanted to have a 'word' with me. 'Would it be all right if he came in for a moment?'

My eyes felt cold springing open. *No.* I gave a violent shake of the head.

The nurse again. No. She was sorry but I *had* to speak to him. He would only be a few moments. It was important.

I felt my eyes strain out of their sockets. Please, please.

The policeman entered. Even now I remember the look on his face: half-nervous, halfstern, mouth moving quickly behind a patchy beard. I refused to register what he said. He brought out his clipboard and gestured towards it. Me. Marina. Joe. A photo of my phone on my bed. Another photo of my laptop in a ring of smashed glass. I felt my breathing become sharp. My throat was closing around the plastic tube. Everything seemed to be too clear, hyper-realistic, the colours of the room garish.

I tried to speak and felt a hot spurt of phlegm choke in the back of my throat.

'There is no need to be alarmed,' the policeman said, looking alarmed himself. The nurse moved towards me and adjusted the tubes. 'The investigation will be over quickly. I just need to ask a few questions.'

My eyes fluttered shut.

'Do you understand?' he said. 'Lift a finger for yes.'

Nothing moved.

'The quicker you cooperate, the quicker this will be over.'

The nurse wiped my face. I heard footsteps outside the room. Shakily I lifted a finger.

He was right about the investigation. It was quick. The Bedes were 'shocked' apparently, but they expressed no interest in pursuing the case. It seemed that no crime had technically been committed in the first place. The police only needed to keep my laptop and phone to exclude the possibility of any other 'incidents', they said. They needed me to confirm the details of what had happened. They needed me to sign a document allowing for the information to be passed on to Facebook and Swipe, so that they could update their future privacy policies. Other than that, they didn't need anything. I was 'free to go'.

Free to go, fine, but I was not really free to live. The tirade against me raged in the papers, on the TV, on the Internet. Some of it was justified – generally I understood why people felt disgusted by me. But a lot of it was abusive, and I couldn't help but think I'd been made a scapegoat for Marina's death. My email inbox clogged with abuse. Death threat tweets circulated. Photos of my face were shopped onto indecent images and shared around the Internet. '*See how she likes her photos being appropriated*', one caption read. It was retweeted over a hundred times before being deleted by the moderators (a screenshot subsequently made its way onto porn sites and illicit forums anyway). Facebook scorched with protestations:

> Let's imagine that a poor middle-aged black guy had impersonated a dead teenager instead of this private-school educated white girl. He would be jailed!!

The like pages poured in demanding so-called justice for Marina.

A Change.org Petition: 'CHANGE THE LAW. JAIL EVA HUTCHINGS'.

At the time I wasn't aware that it was happening – or at least of the full extent of it. I only discovered this weeks later, when circumstances made it impossible to ignore. Then I understood why my parents had been so protective. The incessant phone calls, the emails, the snitching neighbours, the journalists and the death threats … I could see why they had chosen to block me off from the outside world. I could see why I wasn't allowed a substitute phone or to use a laptop.

It wasn't just the use of phones which were prohibited. In the days after the incident, I wasn't even allowed to set foot outside the house without someone (usually my mother) escorting me. This was a method which – despite its Draconian measures – didn't work faultlessly. When I went with my mother to the shops I'd notice the way the neighbours looked at me. Even strangers turned their heads and gave me a querying glance-over. Sometimes I would see a headline that bore my name poke out of the top of the newspaper stand – and though my mother would block my path, seeing it first, I would catch enough of the sentence to extract what was going on. I knew that the outside world was talking about me, that they all hated me. I only didn't know *exactly* what it was that they were saying.

The result of this half-knowledge was that I was not able to properly process what had happened. I spent those weeks in a state alternating between dull acceptance and anxiety – wondering what was being said, and thought, beyond my control.

To distract myself, I thought about the email and password that I had found in Marina's notebook. Luckily my small bag had not been completely confiscated by the police – the pile of books remained where I had left them, scrunched in the bottom of the suitcase. On returning to my house I had lifted them out quickly – and then shoved them under my mattress.

The books were a revelation to me, an obsession even. I was convinced that they would give me full access to Marina's mind. Every day I would retreat to my room and pore over her diary entries. I looked at the dates of her meetings with the professor. I drew out my own notebook, and began to jot them down, analyse them.

Most of the dates were just blank. But there were also those with the asterisk beside them:

2nd October; 29th October; 1st November; 5th November; 10th November; 11th November; 4th December; 13th December.

My eyes flicked between the two sets of dates. It bothered me that there wasn't a clean chronological break between the 'blank' dates, and those marked with an asterisk. If they meant something specific – signifying the recurrence of a particular event, or a personal timetable – then it would mean surely the asterisks would start occurring later. But the first asterisk date was the 2nd of October, which was only a few weeks into term. And then they broke off for a bit, and then they came back ...

It was impossible to follow.

I stared at the numbers and letters, squinting my eyes into fine points, trying to concentrate. I thought about what I had been doing on the highlighted days. Had I seen Marina? If not, what excuse had she given? If so, how had she behaved?

A series of revelations then came to me:

The 2nd of October was the day that we first met. The day I had interrupted the professor.

The 5th of December was the day before Henry's party.

I looked at the email address – thought of the word asterisk – and again I thought about the significance of the symbol. A superstitious chill ran through me.

I flicked to the end of the book and studied it hard. Was that even her handwriting, now I looked at it? The spidery swirls seemed to crawl out from the page. I thought about her fingers gripping the pen as she etched them out, doing that strange thing where her fingertips slipped over the sides, which she said her teachers had told her off for.

Asterisk, underscore, twelve, underscore, two thousand and twelve.

The curiosity twinged – a painful, curling sensation in my chest. I held the book close to my face, counted my breaths. It was a dangerous feeling, it came from the same place that had led me to create the Swipe account. I was suspicious of submitting to it, suspicious of myself and I knew that I should stop.

But when I didn't read the books or think about her, that's when my mind would wander to what people were saying about me, and doing that would invite the fog of faces and words, words of people I had known, or met briefly, or never met. Then I would feel dizzy again, my entire body diminishing, sight darker, everything cold.

One evening, I went downstairs to see what my parents were doing. I asked them when I might be able to get my phone or laptop replaced.

My mother's eyes bulged. 'We found you in hospital,' she said accusingly. '*Hospital*.'

'It's not good to keep me cut off from the rest of the world,' I replied. 'It's not healthy.'

'It is good for you in the short-term.'

'Can I please just quickly check my email on your phone?'

'It's like you think I was born yesterday.'

'It might be—'

'Look, we're not having this discussion,' she said.

My father stared dully at his plate. He looked so disappointed.

Asterisk, underscore, twelve, underscore, two thousand and twelve.

'What I don't understand,' my mother said suddenly, emphatically, as though someone had asked a question, 'is why Northam bothered to stick up for you. Initially, I mean.' She cleared her throat. 'I mean – why *bother at all*? It was obvious you were never going to come back in the first place. There is no way we would have let you.'

Silence.

'It's just ridiculous that they should have "expelled" you. I mean there's no way,' she continued, 'no *way* that you were ever going to be fit to return to university anyway. And not just because of this … silly Swipe business, but because you were in hospital. You were ill. If Northam hadn't stuck their foot in it then none of this would have taken off again. It just wouldn't be an issue.'

The words hung in the air. Out the corner of my eye I saw that my father was still staring at his plate.

I knew that she was trying to make it better. I knew that she was trying to say, in a skewed way, that none of this was my fault and that ultimately it wasn't a big deal anyway. The bigger issue was – quite sensibly – that I'd nearly died from hypothermia. My physical and mental welfare were 'the primary concern here' – not some stupid online stunt I'd performed.

But I didn't believe her. Nor did my father. Nor did the police. Nor did the public.

I went back upstairs to my room.

Alone at last. I peeled back my bedsheets, heaved up the corner of the mattress and inspected the small pile of Marina's books.

The diary had occupied so much of my time that the other books – the academic guides and the philosophy tracts and the novels – had scarcely been touched. Most of them were in tatters from the train journey, with the centre-folds sliding out from the jacket and the corners curled at the edges. But – I noticed, opening one at random – some of them were still readable.

I wrenched the book fully open and flipped onto my stomach. I bent back the spine, and held it in front of me with my neck craned up. I resolved to stay like that, my eyes glued to the page, until I had read every word.

For a few days I continued in that routine. I would wake up and reach out towards the pile of books beside me, grab the closest volume and thumb through to the most recent page. Reading Marina's notes gave me an odd sense of calm. I felt pleasantly disconnected from myself, from my thoughts and from my body. The words were like an escape from my head. It was as though I were communicating with some larger consciousness. I was reaching out of time, twisting the current dimension, reaching backwards somewhere beyond the grave.

I find it hard, still, to patch those days together and understand what I did on a daily basis. But I do remember a day in late March.

The light filtered through the window, making me aware that it was the early morning. I was not sure how long I had slept for that day – it was a bad day, one where I had been unable to get out of bed. My parents had tried to coax me out with food, a board game, or a 'refreshing' walk, but without luck. A book was creased into my face. I lifted it off, thumbed through it for a bit and eventually came upon a poem. The first stanza caught my attention:

What seas, what shores, what grey rocks and what islands
What water lapping the bow

And scent of pine and the woodthrush singing through the fog
What images return
O my daughter.

The title of the poem was 'Marina'. She had not annotated it, or even underlined any sections; but the page was folded over in the corner. I felt that this was a signal. My eyes moved over the next section:

Those who sharpen the tooth of the dog, meaning
Death
Those who glitter with the glory of the hummingbird, meaning
Death
[...]
Are become unsubstantial, reduced by a wind

There came a sound outside the window. A twig snapping, the rustle of a leaf. I snapped the book shut and drew it to my chest. A slow, cold feeling crept up my spine. The hairs on my arms were standing out, pale and thin in the moonlight, and I found myself thinking of that time Marina had sat beside me on the beach. How delicate she had looked. How frightened. The leaves rustled again; a breeze rattled the window. I leaned across cautiously and opened the blind.

'Hello?' I said quietly, into the darkness.

I looked out a little further, poking my head through the frame, so that my neck aligned with the fastening. My skin felt tight.

'Hello?' I said again, this time louder.

Nothing. I listened for a few more seconds.

Still nothing. I closed the blind, returned to my bed, and opened the book again. I tried to focus on reading the rest of the poem:

What is this face? Less clear and clearer
The pulse in the arm less strong and stronger –

There was the sound again. There was something, or somebody, outside the window, I was sure of it. I could hear the sound of footsteps patting along the road. I strained my ears to listen. Then I began to shift my legs, to sit up taller and—

An explosion of glass. The window shattered – BANG –and then came the shadow of a black heavy object, almost in slow motion, making a perfect arc in the air before landing, landing, landing with a thud. I screamed.

'What is going—?'

A light flicked on.

That was my mother's voice. I recognized it instantly, I knew she was there, moving forwards, moving towards me, but I couldn't bring myself to look at her. I could only stare, horrified, at my body in front of me. I followed the line of blood from my hands, down the smears on my legs, to the transparent shards sticking out of the duvet.

In the following moments the house seemed eerily quiet. Everything was very still. I heard the beat of the clock in the next room. The glass lay flat and darkly glittering on the top of the duvet. I became aware that part of my leg was throbbing.

Things changed after the attack. The death threats stopped, there were fewer abusive emails, and the media seemed to view me with more sympathy. Words like 'imitator' and 'stalker' disappeared from headlines. They were replaced by 'mentally ill', or just 'Northam girl'.

I saw this because the police made me read through selected forums, newspaper articles and comments. They said that it was necessary in case I recognized the way certain messages were written. If certain events or details were referenced that I could help shed light on, then it would be easier for them to identify a suspect.

I was – and remain – sceptical of this approach. Very few comments referred to specific aspects of my behaviour at Northam, and even those which did – like the girl who had claimed to have heard me screaming in my room – were too vague to be identified.

None of this was relevant anyway. Even if those comments could be traced, there was no certainty that the person who had thrown the rock through the window had ever posted anything at all. What I'm saying is: the Northam police didn't seem to understand the nature of social media posting. It wasn't a small pool of people from university who were saying hateful things about me. It was a network of complete strangers from everywhere – people I would never be able to identify, who had probably never seen me in person.

Eventually the police rounded up the case as 'inconclusive'. A man in police uniform told me what I already knew, in solemn patronizing tones while wearing a solemn, patronizing expression. He said that someone had posted a screenshot of my house on Google Earth on one of the forums, and that that IP address had been traced back to Northam. Beyond that, however, 'it is impossible to locate a specific device', since everyone at Northam was wired to the same Internet. They said that they would 'keep an eye' on Internet activity, and that we should contact them 'if there were any similar disturbances'. Then they left; the case closed and the police moved on.

They moved on. Good for them. But my leg continued to ache, and so did my head. I had read the death threats sent to my parents. I had read the comments and the news and the letters and the abusive emails. My parents tried to keep me away from it all again, and shut off my access to computers and the Internet and the news. It was too late. I had seen it all.

I was terrified, and I hated myself.

There was a lot of talk about what to do next and where to send me. My parents couldn't afford to move. My grandmother lived

221

miles away, in a tiny one-bedroom flat up the coast. One set of aunts and uncles lived abroad; the other set – my mother's – weren't on speaking terms with us. As a result there was no option but to stay in the house. My bedroom window was taped up. It was decided that I would move to the spare room.

The spare room was a converted cupboard at the back of the house with a bed along the wall, a bedside table and no window. I had slept in it only a few times before, either when I was ill or when relatives were staying over and had to sleep in my room. I did not like the spare room much. The fact it had no window had always unnerved me, and now I was doubly insecure: no window meant no escape route.

I spent my days lying in a mottled dark, a thin artificial beam of light streaming under the door. I stared at the outline of the wall, reassuring myself that I was in a concrete, physical space. I was not dead. I existed in relation to other things, touchable things.

This didn't always work. I had chronic hallucinations involving the attacker. I imagined her – it was always a her – breaking into the house, sneaking through the dark corridors and finding me asleep in bed. I imagined her raising a thick cutlass of glass high above her head, bringing it down quickly and plunging it into my skull. I thought of her hands grappling at my throat and smashing and slicing my face, her teeth coming down to bite great chunks out of skin... and I often woke up screaming, with my mother pressing a hand onto my forehead.

My mother was good at arriving quickly – I'll give her that. Seeing her face would, at first, make me relieved. I'd hear the light snapping on, the smell of sour perfume filling my nostrils, see the familiar features coming into view, and all that was soothing. But as soon as she started talking, I'd immediately feel more anxious. Her tone was shrill and demanding. 'We will come up with a solution,' she would say repeatedly. 'We'll find *a permanent solution*. OK?'

Her voice always had a cracked uncertainty, as though she were trying to reassure herself that those things were true. Then she would look at me meaningfully, waiting for my expression to change – waiting for validation. I would try not to wince at the stinging as she stroked my foot. I always remained silent, with my mouth in a tight grim line.

Once after dinner, when I was sure my parents were fully occupied by the television, I limped along the landing and went into my bedroom. It was colder in there – a subtle, bitter kind of lightness in the air. I stood in front of the smashed window. It had been boarded up with masking tape, but it was possible to pick at the edges and, if I was gentle, then peel it off. I tugged at the corners of the tape. I tugged a little harder. Tiny shards of glass made a tinkling sound. Then the tape stuttered, purred softly, and came off in one thick chunk.

I stuck the tape along the wooden window frame, then looked at the hole that the rock had left. A star of splinters shone iridescent in the moonlight, a gaping black mouth in the centre of the glass. As the wind blew through it the glass teeth seemed even sharper, and I moved towards them instinctively, reaching out my hand, curling it into the gap. My fingers fluttered there for a moment, adjusting to the proximity of sharpness, of danger, then I brought the index and my thumb together, moved them forwards, and sliced them along the ragged edges of the glass.

I felt a sharp jolt of pain, almost enjoyable. I pushed the fingers further against the spike so that the jolt intensified. I kept pushing. I kept it there for as long as I could.

Eventually I retracted my hand and pinched my thumb and forefinger together tightly. The tips felt bloody and smooth. I brought my finger to my mouth and licked it. It was salty, good to taste. I thought about doing that to my entire hand. I wanted to become smooth all over, so that I could curl into a ball and roll away.

***

In a recurrent dream I am back at Northam. It is raining, dark, the trees and buildings are moving silhouettes; everything has blurry edges. I am walking along the moors. I am trying to find Marina. She is not in the library. Not in the silent room; not in the nooks upstairs; not in the café. She is not in the park or by the lake. I walk to the other side of the campus. High in a window – there! There she is! I recognise the pale blue fabric of her dress. I see her pulling up the blind. I call to her.

She sees me, looks alarmed.

'Eva?'

Why didn't you tell me you weren't coming back? I shout. Why didn't you tell me about your drug habit?

'What?'

Why did you speak to Henry. Why didn't you come to me first. Why have you been ignoring me.

'Eva, not now. Leave me alone.'

She repeats that I should leave her alone. She tells me that she doesn't want to hear from me at all.

I tell her that no one cares about her. I tell her she is a fake human. A shallow, empty shell of a human. I tell her to kill herself.

'Everyone thinks you're a whore,' I say. 'That's all you are – a pathetic, shallow, stupid slut. Even your dad probably thinks you're a waste of space. That's why you're here.'

Her face falls then. I see the gold in her eyes flash and disappear. She leans far out the window, puts one foot on the ledge, calls to me.

I do not hear what she says. I turn around, and walk quickly, dizzily back to my car. I get in and slam the door.

Then I wake up.

ii.

On the morning of the 3rd of April, the phone rang. I heard my mother sweep across the room and pick it up. She answered in a tone of strained politeness. Then her voice became louder, affected; occasionally punctuated by a sterile laugh. The footsteps began plodding upstairs. My door clicked open. I sensed she was standing in my doorway.

'How is your leg today, Eva?'

After a pause, I said: 'It's fine.'

'What is "fine"? Better? Completely healed?'

'It's not like it was ever broken,' I said.

'Just answer the question. Is it healed or —?'

'Yes. It feels better. Much better.'

'Show me.'

I peeled back the bedclothes, stuck my calf out towards her. The congealed, bloody bruise had now grown a scab; looked healthy. My mother made a satisfied noise, like 'hmm'. I still didn't look at her. I tucked my leg back under the covers.

'Good,' she said. 'Now listen – there is someone on the phone for you.'

I didn't answer.

'There is someone on the phone for you,' she said again. 'Eva.'

'Who?'

'Just someone who wants a chat.'

The words were meant to sound casual, and when I finally looked up I saw that she was trying to look casual too. Her hip was leaning against the frame, one hand propped above the door handle. We stared at each other.

Both she and I knew that this quite obviously was not a normal scenario: I hadn't been allowed to use the phone myself, and to my knowledge no one had tried to call me since the news had come out. I couldn't remember the last time I had even heard a voice on the phone – Henry perhaps?

I looked at her for a long time, pleadingly. She remained tight-lipped, dangling the plastic towards me. Her body sagged at an awkward angle. I wondered whether she was leaning against the door in that way to stop herself from shaking.

Eventually I took the phone and brought it to my face.

'Hello.' I said.

'Eva.'

A male voice – one I recognized. It had a smooth, glossy quality with a very slight American accent.

'Marcus?'

'Please don't hang up,' he said. 'We aren't angry at you. We don't blame you for anything you've done.'

I sat against the edge of my bed, sensing a numbness creep into my fingertips, up my neck into my face. With one hand, I drew the sheets around me. With the other I pressed the phone deep into my cheek.

'I-I'm so sorry,' I began.

'Please, Eva,' Marcus's voice was gentle. 'You've suffered enough. I'm not calling to reprimand you. The media have been completely unfair, blowing everything out of proportion. It was a silly mistake. No one deserves the abuse you've suffered.'

Abuse. At the mention of that word, my fingernails crept up to the skin at the front of my throat.

'The whole thing,' I said, trying to keep my voice level. 'It was stupid. I don't even know why I did it. I didn't mean any disrespect. I really had no idea that …'

There was a pause, but he said nothing to fill it so I continued: 'Well, that Marina was … I had no idea.'

'Listen, we all make mistakes.' His voice sounded soft, controlled. 'It was a careless and petty error, a human error. You certainly don't deserve to be hounded like this. Marina would have … well, she may have even found it funny.'

I processed his words as the mattress softened underneath me.

'I trust you've recovered from your illness?' he said.

'Yes.'

'And you've recovered from the, ah, break-in incident?'

I breathed hard. 'Yes.'

'I hear you've since remained excluded from the news.'

The news. I thought about the headlines I'd glimpsed during the policeman's report.

DID STALKER EVA HUTCHINGS KILL MARINA BEDE?

The anxiety swelled. It was impossible to concentrate on anything again.

'Eva,' Marcus said, somewhat impatiently. 'You've remained excluded from the news?'

'Yes.'

'What is your plan now?'

'Well,' I said vaguely, 'My leg is healing. I haven't thought much beyond that.'

'Have you thought about where you're going next?'

I paused here and wondered how to answer.

'I've tried to contact firms for work experience. But I haven't had any responses.' I corrected myself: 'Positive responses.'

Marcus paused, and a weight fell upon the conversation. I heard him take in a breath on the other end of the line.

'Well,' he said. 'I'd like to help you in some way. It's not healthy for you to be cooped up like an animal.'

Tears welled up under my eyelashes.

Marcus continued: 'There's no point in someone with your potential wasting their time at home, on their own, worrying about the future.'

He quickly cut to the chase after that: he wanted to help navigate where I was going next. He said that he had a few friends who could use my 'skills', who might help me decide what to do. I could return to university later, he thought, 'though give it a few months, to let the hubbub die down'.

I didn't know what to do with this information. I felt suspicious, first, that he was going out of his way to help me. Then I felt ashamed: he felt *sorry* for me. I was a subject of pity. That was worse than being a subject of hatred.

'It's only a suggestion, anyway,' he said. 'But I think it would benefit you to hear a few plans. I've helped out many people in a tough spot.'

'That's really kind.'

'Yes. Perhaps something in banking or consultancy would suit you.'

I suppressed a scoff at that, but not entirely successfully – a tiny sigh escaped.

'I mean, perhaps.'

It wasn't like I had many options.

'Well what else could we consider, let me think …'

As Marcus continued to talk in this manner, I noticed something else in his tone which disturbed me – a note of impatient aggression, almost, like a bargain had already been struck. I became aware that my mother was still standing in the doorway. Why was she looking at me like that?

'Have you …' I said. 'Have you spoken to my mother about this already?'

Another pause.

Marcus said: 'We have talked briefly about it, yes.'

Of course they had. Of course my mother had snivelled to him about all my problems, of course she'd wheedled up to him to ask for a good word – or, alternatively, perhaps he had contacted her; *out of the goodness of his heart*, to seem like a nice guy. Whichever it was, I was tired of other people offering me help. I was tired of being told how to behave in my life, of having to feel grateful towards everyone pushing me around when I hadn't even asked for their help. I didn't want their help, especially when it was cushioned it in terms like 'opportunity'. It was all so insincere. My parents, Marcus, the papers, the Internet trolls …

A wave of rebellion rose and crashed.

'What about the Marina Bede Foundation?' I said.

'I'm sorry?'

'The Marina Bede Foundation,' I repeated. 'I would love to

help with the MBF. That is, if you need anyone to do … any admin stuff.'

It felt good to say something intentionally inappropriate, to feel the air clam up with tension.

I heard a brief cough on the other end of the line.

'Well, that's … an interesting proposition …' Marcus said, trailing off.

At the same time my mother shook her head: 'Darling I'm—'

'Yes,' I continued, 'I think it would be interesting. As I said before – in my email, I mean – the MBF represents a cause which I really care about. Having been through similar experiences myself, I know how it feels to be in that position – being an isolated teenage girl. Being part of the foundation would give me a huge sense of … um, perspective and redemption.' I paused, then added: 'Doing charity work would make me feel much better about what's happened too. In fact, I think it's … something that Marina might even have wanted.'

I loved listening to myself speak such bullshit with a high, brazen level of selfconviction. It was satisfying to hear. And more than that, it was easy: once I swallowed my pride and tapped into cliché, I realized, I could come across as fairly normal. Yes, churning out dull, pious soundbites and modulating my voice in such a way to seem vaguely sorry for myself, like I'd Learned My Truth – that was the key to being 'nice'. Following this mantra, I outlined other clear reasons for my suitability as a charity worker. I mentioned what I had been through in *my* early teenage years. I laid it on thick, but I also sounded matter-of-fact and therefore – unusually – convincing.

Marcus said nothing, but he listened and made the odd noise to indicate surprise or agreement. In the corner of my eye I saw my mother starting to walk towards me. I tried to wriggle away, but as she came nearer, she bent over me and she grabbed the phone.

The edge of her fingernail caught my palm as she snatched away the plastic.

'Marcus? Marcus, hi it's Linda here. Yes, I'm sorry about that. Yes, she's had a difficult – oh no, no, no not at all. It's so kind of you to even ... yes ...'

I watched her walk out of the room. Her slim neck was twitching a little, and her fingers had turned white with the strain of holding the phone.

'Oh no Marcus,' she said. 'Oh no, no *don't* apologize, it's us, *please.*'

My mother didn't mention the conversation later that evening. She didn't mention it the next day, or the day after that.

But then a funny thing happened. On the sixth day of April, my mother told me that Marcus had called again. There was, in fact, an event coming up to launch the Marina Bede Foundation. Marcus had said that his research assistant wasn't available, and so he urgently needed somebody to help out for a few days. It would just be sorting through paperwork, preparing the decorations, setting out the chairs, making sure it was all in order. And he wanted to know, specifically, whether I would be available. I would only need to work for him for a few days.

'We've thought about it, your father and I,' said my mother. 'The idea seemed strange to us at first, but at the end of the day we think you may benefit from the experience. We think ... well, it might help you see that there is a reality to the situation. There is life beyond this, you see.'

My mother stood in the doorway as she told me this – at a safe distance. I looked at her from my bed. I studied her shy mouth, her neck with its slight forward bent. All of it communicated one word: *defeat*. I tried to suppress a smile.

'I'll think about it,' I said. 'I'll mull it over.'

A short while later, I rang Marcus and accepted.

It seems astonishing to me now that my parents would agree to this arrangement. Even suspicious. Sometimes I look at coincidences like this and I think that they knew.

In the days before I left they both began talking about my future 'plans' with great enthusiasm. They said that my going to Marcus's house presented an *ideal* opportunity. They said that it would mean that I could be away from the 'scene of the incident', by which they meant their house. They said that it would afford me a sense of independence. Crucially, it would mean that I was able to make amends with the Bede family.

'You've spent so long torturing yourself,' my mother said. 'Not everyone is angry at you. The Bedes aren't angry at you, Marcus will show you that. You have to learn not to be so angry with yourself.'

This was a thin argument, and all of us knew it. My parents did not want me to go to the Bedes because they were concerned for me, but because they were concerned for themselves. They wanted to send me *somewhere*, but couldn't afford it. They wanted to alleviate their consciences about what I had done – but to frame it in a way to seem as though they were helping me to alleviate mine. Marcus's offer presented an effective, cheap solution. It was a way for them to send me away, to ease the financial and emotional strain that I was forcing upon them.

But I didn't mind, not really. In fact, I was excited by the idea of going. After all, I had suggested it. For perhaps the first time since I had left school, this suggestion was an active decision: a decision with reasons that I could identify.

The main reason I'd wanted to go had little to do with either being scared of another attack, or being ambitious for my future. It wasn't really because I was remorseful either. I didn't – at this point – feel especially guilty about the Marina impersonation. On that front my emotions had been eroded.

Then why? Because I wanted to be in Marina's house. I knew from Marina's stories about her family that Marcus's house in England, Mosebury Court, was her childhood home. I knew that she had loved the place – she had spent her happiest years there growing up – and it served as the setting for many of her stories

231

about her family. The place where she'd been sent after her mother died. The place where she'd fallen and broken her hip aged 8. The place where, during the summer months, Marcus had played 'Stairway to Heaven' on the ukulele. As a result, it held a special place in my imagination. I wanted to indulge that part of my imagination. I wanted to find out more about her.

I still do, in fact.

Once, early in the winter term, I had sat in my room and typed her address into Google Maps. I'd found the address on her university form. I'd heard so much about her house from her stories that I had wanted to see if it matched up to what my imagination had built. I had wanted to see if, when I zoomed in, I might catch Marina or her father walking around in the garden or the street, caught unawares by the Google cameras. But as it happened, when I put in the address nothing came up. The area was too private. The cameras could only offer a distant bird's-eye view of the village. They must have had some clause protecting it from public view.

The idea that I would now see this house in the flesh – to walk down its corridors, to be among Marina's old things, to see old photographs of her, to live and eat and sleep where she had lived and eaten and slept, to be in the space of the stories she had told me – all of this was irresistible to me. And it might offer, too, an idea of what those asterisks meant.

The following weekend, we set off for Mosebury.

iii.

Mid-April 2014

The question of whether Mosebury Court met my expectations was quickly settled. The answer was: it didn't. My image of the house had been hazy in details but of a specific type: something aged and rambling – probably Georgian – that might fit in a Wodehouse novel. This was not close to the mark.

232

I caught sight of it at the bottom of the hill, and (with distaste) watched it expand as we made our way up the drive. In some respects it could have looked like an eighteenth-century estate – the central building was made of limestone, with a high roof, and thick pillars forming a portico. But when you took in the shambles around it, the overall effect was a mishmash of styles rather carelessly plonked together rather than a consistent – or even coherent – design. Behind the house, in the distance, was a black plasticky pagoda and beyond that, a sleek glass rectangle that I took to be a pool house or sun room. Fountains were dotted about a lush green garden, and in the distance stood a row of marble statues surrounding a pool. As our car creaked over the gravel, I soothed myself by thinking of Marina running around those statues as a child, her hair curling out like tentacles in the sun; her short legs stumbling over the grass.

'Welcome!'

Marcus was stood outside the front door. He wore a shirt loose at the collar, a warm expression on his face. He looked handsome in the sunlight. As he approached our car, his hair shimmered a pale gold and his neck seemed very straight, his clothes very clean. My mother smoothed the edges of her skirt.

'Welcome, welcome!' he said again, the corners of his mouth wrinkling up at the edges. 'Do come inside.'

I got out of the car, twisting my legs carefully to one side, and deliberately avoided eye contact with him. I walked along the side of the car and turned towards the front of the house.

'Marcus this is just *delig*htful,' I heard my mother say.

It had taken me a second to get used to it, but now I had compromised my prior expectations, I sort of agreed with her. It was beautiful and awful at the same time. It possessed the kind of eclectic aesthetic which didn't work at all on paper, but was oddly magnificent when you remembered who it belonged to. That combination of refined taste and sloppy vulgarity seemed to characterize the Bedes. I imagined the child Marina hovering in the spot where I stood then, smiling in her school uniform. One of her socks would be rolling down her ankle, a stray curl would dangle across her forehead, a pudgy hand rising to brush it away.

My mother giggled and said again: 'Delightful.'

I noticed that her voice sounded different. She had leaned in to hug Marcus. Their heads were very close together, and as she drew her neck to the side her curls brushed against his shoulder. His arms fanned out over her back. The cuff of his shirt poked out of his jacket sleeve.

Just then Marcus turned his head and caught me looking at him. He held my eyes for a moment, his brow wrinkling, and then he smiled warmly.

'We've just had the gardener in,' he said. The words were addressed to my mother, but he was still looking at me. 'I hope you won't be too disappointed by the inside of the house.'

My mother laughed a lot at this, more than was normal. I didn't like that. Nor did I like her contrived pout, the flare of her nostrils, the pointed concentration.

'Really, Marcus, how long have you lived here? And all alone, or is your wife …?'

I stared at her.

'Elena is currently in the US,' said Marcus. 'She's looking at some fascinating papers on human rights law actually. Usually I live over there too, but I've taken some time off work to focus on the foundation. And, well, processing everything.'

'Oh yes,' she gasped, 'of course.'

I hung back and I let them talk for a while. I looked at the back of Marcus's jacket. He didn't seem real. Since the funeral, Marcus had felt like an abstraction, someone or something I'd dreamt up. When he turned around again I narrowed my eyes and tried hard to concentrate on individual details to convince myself that he was a physical entity. He hugged me, it felt like an act.

'Don't look so nervous, Eva,' he said. Then he murmured something in Italian which I assumed was a greeting.

Spreading his arms wide, he opened the large wooden doors, ushered us in, and gave us a quick tour of the downstairs section of the house. This had been the family 'abode', he explained, but since his marriage had 'collapsed' virtually no one lived in it. Marcus lived in the US most of the time, so it was only ever inhabited during the holidays, or occasionally by short-term renters.

All the time he talked, he walked a few steps ahead, and the sound of his black glossy shoes clipping against the tiles echoed down the corridor.

I thought it was weird that Marcus referred to his marriage as having 'collapsed', without bringing up the fact that his wife had also died. But it would be inappropriate to pull him up on that, I figured, and I couldn't be bothered to face the wrath of my mother anyway so I let it slide.

'I'm only here now because of the launch,' he said.

To distract myself, I studied the paintings along the walls. They were eclectically, even erratically, arranged – a zigzagging line of gold-framed squares dancing over smooth cream paint. Actually, the paint aside, everything along those walls was slightly out of joint. It was as though there had been an earthquake in a tsar's palace, jolting all the furnishings so that they tilted at a quirky angle. Most of them were paintings of the garden or the house or certain important-looking ancestors. A few of them were old childhood photos of Marina. She sat smiling on Marcus's shoulders; she lay curled up in the arms of an old lady. I suddenly thought of her curled on the pavement. The limbs at uneven angles, the crooked feet, the face mashed to pulp, the blood pooling out of her ear, out of her nose, out of her mouth.

I shook the thought away.

'In this direction is the kitchen,' said Marcus. 'It's a long way down the hall.'

Just then a faded black-and-white photograph, positioned slightly higher than the others, caught my attention. It depicted a group of people stood outside the front of the house. I squinted and attempted to identify them. Marina, with her cherubic pudgy face and a gap-toothed grin; Marcus, young and roguishly handsome, wearing a flat cap. Then there were three other adults – a man and two women, plus two children; a girl and a boy.

One of the women looked disturbingly familiar. I hovered in front of the photograph, studying her closely. She had red hair and a soft, full mouth. I wondered for a moment if perhaps this was Marina's mother – if this was the vilified alcoholic who had died from cancer. Then I looked closer. Suddenly the familiar features came to the fore. The full mouth, the startling blue eyes. I realized that it was the woman I had seen with Henry at the funeral. A child version of Henry – with his triangular face, straight teeth and haunted brown eyes – was stood in front of her.

'So it's just your UK residence?' said my mother. Her voice was nasal. 'I'm sorry but I didn't realize academia was so ...'

'We're very lucky,' Marcus cut in. 'But as I said, we do rent it out. For weddings mostly.'

I stared at the photograph and tried to piece the scene together. The red-haired woman must be Henry's mother. The man stood next to her was presumably Henry's father. Who, then, was the girl at the front of the row? And the other woman with blonde hair – was that Marina's mother? I stared at her profile. She had shoulder-length dark blonde hair, a fine bone structure, large grey eyes. She looked elegant, and I supposed a little like Marina. Yet it was such a different image to the bohemian alcoholic I had imagined.

'Eva,' said Marcus suddenly, 'is your leg all right?'

I looked up. There was a kind of forced, playful expression on his face.

'Yes,' I said slowly.

'Then come along!' he laughed. 'We don't want you to get left behind.'

I laughed back, in a similarly superficial tone, but after that I found it hard to concentrate on what anyone was saying. The photograph had disturbed me – the rest of the house now seemed charged with Marina's presence. I looked at the smooth paint of the walls. I looked at the oak panelling, the gold-edged school portraits of Marina. I imagined her returning here after her first term at Northam – throwing her bag down on the chair, racing to her bedroom.

'Here we are.'

Marcus's voice erupted into my thoughts again. I looked up. His hand was propped against an oak-panelled door, pushing it open. There was the arc of a soft pink palm, curving up to the flash of his signet ring.

'Lovely,' my mother said.

Then I noticed the room he was leading us into – the cream carpet, the double bed, a landscape painting hanging on the wall by the window.

'This will be where you're staying, if you don't mind,' said Marcus. 'It's quite small, and the ground floor isn't ideal perhaps. But it should have everything you need.'

Listening to him say this, it suddenly struck me that I would actually be staying in the house. Soon my mother would leave; I would be alone with Marcus; I would be abandoned in this house; sleeping in this room. Alone.

The room began to spin. I felt sick and dizzy, and the outlines of my mother and Marcus seemed to blur into one another. I looked to my mother, but she seemed very far away, and she was turning, turning away from me. Now she was fiddling with the blind, shaking her hair back and tittering at her own clumsiness while Marcus was showing her how to work it.

Gross. I adjusted my sightlines to the blind, just as the material rolled up and exposed the dark glass behind. I saw my figure

237

dimly reflected there. My round face, my indistinct features. I could only properly make out my matted fringe, and perhaps a pair of expressionless eyes. Peering closer, ever so slightly, I thought I saw glints of gold in them.

After Marcus had showed me my room, we ate a small supper in the kitchen. Then he took us on a tour of the rest of the house. I let Marcus and my mother go slightly ahead of me again, as I wanted to have time to process my surroundings. Everything in that house seemed to carry the ghost of Marina: from the child-hood portraits along the wall, to the stash of old CDs spilling out of the cupboards, to the positioning of the old-fashioned chairs which somehow appeared to emulate her posture. Even in the kitchen, running my hands over the cutlery, I felt a strange proximity to her, conscious of the way that the silver felt against my fingertips, imagining how it would have felt against hers.

I hung back a little further as we ascended the stairs. I looked at the ceiling: a tall dome above the staircase, with a full chandelier dangling from the centre. It was bursting with glass droplets, and as I walked up the stairs I thought I could see my face in each curved bead, stretched out over their surfaces. I thought about how Marina had spent her final weeks in this house. What did she feel then? At what point had she decided what she was going to do to herself?

We reached the top of the stairs, and I could see at least six rooms down the corridor. Marcus took us around each of them. I carefully studied the items inside. There was Marcus's bedroom, which he gestured towards without showing us in. Then there was the bathroom, where the toilet was gilded and a large bath sat in a square in the corner. Beside that was a 'steam room'. Then an upstairs playroom of some kind, and another study. Each of the rooms was painted in the same light grey hue, and had long translucent windows looking out onto the garden.

As we walked back to the top of the stairs, I realized I had only counted five of the six bedrooms. Marcus was talking about something different, and beginning to turn towards the top step. My mother said: 'Whoops,' as her wine glass clinked against the bannister. A droplet of red liquid spilled on the carpet. I saw it; Marcus saw it, and we glanced at each other. My mother didn't seem to notice.

I looked past Marcus, who was still smiling at me. And then I noticed that behind his head there was a dark purple door, slightly ajar. My eyes tracked from the door to Marcus's face and back again. There was a rectangle of Blu-Tack over the wood, as though a sign had been recently removed.

'What's in there?' I asked.

'In where?' he said.

'That room behind you.'

He studied me carefully. His eyes seemed very green.

'Oh,' he said. 'You mean Marina's room.'

He leaned backwards and pulled the door firmly shut.

'No need to go in there.'

iv.

It's hard to visualize all the stuff that happened after my mother left. If the past is a foreign country, then that section of my past is a broad wasteland without landmarks, without marks of any kind. The order of all those conversations and discoveries is impossible to pin down precisely. One thing that I do recall fairly clearly, however, is the work schedule: each morning Marcus would give me a list of things to do, and then leave me in the office. These tasks were manual, tedious, and the first section of the list usually took me a few hours. After that I would have lunch on my own and work again until the late afternoon. I had arrived on Friday night. The event for the foundation was to be held on the Monday, which was a bank holiday.

Saturday was to be spent doing preparatory filing; Sunday

sorting physical tasks such as the table seating and printing off leaflets about the foundation. On Monday the catering staff would arrive and I would be able to go home.

When I first arrived things were predictably awkward with Marcus. We sat in the sitting room and made small talk about the furniture.

I gestured towards an armchair on the opposite side of the room.

'Is that … a …?'

His eyes flashed in my direction.

'Sorry?' he said.

'Oh nothing.'

'Sorry?' he said again.

'I just …' I looked down. 'That's a nice armchair.'

'Yes it is. Thank you.'

'Is it old?'

'What?'

'Is it old, like an antique? Or is it …?'

'That? Oh no, it's one of Elena's purchases. I think we bought it in France.'

'Oh.'

I looked at him – he looked back at me intently. His eyes hovered to my mouth, stayed there for a fraction longer than was normal. Then he looked away.

'Your mother is charming,' he said.

'Yep,' I replied. 'She's a character.'

I felt weird. Being around Marcus was making me uncomfortable, guilty and ashamed, in a way that I hadn't expected. It wasn't a self-hating or repentant kind of guilt, but one that made me feel girlishly defensive. When he looked at me, his eyes seemed to linger. Sometimes he stopped mid-sentence and gazed at me, knowingly, as though I had – unconsciously – given him a signal.

This was distracting and exhausting to think about. I just wanted him to be gone. I wanted to be in the house alone: to walk along its corridors and study the photos, to investigate the attic, to trawl through the old playroom and discover Marina's childhood toys. I wanted to go into her bedroom.

That first night, alone, I lay in my room thinking about Marina. I stared up at the ceiling and thought about the tantalizing proximity of her bedroom. One easy flight of stairs above me. I thought about the purple door I had stood outside earlier in the day and the question of what lay behind was like a sharp, weight lodged inside my brain.

I rolled over and looked out of the window. In the distance, through a thin veil of rain, I could see the row of marble statues filing out against the horizon. They looked somehow menacing, like an approaching army. My thoughts turned back to the attack in my parents' house – to the rock, to the poem, to smashed glass. Swiftly I opened the window, closed my eyes and leaned out. I felt the balmy air on my cheeks. I breathed in, breathed out.

The feeling of sweet warm air against my face sent me into a kind of hypnotic daze. I felt a strange, excitable urgency. I closed the window, climbed out of my sheets and wrapped myself in a dressing gown. I walked across the floor in the darkness. Then I opened my door a crack and looked out.

It was dark in the hallway. Everything seemed very still. I strained my ears but could hear no sound from upstairs. And so I crept out, carefully closing the door behind me, and then made my way down the corridor. I passed the study and turned towards the stairs. My feet pressed into the carpet. I slid the soles along the step, slowly, gently unfurling my injured foot so that it didn't make any sound, and began to ascend.

Outside the rain flung itself with increasing strength against the window. The bannister creaked as I went upwards, forwards. I didn't dare look at the chandelier, but I could hear a faint whisper of beads each time my weight shifted. My toes edged along the carpet.

There was a dim light shining from the bathroom, and I figured that if I opened the door to Marina's room, it would provide just enough light for me to see what was inside. I would only take a glimpse, I told myself, and then go back down to my room. Just a glimpse.

I slid my hand towards the handle and twisted it to the side. It seemed a little stiff at first, but eventually it gave, and the door opened with a small chirring sound. I peered into the room.

Marina's childhood bedroom looked exactly that: like a room for a child. There was an enormous window at one end that opened out onto the garden. The bed sat beside it, then there was a bookshelf, then a large zebra print pinboard scattered with photos and funny little notes. I edged inside, leaving the door open a crack, and tiptoed to the board to read the notes. They were a mixture of the personal and educational: lots of poetry scratchings from Edward Lear and Michael Rosen, but also invites to parties, postcards from her French and Spanish exchanges, Polaroid selfies of carefully made-up girls with luvvie captions scrawled underneath them.

I noted the difference between this room – so personal and kitsch, so crammed full of cutesy memorabilia – and her sparsely decorated, brutalist 'cell' in Northam. It was astonishing. No wonder Marcus had felt so shocked seeing what that place looked like. Whoever had lived and grown up in this room was a completely different person to the one I had known. I realized, looking around, with a sense of sad revelation, that I really had only seen one side of her. Perhaps she really was the sweet and lively girl they had commemorated at her funeral.

A noise outside the window alerted me to what I was doing.

Quickly but quietly I walked back towards the door. But just before I reached it, a wall hanging caught my eye. It sat low down, next to the drawing board: a framed piece of paper with a silver plaque at the top. I squinted through the darkness to read the gold embossed letters:

Darling Marina, Happy 6th Birthday. Love mum

Inside the frame was a piece of parchment paper with writing on it. It was a swirly font, carefully set out within the frame, and as I started to read it I realized it was a poem. My eyes fell to the first line:

What seas, what shores, what grey rocks what granite islands
towards my timbers
And woodthrush singing through the fog
My daughter

I froze. It was the same poem I had read on the night I had been attacked, the same poem that I had found marked in Marina's books. I felt mesmerized by this revelation, convinced that somehow here was the key to something, and I found my fingers reaching out to trace the letters. I continued reading:

I made this, I have forgotten
And remember
The rigging weak and the canvas rotten
Between one June and another September.

There was a creak along the landing. Not from outside this time – but inside the house. Panicked, I looked over towards the door. The light from the corridor had been smothered by a human shadow. It grew taller, longer, and then was still. It hovered for a second. I tried not to breathe, not to move anything, tried to act as if dead. I was so sure that I was going to be found out. But then the shadow shrank again, and moved towards the bathroom. The light snapped off. Pitch-black descended. I heard the floorboards groaning and the wind rattling through the trees outside. The footsteps slowed, shuffled. I heard them go downstairs.

I breathed in a sharp sigh of relief. My palms felt sweaty. I was dimly aware of an animal flapping behind the blind. It cast a strange dark shadow over the room, black on black.

243

Slowly, very slowly, I found my way towards the door.

I made my way down the stairs, stepping over the floorboards cautiously, using the faint glint of the picture framings as a guide in the darkness. When I was halfway down, I noticed a light rising from the entrance to the study.

Very, very carefully, I found my way back towards my room. I leaned my back against the smooth cream wall, feet gliding over the floorboards. As I passed the study, I saw Marcus standing in front of his bookshelf, and the sight of him sent a shiver of terror through me. But I kept moving, as if over ice. I opened the door, slipped inside and closed it firmly behind me. I squeezed my eyes shut.

I couldn't sleep. After several minutes of lying in bed, staring at the ceiling, I walked to the door again and opened it a crack. I looked out to see that the study door, down the corridor, was still open.

Then something moved to my left.

'Can't sleep?' It was a man's voice.

I turned to see Marcus standing a few inches away from my door. The moonlight glistened over his face. His blond hair was uncombed, his eyes bleary. It was so dark, and yet his eyes seemed bright, shining with an electric intensity. We stared at each other. I met his gaze and we both refused to blink.

'I was up, and I saw the light was on in the study,' I stuttered.

There was a Thermos in his hands, shimmering silver in the darkness.

'I struggle with insomnia too,' he said. 'Especially at the moment.'

I didn't know what to say, so I said nothing. The silence stretched between us, and I watched as his eyes tracked from the stairs, to the door of the study, and back to me. He looked old in that light: his hair was so faint that it could have been white, his eyebrows seemed tinged with grey and his wrinkles were etched deep into his face.

'Well,' he said after a while. 'I've just made a pot of Ovaltine. Perhaps it will help you sleep?'

I didn't know what to say. I nodded, and I followed him down the corridor.

In the fresh light of his study, I was able to inspect Marcus properly. He seemed different without his polished shirts, his combed hair, the slick of expensive aftershave wiped over his neck. The sight reminded me, for some reason, of the first time I had seen Marina without her heavy make-up on.

I shuffled in past him and sat on an armchair near the back of the room. He put the Thermos on the desk, unscrewed the lid and began to pour it into two cups. I listened to the thin trickle of the liquid.

I waited for the confrontation.

Instead, without prompt, he said: 'Eva, how well do you know Henry?'

It was an unusual question – and my reaction must have alerted him to the fact, for he waved his hands apologetically and then answered it himself.

'He's a nice boy, I suppose.' He whistled against the rim of his mug to cool the contents. 'Ah, yes, nice.'

I was disarmed by how reluctant he sounded. In spite of myself, I smiled a little.

Marcus caught my expression.

'You disagree?' he said.

'Oh – no, no I think he's … fine.'

Marcus raised his eyebrows. 'I think I catch your drift.'

I was careful not to give myself away. I said nothing.

'We've known him for a while – Henry. He lives around here, you know.'

'I didn't know that,' I lied.

'Yes, well he's a childhood friend of Marina's.'

I listened with a keen ear as Marcus went on to explain Henry's connection to the Bede family. The Bedes and the Bewells had known each other since before their children were born, he said. The mothers – Rowena and Sara – had apparently met at a prenatal yoga class and bonded over the fact that they had the same due date. Sara had given birth to Henry; Rowena had miscarried. Yet the women remained close, and when Rowena became pregnant again the following year, this time with Marina, Sara was made Marina's godmother.

'The families were close after that, but for some reason Henry was always a bit of an odd fit.'

He didn't quite click with the family grouping in the way that the other members did. He tried to get close to Marina at first, but she perpetually brushed him off, and so after that, whenever their families met he tended to sulk in a corner.

'You know,' said Marcus, straightening his neck and mouth in an acute impersonation. 'In *that way* he does.'

I laughed then. I liked listening to Marcus talk about Marina's family history. He was a smart and lively narrator, peppering his anecdotes with jokes and impressions, and his performative manner reminded me of Marina. I also liked the fact that he obviously didn't like Henry. I liked the way that he exposed and laughed at traits of Henry's which had annoyed me too – lampooning, for example, his delight in alienating people; his snobbery; the grandiose generalizations that he wheeled out to intimidate people. That last point had always been a particular source of irritation for me and, more often than not, embarrassment too. I felt that Marcus understood this.

'I think Henry feels threatened by a lot of women, to be honest with you, Eva.' Marcus laughed again. 'Young men – especially those who pretend to be trendy feminists – get defensive.'

While I liked listening to him, however, I found it strange again that Marcus didn't delve more into what had happened to Marina's mother. I could understand that it would have been difficult to talk about, particularly now Marina was gone, but it still seemed odd to avoid the subject entirely when he was talking about the family history.

'I say all this … but I feel guilty about being too harsh on Henry. He's had an extremely hard time. It was just … awful after he found Marina.' Marcus's tone was no longer jokey and flippant, but serious and sad.

The light in the room seemed very bright then. I stared at a spot slightly behind Marcus's head.

Marcus absentmindedly smoothed his dressing gown. He continued speaking, as though in a daze:

'It's so strange to think of what happened, the way that it all panned out.' The words were almost whispered. 'I still feel guilty about it, Eva. I shouldn't have sent him up there. But I didn't know who else to call. It happened so quickly. We had a party on New Year's Eve, then a brief argument … then she was gone.'

The conversation was going too quickly. The words washed in and out of my ears, and I wanted to catch them – to make sure I was processing the right information.

'Do you mean to say that Henry found Marina? That he was the first there?'

Marcus didn't seem to register my words. He carried on, speaking quickly, guiltily:

'We thought that she had run away again. The plan was just for him to go up and bring her back.'

My mind flashed back to the phone conversation I had had with Henry on the day Marina had been found. Had that been the third of January?

'It was a reckless thing to do, perhaps, but he seemed to be the only person who might be able to reason with her. No one else was able to get through to her. Not me, not her mother, no one.'

The lights in the room became unbearably hot. The walls seemed to sway.

'Elena, you mean?' I said.

Marcus looked up at me for the first time since he had started speaking. There was a long silence.

Finally he said: 'Sorry?'

I tried to steady my breathing.

'Elena,' I said slowly. 'Not Marina's mother.'

There was another pause.

'Marina's mother ... your ex-wife ... I thought she was ...'

Marcus was still staring at me.

'Oh,' he said. 'Oh dear.'

He cleared his throat.

'Oh dear,' he said again.

Marina's mother was not dead, as she'd led me to believe. She was alive and well, living in Australia with her new family. She had never even had cancer – only a scare, in 2003. Though she had always been 'fond of alcohol', Marcus said – it was this, he assured me, which had caused them to split up – she had never had any serious health issues while she was living with him. When she and Marcus divorced, she had moved to Australia, where she met her second husband. She had then become increasingly distant with her previous family, and Marina's response was to wipe her out of existence.

Marcus explained all this without looking me in the eye. But I could still tell that it was hard for him. He scratched his cheeks and coughed a lot.

He went on: the lie about her mother had been regular, even notorious. So many people at Northam had heard her mother had 'died' – including, even, Professor Montgomery, despite having met Rowena – that it eventually had got back to Marcus.

'I wasn't surprised,' he said. 'I suppose it was a coping mechanism. By telling everyone she'd died, it gave her a feeling of control over the way Rowena rejected her.'

That word 'rejected' seemed an oddly brutal way to put it, I thought, and I noticed that he'd also slipped into using academic jargon – like a broadcaster. I didn't know how to respond to that. Was this an intimate conversation or an analytical one?

He stood up and move carefully towards the door.

'Come with me,' he said. 'I'll show you something.'

I walked behind him through the hallway, past the gilded photographs, past the portraits, past the little china vases along the mantlepieces. We didn't speak. I listened to the sound of the wind outside, the clip of his feet against the tiles. Until they stopped. Marcus stood in front of a photograph.

'This,' he said softly, 'is the only family photograph in the house. Marina wouldn't allow any others.'

I peered closely at the picture. I recognized the outside of Mosebury Court, the flat cap on Marcus's head, the grin across Marina's face. My eyes fell to the dark blonde woman stood next to Marcus in the photo. I took in her sharp pale neck, her grey-green eyes. But then I saw that Marcus's finger was pointing somewhere else. He was pointing towards the woman the other side of him. The woman who had two teeth slightly protruding over her puckered lips. There was a scarf crossed over her neck, and a plait twisted in her long red hair. She was stood next to Henry.

I realized that it was the red-haired woman whom I had met at the funeral.

She was not Henry's mother – she was Marina's. I had met her. I had met Marina's mother.

The room was cracking with violet heat. The air was thick, too thick. It was like seeing a ghost.

'Are you all right?' said Marcus.

I couldn't answer him. I was distracted thinking of a particular moment, back in November in Northam. I was thinking of the time that Marina had first told me that her mother had died – the confessional, reluctant tone she had affected. Her hand had done that dismissive swatting movement, as though discrediting any emotional slippage – *it's not a big deal*. I remember now how touched I felt seeing that. I loved that she had confided in me. I remember sitting on her bed, stroking her hair gently – all the way from the crown to the curls at the base of her spine. I remember saying that she could talk to me about it, if she ever wanted to.

Thanks Eva, that means a lot.

Her response – indeed her performance – now rang hollow. It hadn't mean a lot. It had meant nothing.

I put my hands over my face to stop the blurring. As I did so I felt my shoulders sliding forwards and beginning to shake. I tried to quell a sob.

'Eva?' said Marcus.

The sob rolled up my throat and came out in a thick choke.

'Eva,' said Marcus. 'Eva, what's wrong.'

I took in a large breath.

'I just think …' I spluttered. 'Sometimes it seems as though we weren't friends at all, that she didn't like me.' I spoke through wet fingers. Some kind of liquid was smearing around my nostrils and the top of my lip.

'Oh,' said Marcus. 'Don't think that. It's shocking, I know. It's a lot to take in.' He hesitated and then said again: 'Don't think that.'

I continued to cry, louder and louder, and as I did so I sensed him coming closer. I felt his shadow fall over me. Then his arms were around my shoulders, his hand was patting my back, and I was leaning forward and crying into his shirt. He smelled warm, I remember: sweet with cologne and dark fresh sweat.

How did I really feel, in light of all this information?

There are four main factors to consider when recalling a situation: 1) what you remember doing 2) what you remember saying 3) what you remember thinking 4) emotional memory. It is emotional memory which is the hardest to verify. When you think back to a specific event, you might be able to remember what you said word-for-word, and what you did action-for-action. You might be able to trace, too, the rational thought process behind it – how you figured out each step of the situation. But it is much harder to pin down exactly how you felt. You might say that a situation made you feel scared. But at what precise point was shock replaced by anger? At what point did fear shift into lust? Even if you latch an emotion to a specific action or a specific word, it is often impossible to figure out where one began to replace the other.

Now I think back to Marcus's question: 'Are you all right?' – and I wonder whether, in fact, I was. The visual indicators are clear: I can remember sobbing into his shirt. I can remember saying that I was upset, that I was convinced Marina had never liked me. But I cannot say how much of my reaction was sincere.

Don't get me wrong – I was quite shocked by the extent of Marina's lying. And I was embarrassed by the weight I'd attached to my relationship with her too. But at the same time – if I'm honest – the fact that she had lied so much made me feel satisfied. It cemented my version of events, my interpretation of her character. Marina wasn't the religious good girl after all. She was nasty and manipulative, someone who pretended to be something else in order to make herself appear more interesting. My instincts had been right after all.

I liked her all the more for it.

I spent the next day at the house, focusing on the tasks that Marcus set for me. They were menial tasks, yes: boring pen-on-paper stuff, sorting admin and sifting through files. Yet they offered a sense of completion. I liked that they could be *done* – that their results were permanent and unchangeable. After the months of worrying, I was grateful to have a distraction from my negative thoughts. It was pleasing to do something straight-forward. It was relaxing being able to concentrate. Other worries, other issues – including Marina's notebook – began to fade away.

That afternoon I went for a walk around the garden while Marcus worked indoors. The weather was just beginning to break, and the spring arrived warm and sweeter than summer. Looking over the horizon it felt as though my whole life were ahead of me: the clouds curling into the hills, the dim dots of light flickering through the hedgerows, the hum of bees around me. I pulled a cardigan over my wrists. Knees stroked the long grass. As evening settled in, the sun fell over the water so that I could see each individual droplet under the surface. I looked at them drifting and blinking against the rim of the basin. I felt happy.

Over the course of that evening I began to get to know Marcus too. I began to see who he was beneath his glossy exterior. He relaxed and fluffed in conversation. He whistled to himself. When concentrating, he would often rub his chin with a clumsy forefinger, or run his hand through his hair, causing it to spike out at jagged angles. I liked him, I realized. I liked these glitches in his refinement. Increasingly when he looked at me I didn't feel the heat of the awkwardness that I had on the previous evening. Instead, I enjoyed his attention.

On the Saturday night we were sitting on the sofa together, watching a film after a long day's work. The actress on the screen had a screechy voice. I remembered reading an essay during a film module about how it had been dubbed over with another actress's voice in a different film. I murmured this to Marcus and we both laughed. Then we were silent.

I could hear him breathing heavily after that. I could sense his presence intensely: the lift of his chest, his mouth parting and sealing shut, every slight furrow in his brow. My eyes flicked towards him – and it was then that I saw that he was staring at my leg. His eyes were trained on a specific point. The long, brown-flecked birthmark on the inside of my thigh. I felt self-conscious suddenly. My fingers inched down my lap, and tugged at the hem of my skirt.

Marcus looked up then. He held my gaze for a second, another second, longer than was appropriate and then his eyes flicked back to the screen. Mine did the same. But out of the corner of my eye I could still see that his wrists were flexing a little – he was tense. I lifted my left hand from my lap and spread my fingers on the sofa beside me.

Suddenly something started to vibrate nearby. I flinched. Marcus's hand crept off his lap and towards the phone on the coffee table.

'Hang on,' he said.

I watched him stand and leave the room. The muscles of his back flexed and contracted under his shirt. There was a speckle of sweat underneath his collar.

I heard him say: 'Colin!' Then something garbled, like: 'How's the research coming along?'

There ensued a muffled conversation outside. I watched the action on the screen. The actress with the screechy voice was gone – now an actor stood in front of a mirror, his biceps rippling, a toothbrush sticking out of his mouth. He put his fingers into a gun shape, lifted them towards the mirror and – before doing anything else –dropped them again. Then he continued to brush his teeth.

Marcus returned a few seconds later. He eyed me curiously as he walked in, rubbing the end of his nose. I sensed an odd change between us. It made me nervous.

'Eva,' he said, like he was tasting the word – trying to figure out if he liked the flavour.

'Is everything all right?' I asked. The corners of my mouth flickered suggestively.

He nodded slowly. His mouth twisted.

'Funny,' he said.

'What's funny?' I was alarmed to hear that a flirtatious lilt had crept into my voice.

'Well,' he said. 'You're a funny creature. Aren't you? You look young, but you have a mature mind.'

Marcus's eyes travelled down my face, down my neck, back up to my chin. I felt my mouth open a little.

'I don't know,' I said, looking away. 'Erm, I don't know what you mean.'

Marcus sat down on the sofa. He was now closer than he had been.

'You just do,' he said.

I sensed that he was still looking at me. I withdrew my hand from the seat beside me and put it on my lap. I stared pointedly at the TV screen.

'You're very observant, very interested in people. Very independent.'

'OK,' I said cautiously.

'I can see why you liked Northam so much, why you wanted to stay there.'

My shoulders tensed. What he'd said wasn't exactly true, but then it wasn't exactly untrue either. I watched the actor on the screen: spitting out the swill of toothpaste in his mouth. Staring at his own reflection. Baring his teeth, creasing his brow.

'You did like Northam, didn't you?' Marcus pushed. 'You liked the campus, at least.'

'The campus grew on me,' I admitted. I was unsure of where this was going, of why he was steering the conversation in this direction. It was making me uncomfortable.

'Yes – and you liked to go walking on your own, around it, seeking things out for yourself.'

'Sometimes,' I said.

'On different parts of the campus.'

I tried to concentrate on what was happening in the film. The actor lifted his fingers into a gun shape again. He began to mouth at his reflection.

'Yes,' I said quietly. 'Especially after I found out about Marina.'

'And before. During the holidays.'

I was silent.

'And during the holidays,' Marcus repeated.

I said nothing. On the screen the actor was talking to himself, louder and louder. His mouth was sloping out of control. His eyes were beginning to bulge out of his face.

Marcus continued: 'You see, I mentioned to Colin that you were here with me, and he asked how you were after … the whole business.' Marcus leaned towards me slightly. 'And then he mentioned that he saw you at Northam station. In January.'

The actor on screen was now fully shouting at himself, his mouth distorted and his eyes crazed. His shouts became shrieks, volume, pitch, madness increasing until it reached fever pitch and he bent forward and shot at the mirror. Bang.

The memory clicked into place. Now I knew what Marcus was talking about. He was talking about the time I'd taken a trip to Northam accidentally: when I'd got onto the train in an attempt to escape from Jonny Wilcox. He was talking about the time I'd seen the professor in the bookshop.

'Oh – right, yes,' I said. 'I saw Professor Montgomery at a bookshop in Northam station very briefly. He was buying a book for his niece.'

'What were you doing there – at Northam?'

I lifted my hand from my lap and moved it slowly towards my opposite forearm. I thought back to the Jonny Wilcox saga; how I could best explain it, without mentioning Joe.

'Well, weirdly,' I said. 'I hadn't meant to go there. It wasn't a planned trip.'

'What do you mean?'

I felt a tiny loose scab under my elbow.

'Er, I was at the station, in Walford. And then I got into a conversation with someone from school – someone I hadn't seen for years.' I picked at the scab. Ridges of hard skin crumbled under my fingers. 'I got distracted … and then I got on the wrong train.'

The skin flaked off in its entirety. A tiny cold dab of liquid slid onto my fingertip. I continued, in a babbling panic: 'And then Northam was the next stop. It just happened to be. Once I arrived, there wasn't a train going in the other direction. So I spent about forty minutes in the bookshop. That's where I saw Mont— that's where I saw the professor.'

I brought my fingertip to my mouth. It tasted of vinegar.

'I didn't even really go to Northam though,' I said. 'Not to the campus. I mean, I got the train straight back to Walford. Then my parents grounded me. I didn't spend any time in Northam over the holidays.'

Marcus shifted towards the television, away from me.

'Your mother mentioned about you driving around,' he said. 'Visiting nearby towns, around Christmas time and New Year.'

I realized what he was getting at then. My driving around in late December; early January. He thought I had driven to Northam at the time when Marina died. Perhaps my parents had told him about my antics. Perhaps he thought I had had something to do with her death.

'Other towns,' I assured him. 'Other towns. Burston, York, Whitby, closer towns. The only time I went to Northam was the trip I just mentioned. It was once, accidentally.'

'I see,' he said.

We watched the rest of the film in silence. When it ended I said goodnight, without looking him in the eye, and went straight into my room.

***

For a long time that conversation gave me vivid nightmares. Occasionally I still have them. I dream of driving through the country lanes. I dream of the raindrops sliding over the windscreen, the wipers squeaking back and forth, back and forth. I dream of the looming towers of Northam. I dream that I am standing outside her window.

I am watching her open the window. Leaning out onto the sill. She looks down at me, her eyes wide. Her eyes laughing.

Eva, she says. Eva. What are you doing here?

My fists clench. I find myself unable to stop the questions. Why haven't you replied to my messages. Why didn't you tell me that you weren't coming back. Why have you been hiding from me. Why are hiding from me. Why are you here.

What the fuck are you talking about? She says again. What are you even doing here?

I tell her she is pathetic. I tell her she has no worth. I tell her no one will miss her and that she has no purpose here anyway. She's worthless, I say.

Stop it, she says. Stop it.

She leans out the window. I keep yelling. She leans further, teasing me.

I tell her I don't care what she does. I tell her I don't care if she dies. I tell her that no one will miss her.

Throw yourself out.

Do it.

Jump.

Her smug expression vanishes. Her features melt away. She leans very far forward. I see her left hand falling out first. The cigarette drops, tumbles down, leaving a long slow trail of smoke in its wake.

In my periphery I see the stick bouncing on the pavement, a smudge of lipstick against concrete. Then there is one foot on the windowsill. The edges of her body blur.

Before anything else happens, I have turned and walked away. I am walking down the path towards my accommodation block. I am climbing into my car, watching the rain slide down the windscreen, the wipers squeaking back and forth, back and forth.

I wake up in a cold sweat, the scene printed on the backs of my eyelids. I have to keep reminding myself that it didn't happen. It didn't happen. I wasn't there.

Still Saturday

Following my conversation with Marcus, it seemed important that I should find out now, more than ever, what it was that Marina was trying to say. I needed to save myself from the conspiracy theories – prove that I wasn't crazy. I sensed that Montgomery was out to get me. Perhaps Marcus was too.

After the film, I did not go to sleep. I entered my room and locked the door behind me. I sat on the bed, and pulled my bag onto my lap. I riffled past the piles of pants, clothes and books, and then – to my relief – saw it was still in there. I drew out the tiny notebook. I thumbed through the pages, noting each of the dates, rolling my mind back to what I had been doing with Marina, if anything, on those days.

2nd October; 29th October; 1st November; 5th November; 10th November; 11th November; 4th December; 13th December.

I stared at the penultimate page.

ast3r1sk_12_2013@gmail.com.

The password: *a5t3r1sk.*

I thought about Marina then, writing in the notebook: the way she would have clutched the pencil and scribbled those symbols down. Perhaps she had done so in this room. I felt a sudden and unexpected tenderness towards her. I thought of the evenings getting drunk together in my room in Northam. I thought of the day we had broken into the professor's office together. And it was then that I felt the familiar stirrings of curiosity about her life.

I'd do it tomorrow, I decided. I'd do it while Marcus was out of his office. I would find some way. I would find some way to get access to a computer. Then I would unlock the account and discover what she had been hiding – or, I thought with a flicker of unease, what her messages were trying to tell me.

vi.

Sunday morning. The air was fragrant and sweet and calm. Marcus and I were in the office together. He was slightly quieter than usual, but his manner was otherwise breezy and friendly – he did not seem to have been affected by the conversation of the previous evening. I was relieved to think he'd forgotten it, but there was also something unnerving about the fact that he was able to move on so quickly.

He told me to sit at the desk opposite, so I did so.

'Now here are a few things to do today. We need to get cracking.'

He pushed a slip of paper in my direction.

18th April 2013 – Marina Bede Foundation Inauguration Dinner
TASKS NEED DOING:
Count table settings
File bank statements
Count leaflets (should be eighteen in total)
Print accounts
Draft emails

'Do the ones at the top first,' Marcus said. 'I'll have to direct you through the bottom section.'

With the thought of the notebook in my pocket, it was difficult to concentrate on work. So difficult. So difficult that I chewed my nails to distract myself. They became raw and ruddy, the cuticles ragged around the nail. When Marcus's back was turned,

I found it impossible to stop myself from touching things. I saw a stack of boxes in the shelves with the words: CHILDHOOD VIDEOS scrawled over them in thick permanent marker and my hands physically itched. I looked at the photos of Marina as a child in arty black and white and stroked my hands over the frames. I liked imagining them in colour, in motion. I imagined her snotty nose running, her pudgy hands wiping, the funny things she would say.

Eventually, Marcus left – another phone call.

'I'll take this outside,' he said. He turned his head as he left the room, frowning at the monitor.

As soon as I was sure that he was gone, I ran over to his computer. The weight of the notebook was heavy in my pocket. I thumbed it a little, feeling the ridges of the pages through the material of my skirt. The screensaver winked at me. I sat down in front of the monitor and brought my hands to the keyboard.

I was alone. I was completely alone in front of the computer. I ran my fingers along the keys experimentally, tracing the plastic corners with my nails. I moved the mouse and the desktop appeared. How surreal it was to be using technology again – I thought – how glossy and smoothly artificial. But no time for reflection – I hastily clicked onto a tab and put in the address for an email server. I tapped in what I could remember, hearing the sing-songy rhythm of the email address pulse through my mind.

ast3r1sk_12_2013@gmail.com

Password: *A5terisk* – no; *a53ter15k*; no. What was it? My hands flurried to my pocket, I brought out the notebook and flicked clumsily through the pages.

I could hear Marcus's voice outside. 'Darling, no that's fine. Look I've got to rush—'

I grasped the page. There – *a5t3r1sk*

I typed it hurriedly into the keyboard. I could still hear Marcus on the phone outside, Elena's vague muttering coming through the speaker, his unsuccessful attempts to cut the conversation short. I typed faster.

Authorization successful.

It took a moment to load, then the inbox appeared. It was full of unread emails, the subject of each simply 'FWD'. I saw the sender initials: 'C.M.'

C.M.

I focused hard on those initials, tried to make them bloom into words …

"Oh yes, that's a good point. Ok, I'll send them today sweetheart. Hang on – wait, yes?"

After a few seconds, it hit me.

Colin Montgomery?

I saw that all the emails had been sent on one date: 13th December.

I grasped the notebook on my lap, and I sped through it to the page which contained the dates of Marina's meetings with the professor.

2nd October; 29th October; 1st November; 5th November; 10th November; 11th November; 4th December; 13th December.

The 13th of December was the final date in that notebook.

Everything seemed very still at that point. Very light, suffused with an ominous energy. It felt as though some instinctive part of me had figured something out, and the rest of me was now playing catch-up, waiting to find out what that was.

I saw my head from behind, staring at the screen. Past that, through the window, I saw Marcus's hand reach through the golden strands of his hair, fiddling with the dark stripe at the root. I could hear him talking: something in Italian, a roar of laughter.

I blinked and tried to focus. An email flickered in another tab.

I shifted slightly, regained my composure, and then leaned

forward in my chair. I put the notebook under the keyboard. I moved my hand over the mouse. I drew the cursor to the subject line of the first email.

Click.

The message of the email was blank. At the bottom of the screen there were two attachments: 'untitled2.jpeg'; 'untitled3.jpeg'. I clicked the first file. A picture began to load up.

It started off as a series of pixels – indecipherable pieces of colour: a flash of blue, a blob of white, a speckle of red. Then they slowly spread over the screen piece by piece until I could see the image in its entirety. Initially it looked like an abstract, maybe some bird's-eye view of a piece of land. But then the pink and brown blotches melded together, their edges sharpened, and the shape appeared to me as a pair of thighs. The strip of paisley blue down the centre: underwear. The tiny tessellations of white-pink: cellulite. Dots of red: a light rash.

I pressed down hard on the 'back' button. My fingers were shaking.

In the distance I could hear Marcus still talking on the phone. His voice was becoming impatient, more clipped, like he was trying to wrap up the call.

I took a deep breath. Then another. I went back onto the browser and selected the next email.

There was text in this email – a forwarded message thread. When I scrolled down I saw the name in the sender box:

hb108@northam.edu
09.37 AM
10/04/2013
Thank you for meeting with me earlier. See below for further 'comments'.
H

The 'comments' he'd referenced contained a number of weird in-jokes: a web of interconnected references – like some sort of high-brow 'banter' trove. There was an obscene pun on an obscure poem by John Donne. A meme about history of art. A satirical cartoon of cereal boxes floating in the air, the caption: 'cerealism'. And then, later, there was a captioned photo: a picture of a girl I recognized from campus. The caption read: 'Spotted: Tess of the Murmurvilles in her natural habitat.' The photo showed her sat on a bench by the lake, with her hand in her hair. She seemed to be looking down, maybe at something on her phone. That was it.

Who was the girl – and why did she look familiar? Wait, I had seen her. She was in Henry's year, I was pretty sure. I might even have seen her at his parties a few times. Had I stalked her on Facebook? I didn't think so.

The professor's reply read:

Ha, ha! Yes very good! Here's the essay I was talking about. Long but worth ploughing through if you can. PS see attached for one I made earlier.

Attached to his email was an edited photo. It was much clumsier, less witty even than Henry's offering. But it was of a similar theme and just as laborious: 'Jane Hair returns to Lowood.' The woman in the photo appeared to be giving a lecture – she had a frizzy bob and a slightly mottled complexion – and as she raised her arm, her shirt had lifted up to show a flash of armpit hair. I recognized her as a lecturer in the English department.

SENDER:hb108@northam.edu
11.14 AM 05/06/2013
Impressed that you managed to get a photograph.
Good sleuth skills.

I scrolled further down the email thread. There were only fragments – not the full transcript of each conversation – but there was enough information for me to see how this sick game might have started, how it might have happened.

SENDER: hb108@northam.edu
12.59 07/09/2013
Here's another one I made earlier.

The photographs in the early emails were all fairly PG. They were taken at a distance, in public places. But the further down I scrolled, the more intrusive the pictures became. The lens zoomed closer. A mole on a neck (**Adrienne's mole**); a ladder in a pair of tights (**Stairway to Heaven**). Then a pair of trousers. A speckle of dirt on the buttocks of a skirt.

And then the upskirt pictures started.

The captions for these were more succinct or entirely absent. The images spoke for themselves.

A pair of thighs. A strip of crotch. Sometimes they were taken slightly further away so that you could see the outline of hands on a lap. An elbow bent, fingers entwined. The shadow of a phone on a skirt.

I clicked onto the next email, and the next. I felt guilty as I did so, as though seeing it made me complicit in the taking of the photos. Yet the sense of voyeurism was ultimately undercut by a sense of mission. I clicked and clicked and scrolled and clicked. An imminent revelation seemed palpable.

There was another conversation; another photo, one far, one near. I clicked past it impatiently. A new picture loaded on the screen.

Then I froze.

The pattern on the underwear I recognized: a distinctive zigzag print with frills around the edges. I thought of that particular night before the Faustus seminar, Marina rolling around in her room after a night out. Falling backwards with her legs sliding apart. A triangle of zigzags. A thin stretch of lace pucked around the edges. I remember I'd felt embarrassed seeing so much of Marina, but also envious – of course she would possess such fine, expensive-looking lingerie.

My face became incredibly hot. I scrunched my eyes into their sockets. I tried to block it out. But even with my eyes shut I could see the photos – they were still there, hot-wired onto the backs of my lids, and as I stared further the pixels seemed to separate, the network of events opened up and suddenly all the wires – all the threads of the last few months seemed to break from each other and swirl towards me. *Henry. The Professor. The photos. The images that Marina had found over Christmas. Before she died.*

Suddenly I heard a door click shut – somewhere in a distant corner of the house. Marcus's leather shoes were approaching, snapping against the tiles. The sound of quiet humming getting louder and louder, closer and closer.

I minimized the tab again and pushed the notebook further under the keyboard. The footsteps stopped. Then the door creaked open. I breathed deeply, digging my fingernails into my knees.

I heard Marcus's voice. 'Cup of tea?'

An outline emerged from behind the door. I knew it was Marcus, but everything about him was distorted. His nose appeared to float somewhere off-centre. His eyes were in duplicate. I felt myself nod.

'Earl Grey, isn't it?'

He was holding the phone, cupping the speaker with one hand.

'Yes please,' I said.

It was surprising to hear my voice: how smooth and confident it sounded. Marcus nodded. I felt myself smile. Then his face disappeared, the door closed, and I heard him resume his conversation. His shoes clacked towards the kitchen.

I stared back at the screen.

I went back onto the photograph and stared at the image, thinking hard. Thinking.

A memory slowly surfaced. I forced myself to confront the

memory, to think about it three-dimensionally. It was from a day in November, after we went to the beach, early in the term. We had arrived back at her room. All my clothes had been soaking and damp. My arms had been shivering. My teeth chattering. Marina had told me to have a shower – my dramatic discomfort was 'irritating' to her – and when I emerged from the bathroom afterwards, I saw that she had left a fresh set of clothes for me. A T-shirt, some tracksuit bottoms. And a pair of zigzagged underwear.

I had given them back. I was sure I'd given those back. Yes, yes, I had. Hadn't I?

I peered closer at the screen. I inspected the tiny red prickles of a rash along the upper thigh. I zoomed in so far that the dots appeared to separate. I moved the perspective a little to the right- and then I saw a faded brown ripple. It was about the length of a thumbnail. It was a birthmark.

This wasn't a picture of Marina. It was a picture of me.

My fingers flew to the keyboard, and I tapped my own email in the sender's box:

eh301@northam.edu

I dragged the mouse to the 'send' button. I hovered for a second and then attempted to push send before—

A shadow fell over the screen.

Marcus's voice: 'Here we are.'

A hand reached forward and pushed a teacup towards me across the desk. Splashes of milk jumped up and slid down the side of the china.

'What are you working on?' Marcus said, ducking his head over the monitor. 'Are you finished printing all that off …?'

Instinctively I minimized the tab. Marcus frowned, set his mug on a coaster and walked around to my side of the desk. He leaned forward toward, pressing a hand into my shoulder.

'I'm not sure your parents would approve of you being on a computer, you know,' he said amiably.

'No,' I said.

'Well why don't you show me what you're doing?'

A silence descended.

'Eva, if you don't show me then I'll have to look at it myself—'

'NO!'

My hand jumped forward – but it was too late. Marcus had grabbed the mouse and clicked on the minimized tab. The conversation looped up onto the screen, showing the photo HD, write large, horribly visible. The close-up of my thighs. My crotch. Marina's underwear.

White-hot embarrassment curled up my neck.

'It's not …' I began.

Marcus looked away

'Oh,' he said tonelessly, into the distance.

'It's …' I began. 'Well …'

I wanted to scream.

What else could I do? I panicked, I wanted to justify myself. And so I told him everything. I told him about the email address and the login. I told him about the records of the dates. I told him about breaking into the professor's office with Marina.

Marina had discovered that Montgomery and Henry were taking photos of students, I said. She had marked the dates in her diary when the professor would be free. She had sneaked into his office before – I knew because, I had been with her once.

The only thing I did not tell him was that the picture was of me. But I had a strange feeling that he just knew anyway – something about the way he was looking at me … I can't explain it, but I could tell that he knew.

Marcus studied my face for a while and was silent. He pressed his finger into his mouth.

'We should call the police,' I said. 'Or at least the university.'

Marcus exhaled.

'I – ah – I don't think that would be necessary,' he said.

'What?'

'I said I don't think that would be necessary. It might be better if the university don't get involved. I can deal with this directly.'

I thought about what I knew of Marcus's previous 'direct dealings' – what he'd also referred to as 'helping people out'. He'd *helped* me out, he'd *helped* Henry out, he'd *helped* Montgomery out.

'I'm not sure that's responsible,' I said. 'We need to do something now.'

Marcus laughed lightly. 'I thought you'd say that,' he said.

I felt a surge of annoyance.

'I mean it,' I said. 'It's important that someone sees this.'

Marcus nodded thoughtfully. He picked up the notebook and began to thumb through it. Then he put it down on the desk, and leaned in towards the mouse. He minimized the tab.

'I agree with you,' he said. 'But we'll deal with it after tomorrow, after the launch party.'

'No. Now. Having an affair with a student is bad enough, but this— This is so much worse. It's a huge invasion of privacy – an abuse of – '

'Yes, as I said, I agree with you, but it's too much to think about now.'

'Give me a phone,' I said. 'I'm going to call the police.'

'Eva,' Marcus's voice was now edged with steel. 'I suggest you keep out of it.'

I began to search frantically for a mobile, for a landline. I opened drawers, lifted piles of folders. There was nothing there. I started to make my way to the door.

'*Eva.*'

Marcus grabbed my hand. I flew around to face him. His face was very close to mine, so close that our noses were nearly touching. I could feel ragged breath against my cheek.

'It's not worth you getting involved,' he said quietly.

'It's a sex crime,' I said.

His fingers tightened on my wrist.

'To push this would only be damaging, to yourself and others,' he said. 'Think about it. No one would believe you, after everything that's happened. The case would be thrown out.'

Perspiration dripped over my eyelashes.

'I'm not sure that's—'

'Anyway,' he continued. 'It's not a good idea to draw attention to yourself. If you get involved in a court case, you don't know what the police might find. They might start asking ...' The corner of his mouth lifted. He finished: 'They might ask what you were doing on the day of Marina's death.'

I froze.

'What?'

His eyes met mine.

'There's nothing I can prove,' he said, 'but it's a bit convenient, don't you think? Your parents say that you were driving around in early January. Colin says he saw you in Northam at the station during the holidays. And then the dates of the Swipe impersonation ... the stealing ...'

'No.'

'Not to mention sneaking into her room.'

'That's insane,' I said. Slowly I repeated: 'That's *insane*.'

'Call it what you like,' Marcus said. 'But where were you?'

A second went by, where I said nothing.

I squeezed my eyes shut. I thought of Marina looking down at me from her window.

'I was at home,' I said.

'Right,' said Marcus. 'And your parents can vouch for that, can they?'

I said nothing. It was a dream, I told myself. It was a *dream*.

'You think it's bad now. You've been feeling *sorry* for yourself about some nasty strangers saying mean things and you think nothing is ever going to get better. It will, actually, but only if

269

you continue to keep a low profile. If evidence emerges linking you to Marina – then you're in real trouble.' He drew back. He gave a little shrug.

'All I'm saying is: think about it,' he said. 'Would it be worth opening your mouth again – drawing attention to yourself – for the sake of a tasteless joke?'

My head was cloudy for a long second, but hearing that final word – joke – I felt a fierce surge of defiance.

'It's ... not a joke,' I said. 'It's not a joke and it's not a game. These are photos of real people – the bodies of real people. I mean, it could be your daughter's body. Don't you care at *all* about Marina?'

Marcus frowned, as though he found me distasteful.

'Do you realize that it's her underwear in that photo?' I said, raising my voice.

Marcus's frown shifted to the floor, his mouth twisted into an 'o' shape. He scratched his jaw with a single finger.

I was pushing it, I knew – I was going above and beyond respectful boundaries, I was about to say something unfair, something speculative, something which could only work to my disadvantage, my downfall, but now there was no way back and I couldn't help myself from carrying on talking.

'Why is it that you're so defensive of Montgomery, Marcus?' I said. 'You two are very close, aren't you? You have shared interests. Not just teaching – other stuff. I've seen the way you look at me, the way your—'

Marcus reached forward quickly then – for a moment I thought he was going to hit me – but instead he snatched at the ends of my hair. He pulled at it sharply, so that my head stretched slightly backwards. I couldn't move.

'Stop that,' he said.

I stayed there suspended, too shocked to speak. My breathing was slow and cautious. I watched his face, his mouth curling into a smile as he gently twirled the ends of my hair. Then, gripping it inside his fist, he yanked sharply and my neck flung backwards. The muscles stretched painfully. I opened my mouth to scream but I couldn't push air out of my lungs. Marcus clamped his other hand over my mouth. He leaned over me, his fingers pushing into my teeth.

'How dare you,' he said. 'You're a guest in this house.'

His face came very close to mine again. His nails dug slightly into my cheek. I struggled to break free.

'When you're in my house you will be respectful,' he said. 'You will behave as a guest.'

I tried to nod but my head was stiff. I tried to speak but I couldn't breathe.

There was a long silence. I felt the intensity of his hatred heating the air between us.

'You stupid girl,' he said. 'You stupid, stupid girl.' His voice was low and controlled, but I could sense it would soon rise to an agitated pitch. 'Your conspiracy theories might seem sophisticated to you, but you're wrong – even wrong about the photograph. Of course that's not Marina. You can see it's not her. There's that very distinctive mark, isn't there?'

My breathing became extremely shallow. From my blurred peripheral vision I could see Marcus's face. The sweat glistening on his cheekbones. The fanaticism in his eyes: detachment.

I thought back to a recent memory. The smell of dark fresh sweat, expensive, strong cologne. An actor on the screen. Next to me, a man in a white shirt. His eyes staring at me, straight down at the long, brown birthmark on my inner thigh.

Now his hands tightened on my hair. 'It's unique,' he murmured softly.

Tears sprang at the edges of my eyelids.

His face was too close, his breath was getting harsher, and I could feel my body coiling defensively. I was preparing myself, steeling myself. I curled my hand into a fist.

What happened next seemed to be the result of two simultaneous movements. 1) I edged my teeth over his fingers and bit down as hard as I could; 2) I jammed my foot into his knee and used the impact to fling myself backwards. Marcus cowered, alarmed, and his hands flew up in a protective gesture. I backed away and then shoved him viciously before running towards the door. But he came back again towards me, this time grabbing at my neck.

'Come here!'

His figure loomed over my head and he reached but I dodged him again, falling back against the shelving unit; scratching my face on the corner of something metallic. I steadied my balance. I drew back my hand in a strong swift pull and blindly, but with all my might, crunched it forward into his face. I felt a moist pop, a sharp sting over my knuckles. Marcus's figure was black and smudgy: a blurred figure with hands over its eyes, staggering backwards.

I did not give myself time to think. I turned and sprinted out of the room, out of the house, out past the rows of statues and along the drive, the sound of my feet beating loudly against the earth.

It was only when I reached the bus stop, far down the lane, that I realized my pockets were empty. I thought then of the draft email, the window left minimized on Marcus's desktop. I thought of the notebook I had left on the desk, pressed flat underneath the keyboard, lying open on the penultimate page.

vii.

Mid-April 2014

The period of my breakdown felt like swimming underwater. When I opened my eyes and tried to process what had happened, I could sometimes make out an image I recognized: Marcus's hand on my shoulder, Marina's eyes under her fringe, the faded outline of my thighs on a screen. The rest of the time I was in complete darkness, trying to shut out everything.

On the day I ran from Mosebury, I was lucky. I was lucky that buses were running that day; I was lucky that I had coins in my jean pocket, I was lucky that Marina's house was high on a hill, so that I could see the surrounding countryside. The other houses. The village shop. The church.

For twenty, maybe thirty minutes, I ran all the way down the road. I ran through cornfields, through sunflower fields, past pea-pickers and strawberry growers, over fences, under fences, through streams, past farm houses and fancy houses. I went past the village shop. I went past the church where Marina's funeral had been.

I arrived at the bus stop. I saw the crusty 21A staggering in, recognized the driver, flagged it down, then I rode it all the way to Northam. From Northam to Walford I travelled via train and from there, I walked home. The journey took six hours in total – from Marina's house to mine. It seems remarkable to me that I had enough energy to stop myself from fainting or throwing up. I don't remember what I thought about.

But I do remember that when I approached my house – the sweet cottage at the end of the lane – that I felt panic rather than relief. I felt another surge of adrenaline. I had only one thing on my mind: *they need to help me.*

As soon as I entered the house I attempted to tell my parents what had happened. I threw open the door, I ran into the hall and set about searching for them, yelling, screaming. When I found them in the kitchen, I paused for a second to collect my breath. I tried to say everything, in order, that I remembered. I really tried to articulate myself clearly: spell out my experience as a compelling case. But it didn't work. As the words came out of my mouth I sensed that my sentences were fractured and that I was not making sense to them, that I was operating on a different wavelength.

It was strange. The shape of what I was trying to say was so

273

clear in my head. I knew exactly what the thought *was* that I was trying to convey: I knew how it sounded, how it looked, what it meant. The perfect version of the sentence was stretched out in a kind of spider-diagram of words in my mind. Yet the way my mouth formed them refused to translate into any kind of coherent meaning. I couldn't make myself make sense.

I watched my parents as I spoke. I saw their expressions of fear and confusion. I saw my mother glancing at my father. She bent forward slightly in her chair; shook her head at the floor. Eventually she broke the silence.

'We know what happened, Eva,' she said simply. 'You don't have to tell us.'

Panic rose in my chest, making my breathing tight.

'What?' I said.

'We're tired of this,' my father said. 'Constantly making us worried. Making up silly stories. It's time for—'

'Don't start reproaching her,' my mother cut in. 'Not now.'

'It's true, Linda.'

'What happened?' I said quickly. 'What's going on?'

There was a beat. My mother looked at the floor for a second, and then spoke.

'Marcus called,' she said. 'Luckily he's not seriously hurt but my god, you could have blinded him. Now the foundation event will have to be postponed. His eye is completely black.'

'Thankfully he isn't going to press charges,' my father added.

'He was – luckily for you – quite good-humoured about the whole thing. But as for your behaviour ...'

'Can you imagine how difficult this is for us?'

The words reverberated around my brain. I blinked hard, tried to forget them, tried process what she said next. Marcus was concerned about me, she said. Yes, he was concerned about me – and although he had tried to see it all within a PTSD frame-work, he thought I needed to see someone. Urgently. I wasn't safe out here. I was unstable.

'He's told us about the Marina obsession,' said my mother. 'The problem is you're a fantasist.'

Marcus had done his research. He had explained to my parents how I'd stolen Marina's clothes and books at Northam – he said he'd found some still in my bag. He told them how I'd snuck into her room without asking him. He had told them how I'd fabricated an 'absurd fiction' about some dealings with Montgomery.

I had nothing to say to any of that.

'We're just …' my father shook his head. 'Sometimes I look at you and wonder if—'

'Wonder what?' I spat.

He sighed, looked at the ground. 'I wonder if you're ever going to learn to be normal.'

My mother started crying then. She said that she was so upset, that she'd been so worried. She said that she felt guilty for not bringing me up like everyone else. She said she'd never known how to deal with these situations, how to deal with me. But talking to Marcus had made things clearer. I needed to go somewhere. Considering my mental history and the current reaction to this it was clear I'd had—

'One of your episodes.'

That sickness again, that creeping dizzy feeling – the sense that I was losing sight of my reality, the knowledge of who I was. All the colours of the room, the faces, the chairs were blurring into one another.

'No,' I said. The tears gathered under my eyelashes. 'It's not that. Please. That's not true.'

'Eva, listen. We know it sounds frightening but we have to address the problem head on. The doctors, and the psychologists, and well, your old tutor. And Marcus. They've all said that what needs to happen is …'

At that moment I caught sight of myself in the mirror. My eyes were bloodshot and my clothes were torn. There was a ribbon of blood across my cheek. The faint outline of a bruise lay under my eye, I was sure of it. I leaned towards the mirror. When I blinked it disappeared.

'... We think you need to go somewhere. We've found a place to send you to, just for a while, it's just a few miles away. It's not like the other place, the one you were before. This is upmarket. It's like a hotel. This one has big grounds, the best care, the nurses are—'

I screamed then. I screamed and it had all come flooding out – Marcus's hand on my shoulder, the funeral, the email address, the notebook, the pictures.

I continued to scream, and when they did not act upon my screaming I began to break things. I picked up a vase and threw it at the wall. I grabbed the frying pan off the counter and threw it against the oven. I loved the sound they made over my voice: a shatter, a blast, a cacophonous thwack. I could feel the impulse building – the desire to destroy things, to hurt someone, hurt myself.

On the floor underneath the wall there was a sea of shattered glass. I thought of my leg. I thought of the rock through the window, the splintered star in the night.

I stopped screaming.

I bent down and picked up a piece of glass off the floor. I brought it up to my fingers, slowly.

'Eva, please.'

Suddenly there was a knock at the door. We froze. My mother opened it apologetically, started to wave the person away.

'It's just my daughter,' she said. 'No, no need to come in. There's something wrong with her amygdala – you know, in her brain? – it was affected when she was an infant.'

'I'm sorry, Mrs Hutchings, I can't take no for an answer. I'm going to have to come in.'

When I saw it was a policeman, I dropped the piece of glass and ran to the door. I began to shout again. I shouted for his help. I told him about Marcus, about Marina, about the professor, and as I did so I found myself unable to stop other anecdotes from creeping in there too – dream anecdotes; drunk anecdotes – so that I no longer knew what was and wasn't real. I shouted at him even while he asked me patiently to calm down, to explain what was wrong.

Finally he shouted, 'All right!' and that was enough to shut me up.

'Eva, I need you to say what's happened *slowly*.'

I closed my eyes.

'Check the inbox now, please,' I murmured. 'Please. There's physical evidence – you can see I'm not lying.'

The policeman paused for a second, then sat down in front of the computer. I breathlessly recited the email address and the password.

He typed them in. He hit enter.

Email address not found.

'Put it in again,' I said.

He typed it again, and this time I watched over his shoulder to check his fingers were tapping the correct keys.

Email address not found.

My breathing quickened.

'They're taking photos of Northam students,' I said quickly. 'Professor Colin Montgomery, Marcus Bede – and others. They're taking photos of female students and lecturers and circulating them over email. And it's … some of them are intimate. I mean really intimate. One of them … I think one of them is of me … Please. We should try to get into their email accounts. Even if the photos are deleted – there must be a way of unearthing previous content.'

I remember the way the policeman looked at me then: the way the corners of his mouth shook; the way one eyebrow drew upwards.

'Those are certainly some serious accusations,' he said. He glanced towards my mother.

'It's *true*,' I said.

I recognized a shrill note of desperation creeping into my voice, and on hearing it my frustration intensified.

'Well I'll be sure to bring this up with my colleagues,' said the policeman, though his tone made it clear he wasn't going to.

The next morning, when they took me to be assessed, I looked out the window and saw the trees and large houses in the distance. I thought again of what Marcus had said about no one believing me. I thought of the notebook, that tiny slim volume which had been left under the keyboard. And I thought of Marcus – how I'd left him, crying in agony, cowering behind the table clutching at his eye.

I wished then that I'd punched harder. I wished I'd punched him hard enough to make him really feel it – to make the bone of the socket shatter and splinter into his brain.

CHAPTER TEN

Early May 2017

i.

LIVE REACTIONS: SHOULD UPSKIRTING REALLY BE CLASSED AS A SEXUAL OFFENCE?

WHAT IS UPSKIRTING? THE MEANING AND LAW EXPLAINED

'IT WASN'T TAKEN IN PRIVATE, SO IT'S NOT VOYEURISM': OUR LEGAL EXPERT OSCAR ELLETSON EXPLAINS

The place they sent me called itself a 'Bertrand Retreat'. It was a sort of rural hotel for rich people with various mental health problems. It wasn't a psychiatric unit exactly, nor was it a rehabilitation centre – you just weren't allowed to leave. I dread to think how much my parents spent on it, but since everyone there was clinically faux-polite and the programme was fundamentally redundant, I expect it was a lot. The staff made a big point about the fact that their "Practice" was modelled on the teachings of a yogi-slash-pharmacist-gone-rogue from the 1970s, which meant

279

exactly nothing to me. All I understood was that the 'guests' were forbidden to go anywhere, although you were granted six slots of visiting hours per week, and occasionally some alcohol, so there was an air of sociability about the place.

Anyway, I don't want to talk about what happened in there.

Two years went by and I almost convinced myself that what they were saying was true. They said that I was crazy; that I had imagined the whole term; that I had been disturbingly obsessed with Marina.

Maybe that last point stands. No one has ever had such an intense impact on me. No one has ever made me question myself to the extent that she did – or made me behave so strangely. I'd be lying if I said I didn't still think about her all the time. The gilded edges of her smile, the dusty ringlets of hair, her strange green eyes staring at a book, glinting with concentration. When I recall our relationship, I try to blot out what came after so that it isn't tainted. I don't ask myself how much she knew about her father's involvement. No. Instead I focus on the memories I have of her face, of the time we spent together: those snapshot fragments lodged in my brain. They are still so vivid.

The days with Marcus are not as clear to me. Those shards of memory come back only in the night, with cold sweat and his oleaginous mouth and the feeling of his hand squeezing my shoulder. I try not to think about that too much.

I try not to think about my parents, either. They were not unsympathetic. They came to visit me often at first, but the more inarticulate I became, the less they seemed to have to say to me in return. Then the visits became phone calls, then the phone calls became shorter and then they stopped completely. It wasn't that we were resentful towards one another, and it's not that I blame them for what happened – there just wasn't anything we had to talk about. Or perhaps more accurately, there was so much that we had to talk about, but I didn't know how, and they didn't know the right questions to ask.

I hollowed myself out emotionally, and didn't contact them when I was deemed fit to leave. Instead I took a train south, far far south – right down to the Cornish coast. I applied for a job there: a gig in property which paid in cash. I lived in a cheap hostel nearby. It wasn't as hard as everyone said it would be – finding work – and it wasn't especially difficult maintaining my anonymity either. I don't think my colleagues ever suspected anything about me. They didn't ask many questions about my past. They thought I was 'cool' or 'aloof' for the fact that I didn't use social media. Sometimes, they would squint at me and ask why I looked vaguely familiar.

'Were you a child actor or something?'

'Is blonde your natural colour?'

'How do you curl it at the ends like that?'

Life like this was satisfying. I ignored current affairs, disengaged from the news, and I didn't reactivate social media or look at my emails. Instead I focused on my work, checking house prices and ringing mortgage lenders. It was oddly easy to focus on these tasks, to make them constitute my existence, to convince myself that this was the only thing worth my attention. I certainly liked making my own money. I met people outside houses and walked them around the premises, showing them empty rooms, selling them stories about the lives they could live in there if they bought them. I was a vessel between people and places, a filler of empty rooms.

Then one day, one of my colleagues mentioned that her eighteen-year-old cousin was starting at Northam. The mere mention of the institution was enough to make my fingers itch – and though I tried to laugh it off, to stay out of the news and the implications of it all, a few days later I sought out an Internet café.

Sitting in front of the computer, I saw some of the headlines. I saw that Marcus Bede had been made Chancellor of Northam. I saw that the Marina Bede Foundation was still going. I saw that the event I had helped Marcus organize had been postponed, but had taken place a month afterwards. I saw that Montgomery still worked as a university professor. I saw that Henry – now in America – was working on a thesis about Mary Wollstonecraft's theory of the sublime. I trawled through the archives, through all the family press conferences, through the online forums, through the snide remarks underneath the articles. I read what my family had said about me since I had been admitted to the ward.

It was hard, processing some of this information, but in many respects it was reassuring to me. Marcus's promotion was a cliché. The professor's continuation at Northam was also predictable. I could have been angered by it but I honestly felt quite liberated. I had feared the worst – I could therefore accept the worst – but there was good news in that people were no longer talking about me. There were no photos of my upper thighs. There were no more death threats. I had escaped my old self – she was dead – and I could continue to live my new life: the one without a past.

That was a year ago. For twelve months I successfully put it all out of my mind. There was the occasional spook – the occasional Northam mention, the occasional reference to 'charities like the MBF' – but after I moved again I hadn't thought very much about any of it. Or at least, I hadn't until recently.

In the last few weeks, the newspaper headlines have reappeared and they are not going away. The stories about Marcus and Marina and Colin Montgomery are ubiquitous. I have seen those dark green eyes glaring out at me from the front page of a newsstand. I have recognised his – their – kindly wizened faces on the TV in the gym. I have seen unnervingly familiar images of Northam across screens and paper. I try to avoid them, to shut them out, but it doesn't work. I can't think about anything else.

NORTHAM EMAIL RING DISCOVERED FOLLOWING TIP-OFF FROM
ANONYMOUS SOURCE

COLIN MONTGOMERY: NORTHAM LECTURER, 54, ARRESTED ON CHARGES OF VOYEURISM

NORTHAM'S COLIN MONTGOMERY PLEADS GUILTY TO CHARGES

MARCUS BEDE – FATHER OF SUICIDE STUDENT MARINA – ARRESTED. LINKED TO MONTGOMERY CASE

'ABSURD FABRICATIONS': MARCUS BEDE DENIES CHARGES OR INVOLVEMENT

HENRY BEWELL DENIES PARTICIPATING IN THE UPSKIRTING RING

BEWELL LET OFF

LEGAL LOOPHOLE? EXPERTS EXPLAIN WHY UPSKIRTING IS NOT A CRIME

Even now, with the print headlines in front of me, I find it hard to read them. The memories all come flooding back. The possibilities come flooding back. I can't look at Marcus's face without feeling sick. Once again I stab the pen into his temple, watch the black ink ooze out.

I am happy that they have been caught – of course I am. I'd thought that I would have become immune to notions of 'social justice', but that's not how I feel. I am, in that sense, very relieved. They should be held accountable for what they've done. This may well result in Marina's retribution: what she intended; what she deserves. And yet … I can't help but be anxious for myself. I can't help thinking that I will be drawn into it again. The attention will refocus on me. Certain things will come to light.

I have had to quit my job. I can't concentrate. I can't think about anything except what might happen, about what might have happened, about what *did* happen and will be shown to have happened. I think about my legs spread wide on the screen. I think about the words Marcus said to me when I threatened to expose him – *what were you doing on the day Marina died?; no one will believe you.* I think of the image – a dream? – of Marina leaning out of the window, turning and smiling down at me. I don't know which parts of it to believe. Nothing feels concrete anymore.

Every day for the last few weeks, I have been sat in the public library with a selective stack of newspapers in front of me. They date from the last few days and pertain mostly to Montgomery. I've been collecting them in my room, storing them up, alternately withholding them and bingeing their contents. I've brought them here to read properly. I know newspapers are old-fashioned, but the Internet overwhelms me. I thought that – due to their specificity – these may be useful to refer to while I type up my version of events. But as it is, I have scarcely looked at them at all.

I stare at the photo of Marina on the front page. Her green eyes glower out at me; her mouth is smudged over with a coffee stain. I dab the newspaper, lean forward and peer at it closely. There is a challenge concealed in that face: an invitation.

Go on, she says. *I'll do it. Don't think I won't do it.*

I know that there is more news out there. Over the last few days, I have seen my own name across the headlines. I have seen my own photograph beside photos of Marcus and Marina and Colin and Henry. I have put off reading those stories specifically – the ones about me – because I dread to think of what evidence will emerge. I dread to think of that photograph coming out – the one of my thighs, her underwear. I dread to think of the other accusations … The things they might say. Will they ask where I was on the day Marina died? Will they force me to testify? Will I be able to say – for sure – that I wasn't in Northam?

I can't put it off any longer. My hands start moving towards the mouse. My fingers begin pushing into the stiff keys. A sea of headlines appears.

I skim them over and click on the sixth link that comes up, recognizing the name in the headline. Then I scroll down and read what he has said about me.

July 2017
Evening Standard

'Eva Hutchings is no Heroine – She Should Have Been
Investigated': Henry Bewell on the Marina Bede
Foundation Scandal

Having been absolved of his involvement in the Northam upskirting scandal, Henry Bewell describes his experience of online abuse, his friendship with Marina Bede, and why he believes that Eva

285

Hutchings was present at the death of his friend.
Words by Harrison Wong

It's been a harrowing couple of months for Henry Bewell. On 25 August, the 24-year-old Northam graduate – who is now studying for a PhD in America – found himself embroiled in the voyeurism scandal involving Northampton professor Colin Montgomery. Emails appeared to show him engaging in a form of 'banter' with Montgomery about female students, which caused media speculation that he had engaged in the upskirting ring himself (the Northam Chancellor, Marcus Bede, has now also been implicated in the proceedings). Due to a lack of solid evidence, Bewell has since been acquitted and the media outlet has apologised. But the online rumour mill is still churning. Bewell continues to be dogged online by members of the public as well as the blogging community, and there is still wild, confusing – and Bewell claims 'hugely unfounded' – speculation as to his involvement in the case. He has decided to speak to the Evening Standard in order to 'put a stop to this madness' and explain on his own terms what happened.

Bewell is evidently nervous when we meet in a West London café. His coat sleeves are rolled back; his fingers clamp around his coffee cup. He tells me that it's been a few days since he even left his house. 'But I don't tend to get recognized in here, so I think we'll be all right.' He speaks apologetically – in a polite, clipped accent – and his manners are impeccable. He opens the door for me, draws back my chair and asks if I want a coffee. He seems tentative and soft. Yet when I bring up the events of the last week – his posture stiffens. 'Enough is enough,' he says. 'The behaviour I've encountered over the last few weeks has been disgraceful. It's been intolerable for me. It's intolerable for my family. And it's disrespectful to the memory of Marina.'

Bewell is referring to the conspiracy theories surrounding the death of Marina Bede, which surfaced after the arrests of Marcus Bede and Colin Montgomery.

'I just cannot understand how we've got to this point,' he says. 'If you consider the kind of detachment that these people have ... The lack of empathy is astonishing. It's as if they are living in their own bubbles, in a completely different reality. They're so detached from the idea that this is actually some-one's life. It's my life. I'm just a normal guy.'

To understand how this happened, it helps to go back and explain the events of the last three years. The tragic story of Marina Bede first hit the headlines back in January 2014, when Marina, a popular, beautiful, high-achieving 19-year-old student, was found dead outside her accommodation block at Northam University. The news that she had committed suicide caused huge shockwaves across the Northam community – and this soon spread to the national headlines. The Marina Bede Fountain was set up in her memory to help spread awareness of depression and coping mechanisms, especially in young women.

'Her father was genuinely trying to help an underrepresented cause,' says Bewell when I ask him. 'He was doing something charitable. I really do believe that.'

Things then took a darker turn when Eva Hutchings, who claimed to be a close friend of Marina's, was discovered to have emulated her online after her death. Bewell says of the affair:

'It was incredibly distressing for her entire family, as you can imagine. ... But of course they didn't escalate the incident. They were busy dealing with other things.'

Bewell says he was too embroiled in his own trauma to be side-tracked by the controversy.

'Marina and I were very good friends,' he says. 'On that morning in January I had been sent to Northam to bring her back home. You see, she'd run away on New Year's Eve, *following an argument with her father. She was in a real state, and Marcus thought that I might be able to talk to her. But …' He trails off and shakes his head: it was too late. When Henry arrived at Northam that afternoon, he found her body lying outside her accommodation block.*

He is reluctant to talk about what happened next in any detail.

'As you can imagine it was very distressing. And so straight after the funeral – I went to Charlton (a prestigious Ivy League).' Bewell tells me that he had to leave Northam for his own sanity, and in order to distance himself from Marina's family. Over the Christmas holidays he had been spending a lot of time with the Bedes and said that the family atmosphere was tense. He was often called over to mediate arguments.

'I was like Marina's carer over that winter,' he says. 'It was a little odd. After her death especially, I needed to get away from them. I had to escape from everything.' He managed to transfer to Charlton for a year, on recommendation from Marcus Bede.

The Bede connection is where things get difficult for Bewell. In May this year, Professor Colin Montgomery was discovered by Northam police to have taken a number of upskirt shots of students around the Northam campus. Email correspondence dating from 2014 showed Montgomery trading pictures of students with Marcus Bede. So how did Bewell come into it?

'It was a complete miscommunication,' he says. 'One message that I'd sent about a female professor from my first year emerged online. I apologise for that now: I can see it was offensive. But I wasn't involved in the personal stuff … I never saw any of the photos.' He trails off here and says that he does not want to talk about the photos explicitly: he only wants to deny that he was involved in their circulation.

Since his acquittal, Bewell has been vocal about his lack of involvement in the upskirting case. This has been seen by many as an unusual, even reckless, decision. Should he not keep his head down? No, says Bewell. In an age where 'fake news' and conspiracy theories abound, it has become necessary for him to speak for himself.

'I tried to ignore it all at first,' he says. 'But it wouldn't go away. And then the death threats started and the coverage became more vicious. I sensed that unless I spoke out then their voices would trump mine. It felt like my identity was getting away from me.'

I ask him whether he thinks that his outspoken position has increased the vitriol towards him, rather than quelled it.

'Possibly,' he says. 'But I need to combat the conspiracy theories myself. I won't let my voice be drowned out.'

The conspiracy network to which he is referring is almost too complex to describe here. But one popular conspiracy theory – and the one he finds most distressing – is that Bewell is guilty of Marina's murder.

When I mention this to Bewell now, he appears both appalled and furious. 'There are timelines which prove it doesn't add up. The autopsy showing time of death. The CCTV of me getting off a train … It was all covered by the media. I shouldn't have to justify this, but it has reached that point.'

The reports are published here. Subscribers can view these in full, with our commentary, by clicking this **link***.*

Although Bewell has experienced distressing abuse as a result of these accusations, I suggest that some conspiracy theories are inevitable, considering how complex the story is. Since the arrest of Montgomery earlier this year, several other people have been implicated, including Marcus Bede, and senior members of the Bede Foundation. The extent of their involvement remains unclear.

Then there is new, disputed 'evidence' from Eva Hutchings's family. Since the news broke, Eva's parents have claimed that their daughter knew about the upskirting ring. They told The Sun that prior to her going to a rehabilitation facility in April 2014, Eva claimed she'd discovered incriminating email correspondence between Bewell and Montgomery. Allegedly, Eva was led to the bank of photographs after discovering a secret email address in a notebook. It is currently unclear when or how this notebook came to be discovered, or to whom it belonged. The existence of both the notebook and the email have been firmly denied by Montgomery and Bede, who also deny Bewell's involvement.

What does Bewell think about the Hutchings' claims, I ask?

'The notebook … Well, no, I never knew of any notebook. I can't really see that that adds anything.' Then the Hutchings are lying? 'Look, I think you have to look at it from a psychological perspective. Eva has been missing for over a year. Her parents are very distressed. They see the ordeal as the trigger for her disappearance. And it's terrible what happened to Eva – my sympathies are with them completely on that front – but what they say cannot be taken as reliable evidence.'

Bewell has consistently refused to defend Eva's position in the case, to an extent perceived by some as irresponsible. Last week, contrarian shock jock Karl Numan sent out an incriminating tweet, in which he accused Eva of having a hand in Marina's death. Bewell has not supported this theory in concrete terms, but he has done little to quell the speculation. Replying to commenters on his blog, he said that: 'I wouldn't say [the theory] is necessarily untrue.' Elsewhere he has described Eva as having 'a sinister side'. I ask him, tentatively, what his attitudes are towards Eva now.

Here Bewell scratches his jaw thoughtfully. 'It's difficult for me to answer that question,' he says. 'The thing is … well the thing is, Eva was in a lot of pain. She clearly suffered. But thinking about it … She was also obsessed with Marina. And when I think about her incessant messages to me during the holidays, and how she hinted that she'd been making random trips to Northam ... I've started to wonder about where she was on the night that Marina died. And I think ...'

He trails off, so I fill in for him: that she should have been investigated for her death?

'Yes,' he says slowly. 'She should have been questioned at the time. There's just so much ... It's all too odd. I know it was ruled as a suicide but the investigation wasn't thorough enough. No one asked Eva where she was the evening that Mari died. If Eva is still alive, she should come forward and explain.' He adds quickly: 'But of course it's not ... Well she has been missing for a long time. I don't mean to cause distress for her parents.'

Whatever the speculative situation with Hutchings, for now the focus is firmly on Bede and Montgomery. Their trial will be taking place over the next few weeks and the Evening Standard will be showcasing a live Twitter feed of the initial court proceedings. Will Bewell be keeping abreast of the outcome?

'I'll have to,' he says. 'I won't be there, of course, but I am keeping track of the case. I can't wait for it to be over ... It doesn't even feel like I've been acquitted, you know? And it won't until it's officially over. I just want to get on with the rest of my life.'

My mouse hovers over the screen.

I thought that reading Henry's article would make me feel afraid. I suppose it should, since now I know that he is out to get me. He is trying to pin me down, to force a confession from me, and to use my supposed guilt to deflect attention away from himself. But I don't feel scared, not really. I am angry.

The photo accompanying the article intensifies my rage. His smug face leers out at me from the screen. I study his cold dark eyes. The lips drawn in a tight smile. To think of those lips touching mine makes me feel physically sick.

I know that he is guilty. I saw the emails. I saw the conversation thread with Montgomery. I saw the pictures that he sent and the captions he posted beneath them. Didn't I?

Quickly I scroll down to the comments. I see the reaction to the article:

I can't believe the press is posting this. It's basically giving a platform to a sex criminal. And he IS a sex criminal. There was insufficient evidence – not no evidence at all. Literally wtf??!

Guilty as hell

So he wants Eva to be investigated, having never been convicted of anything, but thinks that everyone should leave him alone, even though he's been let off !!! Does this idiot have any idea how he sounds?

RE: Does the journalist?

Wow this article really opened my eyes to sympathizing with a 'polite' pervert. Just kidding: this was pathetic and unprofessional.

My fingers detach from the keyboard and move to my lap. My wrists and shoulders feel loose and light. They are on my side, I realize. They are on my side. No one will believe Henry. No one will believe what he has to say about me, or anything else.

I click on a new tab and type in the website address. I put in my password and email address. I thought I had deleted my account, but when I press enter it rolls up anyway. Here is my old life, preserved. Here is a picture of me in that first week of Northam, with my shoulders tensed, my hands awkwardly knotted in the centre of my body. What kind of future did I think I had then?

Caroline Evans is with Eva Hutchings and 5 others at the Bistrotheque, Walford.
Eva Hutchings went to Grime and Punishment at the Cellar.

My eyes move to messages dating from the time that the story of the Swipe impersonation broke. Some abusive, some not; some already read, some not. There are so many from my parents. They ask where I am. They tell me they are sorry.

It is then that I notice a message in the 'other' inbox. It dates from late 2014. The sender appears to have deleted their profile – it simply shows up as a grey 'User' – but I can tell just from the first few sentences who it is from.

Hi Eva

I hope you're well / that your leg has recovered. I was sorry to hear about your mental health issues. I don't know how long you're away for but I suppose you might read this when you're home, and hopefully better ... I know it's somewhat odd to contact you like this. It's very much out of the blue, and I hope you'll forgive me for being so abrupt. But now that Marcus and I have broken up – I felt I had to drop you a line.

To tell the truth, I wanted to say thank you for the wakeup call. The news that you'd stood up to him really made me feel something. It made me realise I could leave. I'd been wanting to for a while, and it took me a few weeks to act on that impulse, but having spoken to my therapist I've established that it was you who set the ball rolling.

There's a line break here, and a short time difference. Then the message starts off again in one long paragraph, as though the sender stopped herself mid-flow and then decided to carry on.

Another thing. A few days before I left, Marcus mentioned your 'conspiracy theory' to me – that thing about a secret email address. It came after something your parents said. I was with Marcus the following week, after you'd been sent away. He was on the phone to your parents and the conversation got pretty heated. I heard some of it from his end, so he had to tell me what it was all about. At the time I didn't take you – or any of it – seriously. I'm sorry about that.

Now I have distance though ... What you're saying does ring true. There are a few things I've been wondering about Marcus in light of your ideas – and there's one detail I think I have to let you know about. The night before Marina went missing she and Marcus had a huge fight. I could only overhear short snippets but there was definitely something about him being a traitor. I got the impression that she found something bad in his study – I was too scared to ask what afterwards, but the argument escalated when she mentioned that she'd 'found out who he really was'. She started screaming at him. Threatening him with something, I'm pretty sure it was something about an email address. I didn't consider this to be significant at the time as she often made comments of that ilk. But it ties into some of what you said.

There is another pause, as though she has reflected on what she's written.

294

*Sorry, I've probably had too much to drink. You
must think this sounds a little crazy. But if it does
make sense – then we might be able to piece some
of it together. What I'm saying is that if you ever want
to meet up and chat, I would be happy to lend you
an ear.*
    Elena

The words are frozen on the screen, and I stare at them for a
long, uncomfortable moment. The possibilities whirl around my
mind. Then they click together, and it begins to make sense.
Marina's strangely close relationship with her father, the adoring
way that she spoke about him – the way she described him as
capable of sorting anything out. Perhaps she thought that he
would be able to help her expose Montgomery over the photos
but – when she confronted him – she was met with the same
violent rebuttal that I'd experienced.

But then …

Another stronger, darker, possibility crosses my mind. *I think
she found something bad in his study* … I don't want to think
about it but it's impossible not to. Perhaps she didn't seek her
father's advice. Perhaps she suspected his involvement in the first
place. Perhaps – despite the lies she'd told herself – she was aware
of a more sinister side to him. Perhaps she snuck into his study,
like she did with Montgomery. And then what she found … Oh
God. I think of the screenshot of me in *her* underwear. Could
that have triggered a miscommunication between Marcus and
Marina? Horror seizes me – a cold, dreadful sensation, like
someone is tracing a knife along my spine. Those photographs
– those awful photographs – on her own father's computer. Is
that what tipped her over the edge?

Without warning my mind rewinds to a memory of my own.
Whether it is a real memory, or the memory of a dream, I'm not
sure. But it's vivid. I see her face through the rain, through the

fog folding over the windowpanes, behind the glass. I see her pulling up the blind, leaning out. I see her frowning, then laughing, then shaking her head sadly. 'Kill yourself,' I tell her. 'Just do it. No one will miss you. No one will care. Everyone thinks you're a whore. Even your dad thinks you're a whore.'

My breath is tight. I squeeze my eyes shut. I squeeze them tighter. I try to block it all out, wipe it all away. The world goes black for a second.

When I open my eyes again I reread Elena's message:

I would be happy to lend you an ear.

That sentence soothes me. Elena believes me. The public believe me.

I wasn't there. They fly out quickly – much quicker than I expected – and fall one by one into a heap on the floor. I lean down, pick one up by the corners, and read the first sentence: 'The first time I saw Marina was in October *2013*. The last time I saw her was three months later.'

I strike out the word 'three' and replace it with 'two'. I'm sure of it now. *I wasn't there.*

For a long time I thought that Marina had destroyed my personality. I thought that an essential part of me – the part that was individual and self-contained – had disintegrated after I met her. She had eroded my sense of who I was.

But now I'm starting to think that Marina did not destroy my personality – she shaped it. Without her, I might have spent my entire life in the shadows, feeding off the energy of other people, always waiting for someone else to show me how to behave. Marina forced me out of my shell. She drew me to see the discrepancies in my own character. And now, having faced up to those, I have finally become a real person. A person with opinions. A person who wants to voice them. A person like her.

I click off the links. I push the stack of newspapers aside and start to assemble my things.

It is time to go home.

AUTHOR'S NOTE

In January 2019, a Bill was passed by the House of Lords to make upskirting illegal in England and Wales. Until then there had been no specific offence for 'upskirting' in England. Cases involving upskirt shots were sketched around definitions of 'voyeurism' or 'outraging public decency'. Voyeurism applied where images were taken of someone in private. Outraging public decency focuses on the idea that the public has been offended (not the harm done to the victim) and so the taking of photos had to be done in public, and usually had to be witnessed by at least two people. In this book, which is set in 2017, Eva reads one headline suggesting that the perpetrators have been charged with voyeurism. In fact, the case would probably have come under 'outraging public decency', since universities are not considered private spaces. But you could argue, for one, that they're not exactly public spaces either.

I'm extremely grateful to Professor Clare McGlynn at Durham University for explaining this to me, and to Gina Martin for her activism. Reading material is widely available online for anyone interested in learning more.

ACKNOWLEDGEMENTS

This book would not exist if Tessa David at PFD hadn't scooped the first draft out of the slush pile in 2017. I can't thank you enough for putting up with my many pseudonyms and ill-conceived pranks. Your patience and tenacity are inspiring.

The tireless work of my editor Charlotte Brabbin has made this a much better book. I'm incredibly grateful for your beady eyes, incisive comments and excellent judgement. Also to Jan Currie and the rest of the KillerReads team.

Other thanks to:

Moira and Nick. Unlike Eva's parents, you are actually supportive and nice. Except for the time you cut off my hair because I was chewing it, Mum, and 'I didn't mean to cut that much off' is not a valid apology. But tuft or no tuft, I wouldn't have been able to finish (or start) this if it weren't for both of you. Thanks for being so open-minded about your wayward spawn, and for laughing at my jokes when no one else does. Thanks also for my good looks.

The Saville Gang: Freddy, Rosa, Oscar and the wickedly talented Tainted Doge. Exceptional thanks to OB.

Al Konstam, for being my plus one at all events, even when the host explicitly says you›re not invited. Pete Saban and his warm bed. Everyone who has ever given me a job.

Charlotte and Toby Smyth, who were both given drafts and did not read them. (I figured you›d feel left out if Millie got a mention.)

Millie Smyth, Katy Fallon and Oscar Batterham, who read a number of drafts several times over and gave thoughtful, extensive feedback.

For anyone struggling with suicidal thoughts, the Samaritans helpline is free on 116 325. There is always another answer. Help can also be found at Rape Crisis (0808 8029999) for those suffering from trauma relating to rape and sexual abuse.

KILLER READS

DISCOVER THE BEST
IN CRIME AND THRILLER

Follow us on social media to get to know the team behind the books, enter exclusive giveaways, learn about the latest competitions, hear from our authors, and lots more:

 /KillerReads    /KillerReads